The Nameless Dead

The Nameless Dead

An Inspector Devlin Thriller

BRIAN McGILLOWAY

WITNESS
IMPULSE
An Imprint of HarperCollinsPublishers

This book was previously published by Macmillan in 2012.

EPub Edition APRIL 2015 ISBN: 9780062400482

Print Edition ISBN: 9780062417336

10 9 8 7 6 5 4 3 2

For Bob McKimm

Saturday, 27 October

Chapter One

THE CADAVER DOG, a small black spaniel, was moving across the field towards the island's edge, its snout pressed close to the ground, its body twisting and flexible as it turned this way and that, following whatever scent it had picked up. It snuffled into the surface vegetation, then cut suddenly left and followed an alternative scent instead. The handler, trailing a few paces behind, did not look up, his attention focused on the animal before him, following its every move with grim determination.

Just beyond them, at the water's edge, gulls wheeled and circled, twisting in the wind. A heavy-bodied heron picked its way along the shoreline, its head angled towards the water, one beady black eye swivelling towards us. Around its feet, the river water lapped onto the gravel shore, instantly disappearing between the stones, then reappearing further down the beach as it drew away from us again towards the Northern side of the river.

The sky above us was heavy with rain clouds, the wind skittish along the river, running down the valley towards Derry. I shivered and zipped up my Garda overcoat.

An urgent yelping broke the silence. The dog had picked up on a scent it recognized. It raised its head and barked sharply, its ears pricked, its tail erect and wagging furiously. Its head lowered, it sniffed again at the ground, then began barking louder, shifting quickly back and forth as it did.

'Apparently they train those things using dead pigs,' Lennie Millar, the man beside me, said.

I looked at him quizzically.

'It's the closest thing to decaying human remains; the smells are almost indistinguishable,' he added.

'I'll never look at bacon the same way again,' I said.

He laughed forcedly.

'Yo, Lennie! Inspector!'

To our right, a few hundred yards along the field, a small mechanical digger sat silently. Its driver, and the man who had been directing him where to dig, had been sifting through the mound of soil at the edge of the hole they had dug earlier. It was the latter of these men, a forensic archaeologist who'd been introduced to me only as Jonas, who had called to us.

'We've found another one.'

Millar and I moved across to where they worked. As we approached, I could see something white against the darkness of the soil in the six-foot hole that they had dug. It was only when I reached the edge of the site that I realized it was a human skull.

A tiny human skull.

Chapter Two

ISLANDMORE IS A geographical limbo: running for about two and a half miles, but less than half a mile wide, the island sits in the middle of the river Foyle, its two lateral shores no more than 200 yards from either Northern Ireland or the Republic. But the island belongs to both and neither; the Irish border, which runs along the riverbed from Derry to Strabane, dissects the island down the middle.

The island had once served as a crossing point for the Derry–Donegal railway. The train had started from Derry City in the North, then travelled along the southern side of the border until, just short of Lifford, it crossed the Foyle via two small bridges, through Islandmore and then on into Strabane.

The problem with such a narrow crossing, however, was that it was exploited by smugglers, either running the railway line across the border with illegal goods and produce or navigating the narrow crossing beneath the bridges in rowing boats.

As a consequence, the bridge on the Northern Irish side, which actually lay to the east of the island, was allowed to fall into disrepair, before it collapsed completely in the 1960s, leaving only a few desultory support pillars jutting impotently out of the river. The bridge onto the island from the Republic, on the western shore, likewise soon fell into disrepair, until the island became separated from both sides and grew wild.

The search team working on the island was part of the Independent Commission for the Location of Victims' Remains. The victims in question were a specific group, collectively known as the Disappeared, individuals who, during the early days of the Troubles in the North, had been targeted because of some slight, imagined or actual, against the local IRA commanders. Some, it was claimed, had proven too friendly with the police or army; some were suspected of providing information or were considered likely to indulge in loose talk. None were ever granted the dignity of proper obsequies, secretly buried in nameless plots, usually in isolated spots around the border, thus condemning the family to double anguish: the loss of a loved one, coupled with the uncertainty of never knowing for sure what happened to them, or being able to lay them finally to rest in consecrated ground.

The Commission team had been on Islandmore for several days now, looking for the corpse of a local man named Declan Cleary. Instead they had stumbled upon a nineteenth-century *cillin*; an unofficial burial site for unbaptized babies.

'Most parishes would have one,' Millar, the Commission's lead investigator on the dig, told me, the first day we had walked the site. 'Often they were found close to churches, but, in fact, an island in the middle of a river would be seen as perfect. The Catholic Church would not allow babies that had died before baptism to be buried in consecrated ground, so families often selected somewhere either close to a church, or on a border or boundary between parishes. Or near a river.'

'Where is the one here?' I asked.

'At the easterly end, on the tip. They always faced east, towards the rising sun. The one here's at least 150 years old but there are more recent remains in it. It's not the first time they've been found. A more recent one was uncovered in Milltown in Belfast not so long ago, just beyond the wall of the existing cemetery.'

I recalled hearing about it; children, trapped in limbo for eternity according to old Church law, who had simply vanished, as if never even born, their burial spots secret, unmarked. I remembered hearing, with much admiration, that the Bishop of Down and Connor, John Tohill, instructed before his death in 1914 that he was to be buried in the field outside the local cemetery, hoping that in doing so, the blessing bestowed on the land during his funeral would extend beyond his site to the children buried thereabouts.

The discovery had no bearing on the Commission's work on the island, so they had reinterred the bodies where they were found and contacted the local priest, Father Brennan. He planned, he said, to hold a Service of Blessing on All Souls' Day, the 2nd of November.

This new skull was different. For a start, it had been recovered on a different part of the island, facing west towards the Republic.

'It's not part of the *cillin*, is it?' I asked.

Millar lay almost flat on the ground, examining the skull in situ. He looked up at me and shook his head grimly.

'It's in the wrong place. But it is a baby, too, by the size of it. Probably disabled. Photograph it, then look for the rest of the remains,' he added to Jonas.

'Why disabled?' I asked.

'You'll see.'

Jonas stepped towards the rim of the pit and began taking photographs of the scene. Then, moving closer, he placed a small strip of paper, marked out with measurements, beside the skull and continued to take shots. Finally, satisfied that he had recorded the skull from each angle, he handed the camera up to the driver and gently lifted the skull out of the Earth.

He held it up towards the light, grasped in one gloved hand.

'It's very young. Another newborn. You can still see the light through the joints where the plates of the skull haven't fused.'

I suppressed a shudder. The bones of the face on the right-hand side looked to have melted into one another, the upper jaw twisted. The hollows of the eyes were abnormally large, wide spaced and sloping.

'There are bones missing from the cheek,' he added.

'Could an animal have damaged the skull like that?' I asked.

Jonas shook his head. 'I don't think so. There are no jagged edges to the bone structure, like you'd expect, no bite marks. Plus, there was a stone over the remains, to keep animals from getting at it.'

He nodded towards the mound of earth below the digger bucket. A large flat stone lay atop the mound.

'We'll work by hand the rest of the way down,' Jonas said to the driver, who nodded and lifted two spades that were leaning against the digger's heavy rubber tracks.

Jonas moved across and handed the skull out to me. I pulled on my gloves before taking it. It was almost weightless, little bigger than an orange. I regarded the hollows of the eyes, the curve of the upper jaw, and tried, without success, to imagine how the child might have looked.

Below me, Jonas and the digger were already removing further bones from the earth and laying them on the ground at my feet.

By the time the light began to die later that afternoon most of the skeleton had been recovered. It had been easier than expected; as the dig progressed, they discovered that the child had been wrapped in a cloth, which still contained the bulk of the remains. Remarkably, the pelvic bones lay inside a dirtied but intact nappy.

The child was no more than twenty inches in length. Jonas had spent the latter hours arranging the bones into some semblance of the correct order, while the digger operator, whose name I learnt to be Mark, continued to recover the bones from the earth. Even in such a state, bare of all flesh, there was something shockingly vulnerable about the infant now lying on the grey woollen blanket in which it had been wrapped.

Jonas lay flat beside the remains, examining each bone. Only when he had finished cataloguing each in a notebook did he stand up.

'We might be best to get a post-mortem on this one, Inspector,' he said. 'There are signs of fracturing on the sternum and the lower jaw. The hyoid bone is also fractured.'

'Strangled?'

Jonas shrugged. 'Or compression over the month and neck. I don't know for sure. A PM will better reveal any injuries. Plus, we'd want a more thorough examination of the facial injuries, the missing bones and that. They're not in the ground.'

'How old are the remains?'

Jonas shrugged. 'We'll not know until we examine further.'

'Might it be a *cillin* baby?'

Millar shook his head. 'The blanket seems wrong. Babies would have been wrapped in white sheets or towels before burial.'

'The nappies a disposable,' Jonas said. 'That means it dates sometime from the mid-seventies onwards.'

Suddenly, across from us, the spaniel began yelping again. The dog handler whistled sharply to get our attention, then, raising his hand high above him, exaggeratedly pointed to where he stood. Three small red flags dotted one of the two-metre-square areas that the men had marked out with bamboo canes on their first day.

'We have another spot by the looks of it,' Millar said. 'For Cleary.'

'Will you start digging today?'

He glanced above him where the sky was darkening.

'It's a little late to start. We'll see the family and tell them we're planning on resuming work in the morning.'

Chapter Three

DECLAN CLEARY HAD been missing since the 3rd of November 1976, when his girlfriend, Mary Harte, had contacted the RUC in Strabane to report that her partner had gone out to the shop the previous night for cigarettes and had yet to return home.

The officer who had visited Harte noted in his report that she was seven months pregnant at the time and that she and Cleary had been dating for no more than a year. With no other reason to attribute to Cleary's failure to return home, his conclusion was that the man had taken cold feet and run out. He had assured Mary Harte of this and suggested that her boyfriend would probably return within the next day or two.

When, days later, Mary Harte arrived at the RUC station in tears, demanding to see the same officer, he offered her tea and sympathy, suggested that Cleary had decided that the impending birth of his child was too much to bear. He was unlikely to have done anything rash – he had left no note, had not displayed any of the usual signs of those contemplating suicide. They would keep an eye on his bank accounts but, with little to his name by way of savings and with no other family alive but for his unborn child, she would have to accept that he had simply left.

Rumours soon began to circulate, though, that he had been targeted by the local Provos as an informer who had given information to the police about IRA activities. As a result, in 1999, when the Independent Commission for the Location of Victims' Remains was founded by the British and Irish governments, Cleary's name appeared among the ranks of the Disappeared. The Commission's task was to gather information about the Disappeared, with a view to the recovery of their remains. Their role, in all cases, was not to investigate the killings or establish motives for them, but simply to recover the bodies and provide those left behind with an opportunity to bury their dead. No prosecutions would arise from any evidence recovered; bodies would undergo a post-mortem to establish cause of death, but no forensic analysis would occur, nor would notes be passed to the police in whichever jurisdiction the body was recovered. In almost all instances, the bodies had been abandoned in the Republic.

In mid-May of this year, the Commission had received an anonymous tip-off that Cleary was buried in the local area. It was not until the start of October, when Cleary's old girlfriend, Mary Harte, and her son were anonymously sent an Ordnance Survey map of the area, with the island marked and Cleary's name written beneath it, that the team visited the island and began running tests. Whatever they had found, it had convinced them as to the reliability of the tip-offs, for they contacted us the following day and requested support from An Garda. As the only detective inspector in the area, I was duly appointed their liaison.

MARY HARTE ANSWERED the door to us when we called at her home in St Jude's Court in Lifford. She had married some years after Declan Cleary's disappearance; her husband, Sam Collins, had been a teacher in the local primary school before retiring. Indeed, he had taught my daughter Penny when she was younger. As a consequence, I had always known Mary Harte by her married name and it was with this that I addressed her.

The woman must have been in her late fifties now; her skin was firm and bright, her permed hair still brown.

'Come in,' she said, holding open the door.

She led us into her living room where her son, Sean, waited on the sofa. He was in his mid-thirties, born eight weeks after his father had disappeared. He sat forward, on the edge of the sofa, his back erect, his hands resting lightly on his knees, which bobbed up and down. He looked up at us as we came in, as if unsure whether to stand, then seemed to decide against it. His hands twisted around each other.

'Is there any news?' Mary Collins asked, standing in front of the fireplace with her hands behind her back, as if to warm them at the fire that smouldered there.

Millar nodded. 'We'd no luck, I'm afraid,' he said. 'We'll start on a new site on the island tomorrow.'

'I thought you said you were sure you had the right spot for today,' Sean Cleary muttered, glancing across at Millar, though not quite looking directly at him.

'We thought we had. We've walked the island and the archae-ologists have identified a number of probable sites, based on sur-face analysis, changes in vegetation, that sort of thing. We just have to work through each until we find him.'

'Changes in vegetation?' Sean asked.

'Any digging, of graves or that, would clear the surface vegetation. As it grows back, it will always be at a different level from the vegetation around it. It's a subtle change; not proof in itself but enough for us to carry out geophysical testing.'

'What's that?' Mrs Collins shifted slightly, as if the backs of her legs were getting scorched. Eventually she moved across to an empty seat in front of the window.

'Resistivity testing, mainly. And magnetometry. Soil displays resistance to electrical current being passed through it. You'd expect all the soil in any one geographical area to have around the same resistance readings. Where a grave has been dug and the spoil returned back into the hole dug, it never goes back in exactly as it came out – the mixing of top soil and deeper soil changes the overall composition and therefore the resistance reading.'

'So you still don't know if Declan is definitely there then?'

'I can't say definitely. There is something there. We had a search-dog out again today and he picked up something around one of the sites we'd identified.'

'You said that yesterday, too,' Sean interrupted, looking between his mother and Millar, as if looking for her agreement.

'There have been other issues with the island and the location we've picked.'

'What issues?'

'We found a child's body in the site we dug today. That had to be excavated and processed.'

'Is it another one of the limbo babies?' Mary Collins asked, her face creased in sympathy.

'We don't know. It's not part of the original *cillin*, but that doesn't mean that it wasn't buried there for much the same reasons. The find was very close to where we believe Declan to be lying. I imagine there may be some scant consolation in know-ing that Declan has not been lying alone these past years,' Millar added.

Mrs Collins smiled sadly, her eyes glistening. I marvelled at her composure, having waited thirty-five years to learn what had happened to her partner, to have come this close.

'What happens when he's found?' Sean said. 'What will *you* do then?' He nodded at me when he spoke.

It was Millar who answered, though. 'When your father is recovered, we'll have to send his body for formal identification. That may take some weeks. We'll also want to conduct a postmor-tem to establish cause of death. Then he'll be returned to you for Requiem Mass and interment.'

'But what about your lot? Will you be looking for who killed him?'

I looked quickly to Millar before I answered. 'I'm afraid not, Sean. That's not how it works.'

Millar nodded. 'The Commission's role is to bring about the recovery of the Disappeared. We have no powers to gather evi-dence or attempt to prosecute those responsible for the death of the body we recover. Nor can anything we uncover be used in court. We will not be passing on any information to Inspector Devlin here. This is a recovery operation only. The legislation is very clear on that.'

'That's balls,' Sean Cleary said suddenly, shifting forward in his seat and standing. 'So whoever killed my father can just sit back and watch on TV while he's dug up.'

'I understand your frustration, Mr Cleary,' Millar said. 'But that is the law. If it's any consolation to you, it was probably one of the people responsible for your father's death who contacted us in the first place. That that individual felt compelled to tell us where your father rested would suggest that it has weighed on his or her conscience these past years.'

'Except you were contacted in May and you waited until now to look for him.'

I could sense Millar swallowing back whatever he wanted to say. I imagined that, in his role, he would come across all forms of response to the work he was doing.

'The information we were given in May was that the body was located near Tra na Cnamha. No one we spoke to recognized the name.' He stumbled over the pronunciation of the name, pronouncing both the 'n' and the 'm'.

'It's pronounced *Crawaa*. Tra na Cnamha means the Beach of Bones,' I translated. 'But I've never heard the name being used for Islandmore.'

'In the eighteenth century, locals called the island Innis na Cnamha. We found it on an old Donegal fishing map in the Linenhall Library in Belfast. It was the name, Isle of Bones, that alerted us to the probability that there might be a *cillin* on the site,' he explained, again speaking to Mary Collins.

She nodded. Sean glanced across at her quizzically.

'We'd only got that name when you told us about the map you were sent. We've worked as quickly as we can. And, again, if the same person sent you the map as contacted us, it suggests that he or she is feeling incredibly guilty about what happened. Thirty-five years on.'

'And that's the best we can expect? That whoever did it feels a bit guilty? My heart bleeds.'

'That's enough, Sean,' Mary Collins said. 'These men are doing their best. They'll bring Declan home. That's all I want now.'

'It's not what I want,' Sean Cleary said, his voice breaking slightly. He was a big man when he stood, just under six foot, though, I suspected, edging near sixteen stone. Despite being in his mid-thirties, though, his voice and manner were a teenager's. 'That's not justice. It's not good enough.'

'It's all we can do.'

'Well, it's not good enough for me,' he snapped, standing and leaving the room.

Mary Collins stood with that, extending her hand to Millar.

'I apologize for Sean. You're doing very good work, Mr Millar,' she said. 'You don't know how important it is. Thank you.'

'We'll work as fast as we can,' Millar assured her.

She nodded, though the increasing glinting in her eyes suggested she could not trust herself to speak further without tears.

'WHEN WILL THE post-mortem be held on the baby?' I asked, when we got back into the car. 'I'll want to get things moving.'

Millar stared across at me, his seat belt still gripped in his hand.

'You can't investigate it, Inspector.'

'But if the PM shows the child was murdered—'

'Even if,' Millar interrupted. 'The same rules apply as I mentioned to the son in there. Any evidence uncovered in a dig for the Disappeared can't be used to prosecute a case, nor can it be investigated or forensically tested. Those are the rules.'

'But the baby isn't part of the Declan Cleary killing.'

'That's not the point. It was uncovered as part of our dig; it can't be investigated.'

'Someone killed a baby. The rules need to be bent a little.'

'No. We rely on people coming to us with information precisely because they know they can do so without fear of prosecution.

Considering the proximity of the sites, and the depth the infant was buried at, theoretically there's the possibility of a connection between the two. If it became known that we were allowing investigations into old killings, our sources would dry up. We'd recover nobody.'

'But this is different.'

He clicked the seatbelt into place. 'You can't investigate the baby, Inspector. That's the law.'

Chapter Four

BY THE TIME I got home, Debbie had dinner ready. Following the accident which had injured our daughter, Penny, a year previous, I'd tried to spend more time at home, stopping off at meal times to see the kids. If I was running late, Debs would hold off on dinner until I was home.

As we sat in the living room after dinner, I mentioned the find we had made on the island and Millar's warning that I could not follow it up.

'The forensics guy they had with them thinks it was a newborn,' I concluded.

'That's horrible,' Debbie said. She was sitting on the sofa, watching the news. Penny lay sprawled beside her, her head on Debbie's lap, while she played a game on her iPod. As Debbie spoke, she ruffled the soft spikes of Penny's hair. She'd had to shave it several times for surgery and it had only now begun to grow out again. In solidarity with her, Debbie had cut her own hair in a gamine style that accentuated how similar the two of them were. 'Was it . . . natural?'

'We don't know yet. They thought there were signs of something. The face was badly deformed, so the child might never have had a chance.'

The comment silenced her for a moment, and I suspected I knew what she was thinking. Finally she said, 'Even if it was natural causes, imagine not being able to bury your child properly, having to hide them on an island. A miscarriage was hard enough to go through, never mind going full term then having to do that.'

Penny propped herself up on her elbows and twisted to look up at Debbie. Despite having had her earphones on, she must have overheard our conversation, for she asked, 'Did you have a miscarriage?'

Debbie glanced at me before answering and, even then, spoke as softly as possible. Penny was 15 now but Shane was only approaching 10.

'He's doing his homework in the kitchen,' I explained, keeping an eye on the hallway in case he should approach.

'When we were first married, we had problems having a baby. It took five years before you arrived. In fact, we bought Frank thinking we couldn't have a baby.'

At the mention of his name, Frank, our Bassett hound, lifted his head slightly off the hearth rug, his heavy wattles of skin drooping beneath his throat. He yawned widely then, satisfied that he was not being directly addressed, lowered his head again to his paws.

'Once I did get pregnant, but we lost the baby early on. I was about five months gone.'

Penny watched her mother as she spoke.

'But, then we had you, so that made everything perfect.'

'If you'd had the first baby, would you have had me then?'

Debs shrugged. 'I don't know.'

Penny considered the implications of the response. 'Do you think about the baby you lost?'

Debbie looked at me, surprised by Penny's interest.

'Sometimes I wonder what he or she would have been like. You and Shane are so different, that that baby would have been a completely different person, too. But I've never regretted that I had you and Shane.'

'What happened to him?' The voice came from the doorway. I looked across and realized that Shane had wandered across and was standing watching us.

'What, love?'

'What happened to him?'

Debbie considered how best to express herself. 'He wasn't well. The doctor told us that he'd be very sick when he was born. God must have decided that he was too good for this world.'

'So where did he go?'

'He went back to God before he was born.'

'He just disappeared?' Shane said.

'Kind of,' I said.

'What was he called?'

'We don't know whether it was a boy or girl, honey,' Debbie said. 'It was too early to tell. He or she didn't have a name.'

The room was quiet. Shane looked from Debbie to me. 'I need help with my maths,' he said finally.

'No problem. Then afterwards, what about a movie night?' I suggested. Debs smiled, though I could tell the conversation was playing on her mind.

We sat that evening and watched a film and ate popcorn, Debs, Shane, Penny and I, with our phantom child somewhere between us, alive again in our minds for the first time in many years. Debbie had not told the children the whole truth. She had not explained to them that the doctors had told us that our child would suffer severe disability. She did not tell them of the terror that thought had held for us, only married a few years. Nor did she tell them of our resolution to face the future with our child no matter what, and the subsequent heartache that we had felt at his loss. And I had never told Debbie, or anyone else for that matter, that my heartache at his loss had been tempered with a degree of relief.

And that I had felt nothing but shame for the unworthiness of that reaction ever since.

Nor could I easily dismiss the thought of the child on the island, the pleading of the hollow eyes, the fragility of the skull. A child deprived not only of sacred burial but even its name.

I was not the only one who had been thinking on our earlier conversation. I piggybacked Shane up to bed after his supper. After he had said his prayers, I tucked him in and kissed him on the forehead. I was turning out the light when he called me back.

'The baby that Mummy lost? Do you really believe that he was too good for this world?'

'I think he was, buddy,' I said, going across and sitting by him.

'Does that mean that I'm not as good as him?'

'Of course not,' I said. 'What I meant was that he was too fragile for life. You're a healthy trout,' I added, laughing lightly.

He was not to be deflected from his questions, though. 'Would you have loved him?'

'Yes,' I said.

'More than me?'

I started and sat again beside him. 'Of course not,' I repeated.

'But you love Penny more than me,' he said, slyly, watching me from the corner of his eye, even as he pretended to be settling down for sleep.

'I don't love Penny more than you. I love you both exactly the same, Shane.'

'You pay more attention to Penny. Mummy even cut her hair the same.'

I laid my hand on his shoulder, but he did not turn towards me. 'Shane, we almost lost Penny when she had the accident. It made us realize how important she is to us. And how important you are, too.'

I'm glad the baby didn't come along,' he said, twisting towards me. 'Then I'd have had to be third instead of second.'

'Shane, look at me.'

He turned towards me fully, but his eyes did not meet mine, settling instead on my shoulder.

'You and Penny? You're both the same to me. Don't ever think differently.'

He considered the response and smiled quickly, but I could tell that it did not reflect a deeper acceptance of my argument. Then he turned from me again.

Chapter Five

THOUGH DEBBIE AND I sat and watched TV together, I couldn't dismiss the island child from my mind. Finally I decided to visit my old boss, 'Olly' Costello. He had been a garda in Lifford for almost forty years prior to his retirement. If anyone knew about the island being used for burials, I suspected it would be him.

He had aged considerably since last I had seen him. He had been the superintendent in the area for years, until the death of his wife during a murder case prompted him to retire. Neither of us had ever discussed that the case had thrown up his possible involvement in the murder of a prostitute in the 1970s.

I had visited him sporadically in the months following his retirement, but our conversation tended to be limited to my reporting what was happening in the station, and I gradually realized that, far from making Costello feel still part of the Guards, it served only to frustrate him and remind him that he was no longer a member of the force. In recent years I had visited him infrequently and was, consequently, a little surprised by the change in him.

He had lost much of the weight he used to carry, his trousers hanging baggily on him when he answered the door. He had not shaved for a few days and his grey stubble seemed to annoy him, for he scratched at his cheek often as we spoke.

'Benedict!' he said. He leaned forward as if to embrace me, but the movement became muddled and instead we moved briefly closer together and patted one another awkwardly on the shoulder. His breath was stale and smelt of illness.

'How're things, sir?' I said, offering him a bottle of whiskey I had picked up in the off license on the way.

'God bless you, son,' he said, taking the bottle, then waving me into the house. The hallway was in semi-darkness, the blinds half pulled. Costello's wife, Emily, had been incredibly house-proud and, in the months following her death, Olly had done his best to keep the place in shape. Over time, however, he seemed to lose interest, particularly when his daughter, Kate, moved to England to work. The carpet in the hallway was faded and threadbare in places. A stack of old newspapers sat beside an old bookcase at the end of the hallway, the shelves of the case buckling under the weight of books.

'How're Debbie and the children?' Costello asked, moving into the kitchen. 'Drink?' he added, raising the bottle before I had a chance to reply.

'No thanks. They're fine. Penny's recovering well.'

Costello nodded. 'The accident. I forgot. That's good.'

He lifted a glass from the sink and rinsed it quickly under the tap, before pouring himself two fingers of the drink.

'You'll take tea, Benedict,' he said. Costello is one of the few people I know who insists on calling me by my full name, rather than just Ben. He drained the glass, then set it down and filled the kettle. While he waited for it to boil he set out a cup with a tea bag in it, then poured a second measure of whiskey for himself, which he cradled as we spoke.

'So, Patterson hasn't destroyed the place yet?' he asked leaning against the kitchen counter. Superintendent Patterson had taken over running the district following Costello's retirement. At the time of his appointment, neither Costello nor I had been wholly convinced about his suitability to the task.

'He's not the worst,' I said. A typical Irish compliment; never quite a positive.

'And what's going on there now?'

'The Commission for the Location of Victims' Remains are doing a dig for Declan Cleary on Islandmore.'

'So I believe. Have they found him yet?'

'Not yet. They did find a *cillin* on one side of the island. They also uncovered a child's body on the other side today. There were possible signs of violence on the body.'

'Is it not part of the *cillin*?' Costello asked.

'It's on the wrong side of the island, apparently. And there are aspects of the burial that don't fit the pattern of the *cillin* burials. I'm told we can't investigate it anyway, because of the legislation governing the digs for the Disappeared.'

'I've never known something like that to stop you before,' Costello said, laughing. He added, 'What about Cleary?'

'Nothing yet,' I repeated.

Costello nodded absently as he sipped at his drink. 'I remember Cleary going missing. The RUC contacted us to be on the lookout for him, but he was already dead at that stage.'

'How did you know?'

'It was after the bridge shooting; Jimmy Callan's boy.'

'Jimmy Callan?'

'A bad bastard, Benedict. He was in and out of jail like a yo-yo during the seventies and eighties. He got early release under the Good Friday agreement. Last I heard, he was back in Strabane and was keeping his head down. He'd not have featured on your radar; his time is past. His boy, Dominic was caught on the river in '76; the Brits executed him; said he was smuggling guns across to the North. Jimmy complained that the cops found nothing on him, but if the son was anything like the father he was up to no good under there. Cleary went the next day; the rumour on our side at the time was that he was passing information to a cop he was friendly with; someone saw him hanging around the RUC station in Strabane. That was the story, but no one ever really pushed it too much. Those things happened then; it was part and parcel of the way things were, you know?'

'Do you think that's what happened to him?'

'God knows. Those people never explained themselves to anyone. Who gave the information to the Commission?'

'I don't know. Someone told them that the body was near Tra na Cnamha.'

'Not Innis na Cnamha?' Costello said, his eyes steely.

'No. Definitely *Tra*. The guy from the dig said it held them up because there was no record of the area being called that.'

'There wouldn't be. The island was called *Innis* – the Isle of Bones – because they used to bury the wee limbo babies there, way back before even the border existed. *Tra* is a different thing. There's only two groups of people who'd use that name: smugglers and net men.'

'Fishing men?'

'Aye. The netters would have run their nets across from the island to the shore after the bridge was brought down there. The smugglers used to have to bring the cattle across the river there, for it was the shortest distance into the south away from checkpoints. If any of the cattle lost their footing in the water, though, they'd never get them back up again. The carcasses would wash onto the shoreline of the island, under where the bridge used to be. The stretch of shore would be covered in rotting cattle bones; it fair ruined the water and the fish stayed clear. Even when all the flesh was gone, the bones and shingle would mix, so as you'd not know which was which. The net men used to talk about it; 'the Beach of Bones', they called it; Tra na Cnamha.'

He raised the glass to his mouth, then paused. 'I'd bet you your tip-off came from either a smuggler or a net man from those days. They might be able to help you with that wee baby you found, too. Try John Reddin; he's in Finnside Nursing home, on the border. He'll be able to help you out. Bring him one of these.'

He raised the glass in salute, then drained it.

'I'll get you that tea,' he said, burping softly as the drink went down.

'John Reddin,' I said. 'Which was he; a smuggler or a net man?'

Costello smiled. 'Both,' he replied.

Chapter Six

THE STORMS OF the weeks previous had abated now, though the first chill of the approaching winter had already sharpened to such an extent that the car windscreen was hoary with frost by the time I left Costello's. On the way home, many of the lampposts I passed bore badly weathered posters advertising a Rally on Lifford Bridge on the 2nd of November, in commemoration of the river shooting which Costello had mentioned. I had already heard more of the details of the incident than Costello had told me.

Dominic Callan was caught in a boat on the river, supposedly carrying guns from the Republic over to the North. He had taken a smuggler's boat and floated downstream, hiding amongst the rushes along the banks of the Foyle. He'd made it almost as far as the Northern side when he was ambushed by a team of Special Branch officers and soldiers who'd been waiting for him along the shoreline.

Those living in the houses along our side of the river, who had an unrestricted view of the scene, said that the boy wasn't given a chance. It was claimed, by those close enough to see, that Callan surrendered, raising his hands above his head. Despite this, he was still shot a number of times in the lower half of his body. He was then left in the boat for three hours until, the army claimed, it was safe to approach. All along the shore of the Foyle his cries could be heard as he died. He was offered neither medical assistance nor last rites.

While the army disputed a number of these claims, there could be little doubt of one salient fact: they had been waiting for the boy, had known that he would be there. Someone had informed on him.

'How was Olly?' Debs asked when I got in. She was already upstairs, getting changed for bed.

'Fine.'

'Could he help you with the baby?'

'He suggested I talk to an old smuggler who used the island as a crossing point after the bridges came down. I'll wait for the postmortem first, to see if there actually is a crime to investigate. Then I might have a word with Harry Patterson and see what he thinks in terms of following it through.'

'Even if there's not a crime involved,' Debbie said, 'you'll want to give that child a story, or a name. Something that can be written above them when you bury them properly, so they don't just disappear.'

I grunted agreement as I got changed. 'Did Shane say anything to you today about Penny?'

She shook her head. 'What about her?'

'Not about her, about him. I think he's feeling jealous of the attention she's getting. He said he was glad the baby hadn't been born because it would have shifted him even further down the pecking-order.'

'That's a nasty thing to say.'

'He's a kid, Debs. Nasty is a given. Maybe we should try doing a little more with him.'

'He's being spoilt, Ben,' Debbie said. 'Penny almost died. We got her back again – there's nothing wrong in us being happy about that. He's being selfish. We can't encourage it.'

I STOOD AT the back door and lit a smoke while I waited for Frank to go out to the toilet before locking him in for the night. He slept in the kitchen now, the old shed where he had slept being too draughty for an animal his age. He struggled slowly down off the lawn onto the path, his thick body seemingly too heavy for his short legs. He was old for a Bassett hound and, in recent years, had slowed considerably. I suspected that the coming winter would be among his last.

I was just putting out my cigarette when my phone rang.

'Devlin,' I said.

'Inspector, this is Laurence Forbes.'

It took me a moment to place the name. Forbes had been a DJ on a local radio station, but had graduated into TV news a few months previous.

'Mr Forbes, what can I do for you?'

'I wondered if you wanted to make a statement,' he said. 'About the child.'

'What child?'

'You found a baby on the island today, I believe,' Forbes said. I wondered how he had heard. The Commission would not have announced the find until cause of death was established.

'Who told you about that?' I asked.

'Sean Cleary,' Forbes said. 'He gave us an interview on the 6 o'clock news about the injustice in the hunt for his father. You'll be able to catch my piece repeated on the bedtime bulletin, if you're quick.'

'I don't have a statement,' I said. 'That information was not for public announcement,' I added, hoping to appeal to Forbes's sense of basic decency.

'It's a little late for that,' Forbes said. 'Switch on the telly and you'll hear about it. Are you sure you won't give a comment?'

'Quite,' I said, hanging up.

The TV in the kitchen was turned on, though muted. It took me a moment to find the relevant channel. I recognized Sean Cleary instantly.

'I'm not happy, no,' he was saying.

'Why?' Forbes asked, the camera focusing on him for the duration of each question. He was in his forties though carried the affectations of men twenty years his junior; his hair was highlighted blond, his skin a permanent glow of bottle-induced tan.

'My father died before I was born. I was never given the chance to meet him, to speak to him. No one ever told my mother or me what happened him, or why they took him from us. We didn't even know for sure that he was dead. We've been living in a state of . . .'

'Limbo?' Forbes suggested.

'Aye,' Cleary said. 'That's just what it has been. Now the men who did that, who took my father from me, think they can just wash their hands of it.'

'You've had thirty-five years of wondering about your father, isn't that right?'

Forbes angled his head sympathetically, even as he stoked Cleary's anger.

'We still don't know for sure why my father was killed. I don't believe that my father was a tout. So, I want whoever reported his burial-spot to the Commission to meet me; I want them to tell me why my father had to die. People know where I live.'

Forbes nodded. 'You need the closure, isn't that right?'

The word closure itself was enough to make me switch off the set. I wondered how Millar would feel about Cleary's interview. While not criticising the Commission, he was clearly angry at the legislation that allowed his father's killers to escape justice.

As I reflected once more on the nameless child that had rested on the island for so many years, I could begin to understand his ire.

Sunday, 28 October

Chapter Seven

'THE INFANT WAS newborn; the remains date probably around thirty to thirty-five years. There are signs on the skull of an assisted delivery, probably using forceps. The craniofacial abnormalities are consistent with Goldenhar syndrome, which would have also brought various associated difficulties.'

Lennie Millar paused reading from the post-mortem report. Superintendent Harry Patterson, who had been doodling on the file pad in front of him on his desk, looked up. It was clear he resented being brought in to the station on a Sunday, but Lennie Millar had insisted that the dig would continue and had requested we meet him to discuss the pathologist's preliminary findings from the previous evening. Millar had been waiting outside the station when I came back from early Mass, keen to get started on the day's dig.

'What is Goldenhar syndrome?'

'It results in all kinds of birth defects, basically. Facial deformity, hearing problems, cleft palate, missing eyes at times. It also can cause spinal problems; vertebrae fusing together, that kind of thing. It would not, however, necessarily lead to death.'

'So, what killed him?'

'Her. The child was a girl. She was throttled.'

Patterson began tapping the top of the pen he held against the pad. 'So, she was murdered.'

Millar glanced down at the report, though the answer was clear.

'Yes. I need to speak with our own lawyers to see where we go from here. At the moment, my inclination is that you can't investigate this. The legislation is very clear: "Any evidence obtained, directly or indirectly, shall not be admissible in any criminal proceedings."'

'This isn't evidence. It's a child,' I said.

'"Any human remains or other item found resulting from a dig shall not be subjected to forensic examination or testing." I didn't make these rules, Inspector, I'm simply telling you what they are.'

'I understand that,' I said. 'But we can't just ignore the killing of a child.'

'A disabled child,' Patterson said.

'I'm not sure I would term the infant as disabled,' Millar said.

'You said it was deformed,' he said. 'To a young mother, look-ing at a baby like that, she'd probably think it disabled.' For a moment I thought he was supporting me, until he stood up from his seat and moved across to the window.

'This child was born disabled. Someone either didn't want it or couldn't cope with it. Thirty odd years ago. What good is going to come from raking over that now? We can't prosecute anyone anyway, isn't that right?' He gestured towards Millar as he spoke.

'You'd need to check, but I'd be surprised if the Director of Public Prosecutions would proceed with any case considering the wording in the legislation. Wording that has never been tested in court.'

'Just because the child was disabled doesn't make it any less valuable than anyone else,' I said.

'I'm not suggesting that,' said Patterson. 'But what do you want to find, Ben? Some wee girl who couldn't cope? Saw that face and panicked and did something unimaginable? Will it mean anything to haul that up now? Christ, the person who did this could be dead.'

'It's not about who did it, Harry,' I said. 'It's about the child. She deserves something. A name, at least.'

'The best we can do for her is have her buried somewhere proper. Or inter her in that *cillin* you found, with the rest of those youngsters.'

'I'm not saying I agree with not following this through,' Millar said softly. 'I'm frustrated, too. But I'm telling you the law as it stands. I have to think about the Commission; the amnesty against prosecution is necessary if our sources are to keep helping us locate these individuals.'

Millar was cut short by the shrill ringing of his phone. He excused himself and moved outside to take the call.

'So you leave it alone now,' Patterson said to me. 'Let them get Cleary off that island and things might settle. We've this bloody rally on the bridge on the 2nd, too. If you ask me, they should stop pissing around with Parades Commission up in the North deciding on this, that and the other, and just ban the whole bloody lot of them. That's the problem with the North – there's a bloody commission for everything.'

Millar walked back into the room, having caught the final few words of Patterson's comment. 'Well, *this* commission has a problem. Someone has gone onto the island and burned out our diggers.'

Chapter Eight

NEWS OF THE attack travelled quickly. Less than half an hour after Millar and I reached the island, a blue car trundled across the temporary bridge the Commission team had erected and pulled to a stop next to our cars. I recognized Laurence Forbes immediately.

'It's the press,' I told Millar. 'The guy who interviewed Cleary last night. Do you want me to chase them?'

'We'll maybe use it to our advantage,' Millar said, and headed up the embankment onto the roadway where Forbes and his cameraman stood.

Standing downwind from them, over the course of the next few minutes I could catch snippets of Millar's responses to Forbes's questioning.

'. . . attack is ridiculous. We have no interest in prosecutions. We can't prosecute. Any information given to us is entirely confidential. No one has anything to fear from our dig; it's about recovering the remains of Mr Cleary and allowing his family the opportunity to grieve, to have a proper Christian burial, to have a grave to visit.'

'To bring closure?' Forbes added, obviously so pleased with having thought of the word that he decided to use it again.

'Quite,' Millar replied. 'Our only concern is to bring the Disappeared home again. There is no other agenda. So the destruction of these diggers is simply an act of wanton vandalism. People have nothing to fear from what we are doing.'

'So how do you respond to the complaints Declan Cleary's own son has made regarding the process?'

'I understand Mr Cleary's sense of frustration,' Millar said. 'We are, however, bound by the legislation. Our role is recovery of bodies and nothing else. So while I empathize with Mr Cleary, we are simply doing what, by law, we must do. I hope that, if we do recover his father, that might bring him some sense of comfort.'

'And any comment on the reports of the child's remains found here . . .?'

I saw the cameraman angle away from Millar, focusing just past his right-hand shoulder. I followed his gaze and saw, in the near corner of the field running below us away from the road, the two burnt-out diggers.

They had been relatively small machines, more useful for targeted digging than for mass earth removal. The remaining chunks of glass where the windscreen had been were yellowed and hung from the rubber stripping which had once sealed the window to the frame. The interior cabin had melted out of shape, the black plastic of the dash now hardened blobs on the outer body of the machine where it had dripped from the opened doorway. Blackened springs and pieces of charred sponge cushioning, trapped in the once molten plastic, were all that remained of the driver's seat.

'Bit of a tit, that one,' Millar said, walking over to me as he nodded back towards Forbes, who was standing with his cameraman, recording a top and tail to the interview. Forbes was being directed to stand in such a way that the diggers would be visible behind him.

'Has anything like this happened before on a dig?' I said, nodding across to the remains of the diggers.

Millar shook his head. 'There's never been any animosity to what we do; in fact we've got to the point where we hardly need to have police about on site. People leave us alone.'

'Why this time? Did his interview with Cleary cause it?'

Millar glanced across at Forbes. 'Possibly. Maybe it drew attention to the fact we were here; some kids might have decided to do some damage. It just sets us back a day. Everywhere will be closed today. We'll have to hire in two diggers from Strabane tomorrow, and two new ditching buckets.'

Presumably he could tell from my expression that I didn't understand, for he continued, 'We can't use buckets with teeth on them when we dig, for obvious reasons. Ditching buckets are flat edged; they scrape off around five inches of surface clay at a time. The ones we had fitted to our diggers may not fit the new machines.'

I nodded as I offered him a cigarette. 'Whereabouts was the *cillin* found again?'

'I'll show you,' he said.

We took the 4x4 across the length of the island, the drive taking a few minutes on the potholed pathways which served as roads. The field in which the *cillin* lay was at the extreme tip of the island, a promontory stretching into the Foyle. As I stood I silently understood the impulse which had driven the bereaved to select this spot as the final resting place of their loved one. The sun had broken through a bank of clouds to the east, as if to shine directly on the spot, its brightness caught on the river's surface and shattered into many pieces. The river's current here, where its streams merged, having been diverted around the island, was slow and lazy, the reflected sunlight winking against the light breeze. The banks of the river on both sides were low-lying, running down to mudflats along the river's edge. The fields beyond were flat and grown to meadow. A single hawthorn tree stood in the centre of the field on the Republic side.

'The border runs right through this spot,' Millar said after a moment. 'It runs up the centre of the river, then cuts diagonally across the island here, presumably along the line of the old railway. It really is neither here nor there.'

'Limbo,' I agreed.

The peace was broken by my mobile ringing. I found myself apologizing to Millar before answering it. I glanced at the screen and noted that I had missed a call already, the signal strength on the screen a single faltering bar.

'Ben? Jim Hendry here.' Hendry was a DI in the Police Service of Northern Ireland, across in Strabane.

'Jim. How're things?'

'I tried calling a few minutes ago but it went to voicemail.'

'I'm on Islandmore, over at the Cleary dig. I must have lost reception.'

'Anything found yet?'

'Nothing. The diggers were petrol bombed last night following Sean Cleary's interview. Everything has been held up. I hope he's happy.'

'I doubt it. He's over here. And he's dead.'

Chapter Nine

HENDRY WAS WAITING for me at the police cordon at the entrance to Beechmount Avenue, just off the main thoroughfare of Melmount Road in Strabane. He wore a loose-fitting suit that served only to accentuate his wiry frame. He raised one hand in salute when he saw me approach, the other hand tugging at the edges of his sandy moustache.

'He's in the playground,' Hendry said, as I ducked under the cordon and followed him along the road.

'What happened to him?'

'Looks like a shooting,' Hendry said, glancing back at me.

'Who found him?'

'A young mother, bringing her kids in for a run-around this morning. He's down at the back.'

'How did you ID him so soon?'

Hendry shook his head. 'Apart from his appearance on TV last night? We found his wallet lying a few feet from the body; emptied apart from his supermarket loyalty card which had his name.'

As we walked, I glanced across to my left. The entire far side of the street was now derelict wasteland. A factory had once stood here but, since its demolition some years earlier, the spot had not been redeveloped. The entrance gates remained locked, but had since been bent off at the hinges on one side to allow the local kids access to the site. A gate hut at the entrance remained, the door burned away. Graffiti was scrawled over its walls, blue bags of empty beer cans piled against the wall nearest us.

'Have they still not done anything with that place?' I asked, nodding across.

'No,' Hendry said. 'It's a bloody pain. Youngsters use it for a drinking den. Plus the Halloween bonnie's in there.'

Traditionally, bonfire night, both North and south, is held not on November the 5th, but on October the 31st. At the centre of the old factory site a pyramid of stacking crates, wooden planks and old tyres rose about thirty feet into the air where the local kids were constructing this year's bonfire. I knew from reports in past years, though, that what started as a good-humoured evening often turned into something more sinister as the night progressed and the young families dispersed and were replaced with drinkers.

We reached the gate of the playground. I noticed now that the railings along either side of the gateway had been covered by heavy white tarpaulin to block from view the sight that lay beyond.

'There's a church just up the road. The post-Mass exodus will be starting soon and we need to restrict the view,' Hendry explained.

I followed him in through the gate. The playground was relatively small and shaped like a dog's leg. At its centre was a large cruciform multicoloured climbing frame with steps leading up one side and a slide running down the other.

I felt the give of the rubberized tarmac matting as I stepped onto it. To my immediate left a tired-looking wooden hippo hung awkwardly at an angle atop a thick painted spring. A swing-set to our right creaked in the wind, the breeze causing the chains of the seats to rattle in mild complaint against the metal A-frame. As we followed the bend of the park, which sloped gently down, I saw Sean Cleary.

At first sight he might have been asleep. He was on his side on the bench at the rear of the playground, his right arm pillowing his face from the wooden slats on which he lay. His legs were pulled up onto the seat, his feet crossed at the ankles. However, his eyes were open, unfocused, already clouded. His stubble seemed unnaturally dark against the pallor of his skin.

Beneath the bench, his blood had settled into a gelatinous puddle, though as I approached I could see that someone had stepped in the pool to the left-hand side, for the surface tension at that edge had broken and a second, smaller pool had run off.

Scene-of-crime officers worked around the body, one using a still camera to record any evidence while a second video-taped the entire process. At the centre of it Sean Cleary lay, unmoving.

'Poor bastard,' I whispered.

'The uniform who was first on scene called it in as a robbery,' Hendry said. 'There was no phone on him; the wallet was emptied and dumped over there.' He pointed to where a small marker stood beside the brown leather wallet.

'Any money?'

'Nothing.'

'What about cause of death?'

'Wounding to the right side of the skull. The ME's already confirmed death but said he didn't recognize the wounding. He thought it was gunshot, but there are multiple small wounds and reddening of the skin he thought unusual. We're waiting for the pathologist to get here.'

I glanced around at the houses surrounding us. In one or two in the block running behind the park, I could see the occupants standing at rear windows, watching down on us.

'No one reported hearing gunshots?' Hendry had mentioned a parent had found the body earlier that morning. Had Cleary's death been a shooting, someone would have heard the shots and reported it.

'No one,' Hendry said. 'But that doesn't mean anything. If the killer's connected to any of the splinter groups doing the rounds, potential witnesses might be too afraid to report anything.'

'Those days are past,' I said.

Hendry raised an eyebrow. 'Do you think?'

As we spoke, I stared across at the old factory site. To one end of the site, the rubble from the building's demolition had been piled up into a small mountain of hard-fill. It backed onto the rear of the shops and post office I had passed on the corner. I could see where skaters had set up planks of wood on milk crates, makeshift ramps to practise jumps. To the far right, almost in line with the playground, sitting to the immediate right of the bonfire, I could see a circle of milk crates set around the charred remains of a fire. I thought I could still see wisps of smoke drifting up from the ashes.

I pointed across to it and said to Hendry. 'Is that fire still lit?'

Hendry followed the direction of my finger, squinting against the light.

'Let's find out.'

THE GROUND WAS littered with shattered bottles, pieces of rock, twists of charred wire from previous fires. The numbers of beer cans, in particular, proliferated the closer we got to the remains of the fire. Sure enough, as we approached, we could smell the sharpness of burning wood being carried to us on the breeze. The fire was almost dead, the last few pieces of plank lying among the embers blackened but for the edges, which were still glowing with a dying light.

'Someone was here last night,' Hendry said. 'Potential suspects.'

'Or witnesses,' I said.

We stood and looked across to the playground. From this angle we could see where Sean Cleary lay. The gate was open, the SOCO team in their blue forensics suits clearly visible where they worked at the body.

'Local kids, probably. We'll need to come back at night when they're here again and see what we can find,' Hendry said.

At that, a black van pulled up, blocking our view of the play-ground, and the forensic pathologist, David Ryan, stepped out.

Chapter Ten

WHEN WE MADE it across to the playground, he had already begun his preliminary investigation. He'd set up a thermometer to measure the ambient temperature before he checked the body temperature. As we approached, he was attempting to flex Cleary's arm, measuring the level of rigor mortis.

He jotted down a few notes in the black book lying on the ground beside him, then, laying almost flat on the ground, examined the underside of the bench. He pushed himself up slightly on his hands and leaned over the blood puddle.

'Someone stepped in his blood,' he said, without looking back at us.

'I know,' Hendry said. 'One of this clumsy lot, no doubt.'

'When was he found?'

'About ten.'

The pathologist shook his head as he stood up.

'The blood has pooled where the surface tension was broken. That means it was still low viscosity. Whoever stepped in that did so within maybe an hour of death.'

'His killer?'

He twisted his mouth as he considered the question. 'I couldn't say. You'll get a decent print from it, though. If the blood is on the bottom of the shoe, you'll find prints for a few yards from here.'

'How long since time of death?' Hendry asked.

'Maybe five hours to eight. Sometime between two and five, I'd say. I'll know better when I get him on the table.'

Ryan pulled a pair of glasses from inside the forensics suit he wore, then sealed it up again. Putting the glasses on he moved across to the top of the bench where Cleary lay. He raised Cleary's head slightly and began examining the skull.

'Lift this,' he said.

Hendry and I moved across to the body, Hendry handing me a pair of gloves. Standing either side of Ryan, who knelt again beneath us for a closer view of Cleary's skull, we held the head gently between us.

Hendry winked at me as we did so.

'So how's it looking, doc?' Hendry asked. 'Do you think he'll pull through?'

'It's unlikely,' Ryan replied, deadpan. 'Someone's shot him.'

'The ME thought that. But he said the wounding was unusual. He wasn't sure.'

'Turn his head a little,' Ryan said. He reached across for a thin throat probe, then used it to brush back Cleary's hair from the wounding. From such close proximity, I could understand the confusion. There seemed to be several small wounds, closely packed together, all quite deep, but encircled by a red ring on the skin, perhaps two inches wide.

'There's none of the burning one would associate with a gunshot wound at close range. But the relative tightness of the wounding pattern would suggest this was a close-range shooting.'

'So?'

'So, I'd say your killer used a silencer. And not a particularly good one; either old or homemade.'

'Why?'

'The baffles inside a silencer help to trap the expanding gas as a bullet is fired,' Ryan explained, sitting back on his haunches. 'That stops the sound, but also slows the bullet. If the baffles aren't aligned properly, the bullet can strike them inside the barrel and shatter. In that case, you get this kind of pattern; several tiny bullet wounds from each particle, rather than a single bigger wound. Misaligned baffles suggest something old or homemade.'

'The silencer would explain the lack of burning tattoos on the skin too,' Hendry offered.

'And the lack of reports of gunshots from last night,' I added.

Ryan nodded. 'Silencers tend to leave erythematous wounding rather than abraded, at close range; the disproportionately wide red ring on the skin is typical of it.'

'I was just thinking the same thing,' Hendry said to me, earning a dirty look from Ryan.

'You can put him down now,' he said, grunting softly as he stood. 'Of course, the redness also suggests vital reaction; his body trying to heal itself. It wouldn't be so pronounced in immediate death.'

'Meaning?'

'He didn't die instantly. He was alive for sometime after he was shot. Maybe ten or fifteen minutes. Maybe more.'

'How would a gunshot wound to the head not kill him instantly? Especially if the shooter is skilled enough to be using a silencer.'

'Probably the bullet shattering before impact,' he said, his hands at his side.

'Wouldn't people have heard him screaming, if he took that long to die? There are houses all around.'

'The force of the shot may well have stunned him, then he died slowly over a period of time. But I suspect we'll find he bled out as the heart kept pumping.'

A SOCO who had been working to our left called Hendry across.

'The wallet, sir,' he said. 'We've pulled loads of fingerprints from it.'

Chapter Eleven

HENDRY AND I stepped out of the playground while the SOCO team got to work, combing the site for evidence. We stood in front of the tarpaulin while I had a smoke.

'So what's the story on the dig for his old man?' Hendry asked.

'They got a tip-off a while back. They've walked the site and brought in a dog. They were planning on digging today but their diggers were burnt out last night in an arson attack.'

'On the same night Cleary himself was shot? No such thing as coincidence.'

'Did you see his interview?'

Hendry nodded. 'Quality viewing.'

'We thought the attack on the island might have been prompted by it.'

'So might this. Maybe someone did get in contact with him. Someone who wasn't too happy about the case being reopened.'

'Yet the Commission were tipped off. So someone involved in the killing wanted to come clean.'

'And someone else didn't.'

I reflected again on what Costello had said to me the previous evening.

'Do you know Jimmy Callan?' I asked. 'His name was mentioned in connection with Declan Cleary's killing in '76.'

Hendry shook his head. 'He was a suspect, mind you, but he was a guest of Her Majesty's at the time. Of course, that doesn't mean he didn't order it from the inside. He was heavily involved back then; he'd have had any number of people lining up to do it for him.'

'Would he kill the son for asking too many questions?'

'Why don't we ask him? I'll come with you if you're going across to Lifford to inform next of kin about this.'

'Me? I'm telling Mary Collins her son's dead?'

Hendry smiled. 'I thought you'd never offer.'

JIMMY CALLAN'S HOUSE was located on the Park Road in Strabane. The area was low lying, running parallel to the River Foyle. At high tide, during the autumn rains, the fields bordering the river became little more than floodplains for months on end. As a consequence, the area had not been developed for property to quite the same extent as other outlying areas of Strabane.

Callan's house was on our left-hand side as we drove down the road. It was an old cottage which seemed in some need of renovation, especially when compared with the much grander affair which squatted next to it.

Hendry pulled into the driveway of Callan's and, as I knocked on the door, I saw him shift across to the front window and look in, leaning against the glass, using his hand to reduce the glare.

I knocked a second time, but there was no response.

'Let me try,' Hendry said, coming over to me. 'It might not be locked.'

He began to fumble in his pocket for a bunch of keys, rattling at the handle as he did so.

'Can I help you?'

When we looked across to the source of the shout, we saw the occupant of the big house next to Callan's standing at the wall which separated the two properties.

'We're looking for James Callan,' I called.

'What's he doing with those keys?' he shouted, nodding towards Hendry. The man was stout, grey haired, in his sixties, I guessed, but his eyesight was sharp. 'I'll call the police.'

'I am the police,' Hendry called back, pocketing the keys and leaving the doorway.

The man snorted disdainfully. 'Figures,' he muttered.

'We're looking for James Callan,' Hendry said again. 'Have you seen him?'

'He's not in,' the man replied.

'We've established that,' Hendry said. 'Have you seen him recently? Do you know where he is?'

'He left this morning,' the man said.

'Did he say where he was going?'

The man shook his head. 'He'd a bag packed, though, so I'd say he'll not be back for a bit. He asked me to put his bin out at the weekend and keep an eye on the house for him.'

'How did he seem?'

The man frowned bewilderedly.

'Was he relaxed, like he was going on holiday? Anxious? Panicked?'

The neighbour considered my question for a moment. 'He seemed a bit flustered. Like he didn't want to hang around too long. He left me money to pay the milkman for him and wouldn't wait for me to give him the change. The incident last night can't have helped.'

Hendry and I stopped and turned towards the man. 'What incident?'

'I shouldn't get involved,' the man began, moving closer to the hedge and, thereby, inviting us to do likewise. He glanced at Callan's house as if afraid that Callan might somehow be listening, even though he was the one who had told us it was empty.

'There was a young fella here last night. He and James got into a row about something. We could hear it through the wall.' He wrinkled his nose in disdain. 'The walls between the houses are very thin,' he added.

'What were they rowing about?'

'They're not that thin. I could hear raised voices and that, but God knows what it was about.'

I sensed there was something the man wasn't telling us, something significant that he was holding back for a finale.

'But did you recognize the person with whom Mr Callan was rowing?'

As the neighbour glanced around again for listeners, Hendry and I leaned further forward. 'I don't know his name,' the neighbour said, 'but I did see him again. He was on TV last night, being interviewed about that dig going on over on the island.'

'He was here last night?' Hendry asked. 'At what time?'

'Around eightish, it must have been. The wife was watching her soaps and I had to get her to turn them down to hear.' He blushed slightly. 'I mean up, to hear them better over the shouting.'

'What time did he leave?' I asked.

'Maybe five, ten minutes later. He arrived in a taxi, but he walked back down the road again afterwards.'

'You're sure about this?'

The man nodded.

'You've been very helpful,' Hendry said. 'We might have to send someone out to take a statement from you. We'll just check around the back.'

The man stared quizzically at Hendry, clearly wondering why the need for a statement. By the time he'd see the lunch-time news, he'd work out why.

As we moved around the side of the house, Hendry checked each window in turn. 'Looks like there's no one around, right enough,' he commented.

We'd reached the rear of the property. Callan's garden was separated from the river by one small field. From his back fence, we could see across to Islandmore, past the metal girders jutting out of the river, to where the burnt-out remains of the Commission's diggers stood.

'Maybe the sight of the digging spooked him,' I suggested. 'If he was involved in Cleary's disappearance, it would be difficult to stand and watch from his back window while the body's being exhumed.'

'Either that or he followed Cleary's son after he left, shot him well away from his own house and he's gone on the run. Either way, he's guilty about something.'

Chapter Twelve

MARY COLLINS OPENED the door almost before I had rung the bell, and I suspected that she had been watching our arrival. Indeed, with the dig going on for her missing partner, I suspected she had simply been waiting for news. I did not imagine that she could have expected the news we were bringing.

'Inspector Devlin,' she said to me, then smiled at Jim Hendry. 'Hello,' she said.

'This is PSNI Detective Inspector Jim Hendry,' I said. 'Can we come in, Mrs Collins?' She smiled anxiously when I spoke.

'Have you found him? Have you found Declan yet?'

'We're not here about Declan, I'm afraid, Mrs Collins. We'd best go inside.'

Her smile faltered. 'What's wrong? What's happened?'

'We have some bad news, Mrs Collins,' Hendry said, his cap clamped tightly under his right arm. 'We're here about Sean.'

'Sean's not here; he . . .' she glanced backwards into the house, as if Sean was waiting inside. Then she turned again, her face drawn, the terror of the situation only beginning to hit her. She covered her mouth with her hand, shook her head. 'You're not . . . you . . . Has he been hurt? Where is he?'

'We'd best go inside,' I repeated.

She turned from us, moving up the hallway. Suddenly she lurched to one side, her legs collapsing under her. I only managed to grip her under her arms to prevent her falling. Hendry shifted quickly in beside me and, together, we hoisted her to her feet and brought her into the living room. We lay her on the sofa, all the time speaking to her, encouraging her to come round. Her skin was pale, her face clammy with sweat.

'I'll get an ambulance,' Hendry said, taking out his phone.

Mrs Collins began to revive, moaning softly. I could see her eyelids flutter quickly, could see the shifting of her eyes beneath the thin film of their lids.

'Give it a moment,' I said. 'She's coming round.'

After a few minutes, she had recovered sufficiently that she could sit up, though we insisted that she keep her legs up on the sofa. Hendry fetched her a glass of water.

'I'm sorry,' she repeated. 'I don't know what . . .' her voice faltered into a mumble.

'Would you like us to contact someone for you, Mrs Collins?'

'My husband,' she said. 'My husband is out golfing. His number is on my mobile, on the . . . thing.' She waved her hand vaguely in the direction of the corner where a coffee table stood, the mobile phone atop it.

'What happened to Sean?' she asked. 'I thought you were here about Declan. I thought you'd found him. But not Sean. Where is he?'

I glanced at Hendry. 'I'm sorry, Mrs Collins. Sean's been found over in Strabane. He's dead.'

HER HUSBAND ARRIVED twenty minutes later; a short, wheezy man, his eyes wide and guileless, his face flushed from his morning exertions on the golf course. He sat on the sofa next to his wife and held her while she spoke, shaking his head and staring with the vacant expression of one who has become observer rather than participant in his own family's story.

'Sean never knew Declan,' Mrs Collins said. She clenched her sodden tissue as tightly in one hand as she gripped her husband's hand in the other. 'I always regretted he never knew him. Not that he needed a father,' she added, nudging lightly against her husband, having remembered that he was sitting next to her. 'Sam always did right by Sean.'

She smiled briefly at her husband, then continued. 'I was expecting when Declan went missing. Seven months gone. When he went, I thought he'd run out on me; taken cold feet.'

'Did he give any indication that he was likely to do so?' I asked.

She shook her head. 'He was decent. Not the brightest, maybe, but decent. He was worried about providing for us; those were his words. He was an orderly in the old St Canice's. It didn't pay very well; he was panicking a bit about how he'd afford to look after me and a baby.'

Hendry raised an enquiring eyebrow.

'St Canice's was a mother-and-baby home,' I explained.

'He was hoping for better,' she went on. 'Then he just vanished.'

'Disappeared,' her husband added, then blushed at having interrupted.

'Sean never asked about his daddy until he went to school. I told him he had gone away. I couldn't say he'd died, for he'd have asked to see his grave and, well, there was none. Then I met Sam and decided to marry. I gave Sean the choice of using his daddy's name or Sam's and he stayed with Cleary.'

She glanced at her husband and added quickly, 'Not that he didn't love Sam. He was younger and, you know, wanted to stay loyal or something to his father.'

'I understand,' I said. Collins rubbed his wife's hand soothingly as she spoke.

'Do you know where he was last night?' Hendry asked. 'Sean?'

Mrs Collins stared at him blankly for a moment, the shift from past to present taking a little time to register with her.

'He went out to see someone,' she said. 'He'd become fired up about his daddy's body being looked for. He'd always known he was dead, but when the dig started, it made it more . . . real for him. I think it was the first time he thought of it as having actually happened.'

'Do you think he was trying to find out what happened to his father?'

She shrugged. 'After we met the people from the Commission and passed on the map, they told us about the call they'd got. Sean got so angry.'

'Because of his father?' I said.

'Kind of. More about the fact that they wouldn't investigate it. They told us their job was to recover the body, not to find who killed him.'

'Sean couldn't quite accept it,' Mr Collins said. 'He resented the fact that he never had a chance to meet his father. That and the fact that someone might get away with murder.'

'I told him, enough stuff has happened, enough bad stuff and suffering and pain, that it would do no good. What does it matter now if they lift some poor young fella, doing as he was told thirty years ago? It'll not bring Declan back. He's gone, life changed, moved on without him,' Mary Collins said.

'Disappeared,' Mr Collins said.

'Has Declan any family living?'

Mrs Collins shook her head. 'Both his parents were dead when I met him. He'd no other family. Just Sean. Only Sean.' With that, her sobbing began again. She bowed her head, her husband angling his against hers, embracing her tightly, his arm around her shoulder as he whispered in her ear the perennial mistruth that everything would be okay.

Chapter Thirteen

I DROPPED HENDRY back across to the North. As he got out of the car he mentioned that they would be running a reconstruction of Cleary's final movements on Beechmount Avenue the following evening, if I wanted to come across.

The clouds were gathering overhead as I crossed the border into the Republic again. I noticed more of the posters advertising the rally on the 2nd of November hanging from the lamp-posts, tattered from the high winds of early October. As I slowed to read one, I spotted the entrance to Finnside Nursing Home behind the Community Hospital just to my left. Patterson had told me I couldn't investigate the death of the island child. But that didn't mean I couldn't talk to anyone about it. I swung right and stopped at the Off Sales, then cut across the road into Finnside.

It had been some time since I was last there, but once inside the door I recalled immediately the familiar smell of disinfectant and urine, which the owner had attempted to mask with incense sticks and votive candles, their collective scents and smoke drifting ceiling-wards as if in offering.

I stopped at the office to the left of the foyer, where the owner, Mrs McGowan, was sitting in discussion with one of the staff. The decor had changed little since last I had been there; the carpet was still wine red, the walls painted neutral shades of magnolia and yellow and hung with prints of Constable landscapes. I also recalled with some sadness that, during my last visits here, I had encountered a young woman named Yvonne Coyle who, it transpired, had been responsible for the deaths of several people and had ended up dead herself inside the ruins of the Borderlands dance hall a little further along the road from here.

Mrs McGowan came out to see me, closing the door behind her, leaving the staff member sitting in her office.

'I'm here to see John Reddin,' I said, after we had exchanged pleasantries.

'He'll be up in the lounge,' Mrs McGowan said. 'We've a band playing on a Sunday afternoon; Mr Reddin never misses it.'

I followed the corridor along the direction she had pointed. It was a relatively large lounge, over-furnished with mismatched easy chairs, most high backed, and several bookcases of large-print books and tattered paperbacks. At the far end, in front of a large TV, two musicians were setting up to perform; one was connecting leads to the back of a keyboard while the other was busying himself with tuning his guitar.

There were already almost a dozen of the home's occupants sitting in the room, connected by their seeming isolation. A nurse was moving amongst them with a tray of small plastic tubs containing a variety of medicines. With each person she carefully selected the tub, watched as they took the tablets, then marked it off on a sheet of paper sitting on the tray, before moving on to the next person.

'Excuse me,' I said. 'I'm looking for Mr Reddin.'

She stared at me appraisingly. 'You're not a relative,' she said.

'I'm a Garda inspector. I was hoping to speak with him for a moment.'

'That's him across there,' she said, nodding towards the far corner. A man sat upright in an arm chair. He was heavy bodied, his face jowly and ruddy, his hair thick, its whiteness slightly yellowed like wild-sheep fleece. He tapped on the arm of the chair as if in anticipation of the rhythm of the music he was waiting to hear.

'Mr Reddin,' I said, moving across to him. 'I'm Garda Inspector Benedict Devlin. I was wondering if I could speak to you.'

He looked up at me. One of his eyes was clouded in the centre, as if thick with cataracts.

'Come closer,' he said.

I squatted down to his level, near the seat. 'I'm Inspector Benedict Devlin. Chief Super Costello suggested I speak to you.' I handed him a brown bag containing a bottle of whiskey, as Costello had suggested.

'Old Elvis isn't Chief Super anymore,' Reddin said, wagging his finger at me. He slipped the bottle from my grip with his other hand and hid it down the gap between his leg and the arm of the chair. 'Once a smuggler,' he commented, winking conspiratorially. I had assumed that his presence in the home was due to mental degeneration, but it seemed I was wrong.

'So what can I help the Garda with?'

'Tra na Cnamha.'

He nodded, his good eye rolling to the side, as if he were trying to recall the place.

'Declan Cleary.'

'You knew he was there?' I said.

'I heard on the TV today,' he said. 'What can I help you with?'

'The person who passed on the information about Cleary's body being on the island referred to Tra na Cnamha. Costello said the only people who knew that name would have been smugglers and net men. There aren't that many of either left. He thought I should speak to you.'

'The old smugglers have all gone – all the stuff across the border now is organized criminals' doing. Not like us; what we did was harmless. Foodstuffs and that.'

I decided not to get involved in arguments about so-called victimless crimes.

'You started young in them days,' he said, laughing lightly. 'Me mother took me across to Strabane when I was just a wee'un. She'd be over to buy sugar; you could bring a two-pound bag back with you, but not tobacco. The shops in Strabane used to hide a couple of ounces of shag inside the sugar bags. And my mother used to tie her stocking to the inside of me belt, running down inside me legs. You'd get them filled with flour and sugar and that; or butter, flattened and pressed against your thighs when you walked. The customs must have known, the shuffling of all the kids across the bridge like they was desperate not to wet themselves. Now it's drugs and oil and that. It's not the same.'

'Who would still be around from the early-seventies?' I asked.

'Smugglers?' Reddin said. 'Not many. There were only three or four of us running the border by that stage anyway; the Fisheries men confiscated all the boats. Then when they shot that young fella Callan under the bridge, well that stopped everyone. Being caught bringing across a few cows was one thing; being shot for a Provo was something else.'

He leaned past me and winked sharply at someone. 'All right, Maisie,' he said. 'I'll be looking a waltz later, whatever time the boyos get started.' He smiled wolfishly.

I turned to the recipient of his request. Opposite us sat a small, frail woman, her skin fine, her hands small and neat where they folded on her lap. She raised one slender hand and shooed away the comment. Despite that, her face was bright and keen, her smile at the comment radiant.

'She's a lovely old girl,' Reddin said. 'Poor woman, no one ever visits her. I'm here five years, I've never once seen any of her family come near the place; even at Christmas. They just let her vanish.'

'How about you?' I asked. 'Do you like it here?'

'It's all right,' Reddin said. 'My eyesight kept going, and I couldn't gauge things anymore. I'd be pouring tea and not know I'd missed the cup till I'd scorched me feet with the boiling water.'

'I'm sorry to hear that,' I said.

Reddin shrugged. 'There's worse things happen to people. The band will be starting soon, son, so you may finish your questions.'

I nodded. 'I appreciate your speaking to me. Can you think of anyone from that time; net men or smugglers who would still be about?'

Reddin's clear eye swivelled toward me. 'I thought anything that went to the Disappeared crew couldn't be investigated.'

'It can't,' I said. 'They found a child on the island. That's what I'm more interested in.'

Reddin nodded. 'The place was coming down with them; wee limbo babies.'

'This one is different. From the late-seventies probably. We think it was murdered.'

Reddin squinted slightly, as if trying to focus on something.

'The bridges were down by then. Whoever took that child onto the island needed a boat. Net men and smugglers would be the most likely to provide transit across,' I explained. 'They would know who brought the baby across. It was buried in another part of the island from the rest of the *cillín*.'

'The same goes for Cleary, too, if you find him on that place – someone would have had to bring him across, too. Someone could get into trouble for that,' Reddin said shrewdly.

'No one can be prosecuted in either case. To be honest, I just want to know what happened to the child. I want to find out her name. So she doesn't just disappear.'

Reddin considered the response. 'In terms of smugglers, the only ones I knew of left were Pete Cuthins and Alex Herron. The net men were different. Their numbers have been dropping constantly; the Fisheries stopped them as well. Bloody stupid, too. You can have a thousand people with rods fishing above the Lifford bridge, but the net men fishing for a living beyond the bridge is having their licences cut every year. There would only be three left I can think of: Tony Hennessy, Finbar Buckley and Seamus O'Hara.'

'Thank you, Mr Reddin,' I said, as I jotted the names down.

'O'Hara might be able to help you best. He was the ferryman, you know?' He winked blindly as he spoke.

'The ferryman?'

'From when people used the island for their babies. A *cillín*.'

I nodded, worried that the conversation was simply going to be repeated.

'It means little church, did you know that?' Reddin said, raising his chin interrogatively.

'I didn't.'

'O'Hara ferried across the babies. To bury them. The church knew all about it; they were happy for him to do it.'

I could see that Reddin was no longer looking at me, his vision seemingly locked on something in the middle distance, which I knew he could not see.

'I used him once. The missus lost one of ours. He came too early, hadn't a chance. I called the priest but he wouldn't do anything for us. He said a quick prayer. We asked him to baptize the wee critter. Padraig, we wanted to call him, but he wasn't allowed, he said. "Put him in a shoebox, with a scrap of white wrapped round him and take him to Seamus O'Hara. I'll tell him to expect you; down at the island."'

The whiteness of his eyes shone through the tears that had gathered over them.

'It was a spring morning, the mist on the river just beginning to burn off. I carried him down there, the shoebox under me arm, like a lunchbox, like I was going to work for the day. Marion wanted to see him one more time; she wrapped him in a white sheet. We blessed him ourselves, with holy water. I didn't give a tinker's curse whether it was right or wrong. We christened him ourselves, then we laid him in the box like he was sleeping. Marion wouldn't let me dry the water off his wee head. I could still see the dampness of the cross we'd made with our thumbs when I reached the island.'

He turned towards me, lifting his hand and wiping his eyes.

'O'Hara was there. Him and his boat coming across through the mist. "I've it dug already," he said. "I'll take care of it." I wanted to go with him, but he wouldn't let me. "You can't cross over," he said. "Don't be fretting about it. I'll look after it for you." I had to hand him over the wee boy, laid the box on the floor of the boat.

O'Hara stood there waiting, until I palmed him a few florins. Then he pushed away from the bank. I never saw where he laid him.'

He raised his head as if to stymie any further tears. 'I'll tell you one thing, though. That wee lad is with Marion now, and the two of them are looking down on me, waiting for me to join them. Padraig was on God's right hand the day he was buried, baptized or not, and no bastard will ever tell me otherwise.'

I laid my hand on Reddin's arm. 'I'm sorry, sir,' I said.

My speaking seemed to bring him back to the present, for he wiped his face quickly with the sleeve of his cardigan and turned to me. 'I didn't give you those names,' he said, raising a finger towards me. As he spoke he looked past me, waving and smiling genially to one of the other residents who was being led into the room.

'Your eyesight seems to be okay now,' I said, following his gaze.

'I've no bloody idea who they all are,' he muttered, blinking like Tiresias as he continued to wave. 'They're all just outlines. I imagine they're good-looking, which helps. I know Maisie, for she always sits in that seat. The rest of them are a blur.'

Chapter Fourteen

My sergeant, Joe McCready, was standing in the small kitchen in the station in Lifford when I stopped off on the way home. He was pouring himself a coffee with one hand while his other held his mobile.

'That's fine, I think. Didn't he say that was okay?' His tone was nervous, the speech hesitant, unconvinced.

I could hear the ghost of the voice on the other end of the call while I poured myself the final coffee from the flask.

'Maybe you should phone and double-check with him.'

He nodded, though the speaker could clearly not see the gesture. 'I'm not worrying,' he said. He shifted away from where I was standing and lowered his voice. 'I just want to be sure everything is okay.'

I took my coffee and walked down to the office where we worked. It had once been a sizable cleaning store but had been converted for a murder enquiry and had never been changed back again. As I sat down, the door opened and McCready followed me in. Outside I could hear the main phone ringing.

'Everything all right, Joe? I thought Burgess was the only one in today.'

He nodded. 'I've bits and pieces of paperwork to do. I fancied getting out of the house for half an hour, to be honest.'

I nodded at the phone still in his hand. 'Things getting a bit heavy?'

'Ellen's having contractions. But it's too early. She says they're Branston Hicks.'

'Braxston. I remember Debbie having them.'

'They're okay, aren't they?'

I nodded. 'She's how long left?

'About six weeks.'

'They're perfectly normal.'

During the conversation, our desk sergeant, Burgess, had pushed open the door. He held a Post-it note in his hand.

'I'm too long in the job when the station chat is about babies,' he said, without humour. 'This one will be right up your street. It's the partner of one of the Cashell girls. He asked for you directly, Inspector. Apparently his missus's hearing a baby crying in her baby monitor.'

'What?'

'I don't make the calls, Inspector, I just answer them. He asked for you by name; what do you want me to do?'

THE LAST TIME I had seen Christine Cashell had been a year or so after I'd investigated the murder of her sister, Angela. Christine's father had been a career criminal, a petty thief and enforcer whose actions had resulted in the death of his daughter. Christine had had a baby then and was working in the local pharmacy, despite being only in her late teens; she would now be in her mid-twenties.

When we knocked at the door, it was a young ferret-faced man who answered, snuffling into his hand.

'Are you Devlin?'

'That's right. This is Garda McCready.'

He raised his head in acknowledgement of Joe, then nodded at me. 'She wants you.'

He stood back to allow us to enter the house, pointing across the hallway to where a door lay ajar. We passed him and went into the room. Christine was lying on the sofa. Though older, she had not changed that much physically. Her red hair was still striking in its lustre, her expression still one of defiant vulnerability. But, when I saw her now, it was clear something fundamental had changed, something had broken inside her.

She smiled when she saw us, though the gesture did not reach her eyes, which were puffy and raw with crying. I noticed that a baby monitor perched on the arm of the sofa by her head, its hiss a constant, unbroken soundtrack to our conversation.

'Hello, Inspector.'

'Miss Cashell. Or are you *Mrs* now?'

It was Christine's partner who responded. 'Christ, no,' he said quickly. 'We're not married. We've moved in together.'

Christine looked at him and I suspected for a moment that the speed of his denial had hurt her.

'You wanted to see me, Christine.'

She nodded. 'Thanks for coming out. I wondered if you were still about.'

'Is everything okay?' The man's fidgeting, her recent tears, his nervous pacing near the doorway bore all the hallmarks of the aftermath of a domestic-violence incident.

'She's hearing a baby crying. In that thing,' he nodded towards the monitor. He snuffled again into one hand, rubbing at his nose, then wedged his fist into his pocket again.

'What's your name, sir?'

'Andrew,' he said, pausing in his pacing. 'Andrew Dunne.'

'Would you like to sit down, Mr Dunne, and tell me what's wrong?'

He stared at me a second, as if reluctant to capitulate to my request. In the end, he moved across to the armchair in the corner and rested one buttock on the arm of it in a vague compromise.

'She says she's hearing things in that thing. A baby crying.'

I nodded, looking at Christine. She returned my glance, her eyes a little wide.

'Is that not normal?'

'It's not my baby crying.'

'And where is your baby?' I said, smiling. I glanced around the room, half expecting to see a child sleeping in a carry-cot, but could see none. I nodded to Joe who drifted out into the hallway to take a look around.

'My baby's Michael.'

I nodded. 'That's a nice name. You have an older child, don't you?'

Christine smiled briefly. 'Tony. He's at school.'

Dunne stood again. 'You need to do something. She's balling her eyes out constantly, hearing a baby crying in that thing.'

'Someone hurt it,' Christine said.

'What?'

'Last night. I heard the baby crying,' she explained. 'I heard him crying. I thought he was Michael. I asked Andrew to check but he wouldn't . . . you wouldn't check.'

'It wasn't Michael crying, Chrissie,' Dunne said. 'I told you that.'

'He cried on and on. Then I heard someone shout at him. I think they hit him. He didn't cry after that. I've been listening all night, but he won't cry.'

'And you're sure it's not your baby.'

'It's not our baby,' Dunne replied tersely, gritting his teeth. 'I told her that. It won't go in.'

Joe McCready wandered back into the room. He looked at me and shrugged lightly.

'Where is Michael now?' I asked again.

Dunne shook his head.

'He's sleeping,' Christine said.

'Jesus,' Dunne snapped, suddenly leaving the room.

'Are you okay for a second, Christine?' I asked. 'Garda McCready will take a statement from you.'

I nodded to Joe, who moved over and sat on the edge of the sofa beside Christine. She smiled wanly, lifting the monitor and cradling it in her hand, her eyes fixed on the display.

Dunne was in the kitchen when I went out, lighting a cigarette.

'Is there something I'm missing?' I asked.

'She's the one with something missing. A fucking screw,' he said, pointing towards the living room.

'Maybe keep your voice down, sir,' I said. 'You might wake the baby.' I had meant the final comment to be light hearted. It had the opposite reaction.

'There is no fucking baby,' Dunne spat, flecks of saliva catching in the faint moustache of hair on his upper lip.

'What?'

'She lost her baby. Stillborn. There is no baby, there's no crying, there's nothing. She lost the baby, now she's lost her fucking mind.'

'Why is she listening to the baby monitor, if you don't have a baby?'

'Because she's nuts,' Dunne stated, as if talking to a child. 'She bought it before the baby came. I came in one night and she's sitting with it on. In case Michael cries; I'm up and down those fucking stairs every ten minutes checking on an empty room for her.'

He stared at me plaintively, a thin column of ash dangling from the end of his cigarette. It dropped onto the floor, shattering lightly on the linoleum.

'I never signed up for all this . . . shit, you know,' he said, his anger spent now. 'I just wanted to do right by her.'

He slumped heavily onto the seat by the table, propped up his head on his hand, his elbow resting on his knee. He took one drag from the cigarette, then stubbed it out on the saucer he was using as an ashtray.

'I'm sorry,' I said.

'Everyone's sorry,' he replied bitterly. 'Doctors, nurses, priests, everyone's sorry.'

I stood a moment before excusing myself to go back in to Christine who, no doubt, had heard the entire exchange.

'I didn't mean none of that,' Dunne said behind me. 'Sorry I took it out on you.'

I nodded, then moved back into the living room as Christine wiped her eyes free of tears. Joe McCready looked little better and I realized that, for a man worried about his pregnant wife, this call-out might not have been the best for assuaging his fears.

'I'm sorry for your loss, Christine,' I said. 'I truly am.'

She wiped her nose with the back of her hand, sniffed loudly. A final tear trickled down her cheek and she wiped it away, too.

'I'm not mad,' she said. 'I did hear crying. Someone hurt that baby. You believe me, don't you?'

She looked from Joe to me and back, willing us to believe her.

'Of course,' I said.

But she must have read something different in my eyes, for she turned from me.

'I'm sorry I bothered you,' she said. 'I thought you'd care.'

DUNNE STOOD AT the doorway with us. The darkness had thickened, but the street lights along the pavement outside offered no light, being little more than decapitated poles with occasional wires hanging loose from the top of them.

'This place doesn't help,' he said, raising his chin slightly as he gestured towards the estate beyond.

I could understand his concern. Island View, where they lived, was one of a number of ghost estates along the border; housing developments begun just before the property bubble burst and never completed. The skeletal outlines of the houses standing around us were not the only unfinished element of the estate; the road was potholed and weedy, the pavements loosely comprising hard-fill but no tarmac.

The houses were in varying states of completeness. Island View was begun during the final yelps of the Celtic Tiger by a speculator who convinced the banks to loan him enough to build eighty houses. The money had run out halfway through, the contractors folded, the developer long since fled to the North, where he had claimed bankruptcy to avoid having to pay any of the men who had worked on the houses. It was just as well; the development had been built on the expectation of the continued influx of immigrant workers to bolster an Irish workforce wealthy enough to be choosy about the employment they would seek. The death of the Tiger had seen the workers leave again, and the jobs no one would take became the jobs everyone wanted but no one could get anymore.

Only thirty of the houses had ever been fully finished; they sat along the first street of the estate, near the road, completed early to attract potential buyers to set deposits on the houses further back, out of view, squatting spectrally in the dark. In addition to the €400,000 each of the thirty buyers had paid for their homes, there were unforeseeable additional costs: the empty houses further back in the estate were a magnet for couples seeking quiet spots for half an hour, or kids, too young to get into the bars, looking for shelter as they drank their carry-outs on a Saturday night.

'It's a rough-looking spot, all right,' McCready said.

'It's a shit-hole,' Dunne said. 'The builder used the cheapest stuff he could get in the houses. We were in a month and the plaster started falling off the ceilings. The bloody door locks were so cheap we found out our door key could open all the neighbours' houses as well, and theirs ours.'

'Builds neighbourly trust, I'd imagine,' I said.

'Can they do nothing to get it finished?' McCready said.

'Who? The Council?' Dunne snuffled into his hand, rubbing his nose vigorously. 'They won't even fix the shitters.'

Of all the problems facing the inhabitants of Island View, the worst by a stretch was the fact that the sewage-pumping station had broken soon after the developer had fled the jurisdiction, meaning that the effluent of the households pumped out of a pipe to the rear of the estate into a mound in the corner of a field.

In autumn, sodden nappies and the detritus of each household floated in the pools created by the heavy rains. Even that, though, was preferable to what happened to the same area in the heat of summer.

'It's not right,' Dunne added. 'Christine shouldn't have to live in a place like this. I wanted better for her. You know?'

I nodded, my estimation of the man rising significantly.

Chapter Fifteen

As we reached the main road, having left Christine Cashell's, a red BMW pulled in past us and continued on towards the back of the estate. I was fairly certain I recognized the driver.

'I want to check something for a minute, Joe,' I said, doing a U-turn and following the car.

The driver of the BMW was a local thug named Peter O'Connell. We'd been aware of O'Connell for months now; he'd slotted into the gap left by Lorcan Hutton, one of our most proficient drug dealers, who had been murdered a year previous.

We followed at a distance, helped somewhat by the fact that I was driving my own vehicle rather than a marked squad car. Finally we saw the flash of the brake lights as the car pulled up outside number 67, one of the unoccupied houses to the rear of the development. It was in relatively good repair in comparison with the shells surrounding it; notably it was one of the few unoccupied houses that had managed to maintain all its windows unbroken.

O'Connell climbed out, shutting the door and locking it with his key fob. He was a tall fella, just shy of 20, his face still red and pock-marked from adolescent acne, his hair spiked and tipped. He glanced around, then placed one finger tight against his left nostril and snorted the right one clear of mucus onto the pavement. Pinching his nose between finger and thumb, he wiped it clean, then rubbed his hand against his trouser leg. He hoisted at his belt, pulling his trousers fractionally closer to his waist. Such was their style, they dropped again towards his hips, exposing the white of his underwear. He stuffed his hands into the pockets of his top, then sauntered towards the front door of the house, exaggeratedly rolling his shoulders as he walked.

At the front door he withdrew a bunch of keys from his pocket, selected one and opened the door. A moment later the room to the rear of the house illuminated. The houses had not been wired for electric this far into the estate, which meant he had lanterns in the house.

'Do we go in?' McCready asked.

'Let's give it a moment,' I said. 'I want to catch him in the act.'

'Are you waiting for Morrison?'

I shook my head. 'Morrison won't turn up here,' I said. 'He's too smart to get his hands dirty. But I'd guess O'Connell is using this as his office, so we can expect callers.'

'Even if we get O'Connell, Morrison'll have someone else out here selling tomorrow,' McCready said.

I nodded. 'Perhaps. But for tonight, O'Connell getting taken will royally piss him off.'

McCready smiled, but I could tell he was questioning the value of what we were doing. O'Connell was selling drugs, but he was doing so with the permission of, and paying commission to, Vincent Morrison. Morrison had cleared the decks of drug dealers along the border in a previous case I had worked, persuading a dissident paramilitary group to take out his competition, so that he, ultimately, controlled drugs in the borderlands. Two factors complicated things: firstly, we could not prove that he was behind the drugs. Secondly, and more problematically for me, Morrison had saved my daughter's life following a riding accident, by taking her to hospital. The depth of gratitude I felt for his having so done was surpassed only by my determination to bring him down over his drug dealing.

A few moments later a Ford Fiesta pulled up in front of the house. As best we could tell, despite the mist of condensation on the windows, there seemed to be three young men in the car, the thumping of the bass beat from the radio audible even from our distance. They parked up and one got out, glanced around, then swaggered up to number 67, banging on the door with his fist three times, then stepping back. O'Connell came to the door, his rolling gait visible in silhouette against the lantern he'd lit when he entered the house. He opened the door, and the two slapped hands then slid them apart, tugging one another's fingers before separating. They banged shoulders lightly in embrace, then both went into the house.

'I'll go in,' I hissed. 'You take the two in the car. Keep them quiet; we need O'Connell with drugs.'

We got out of my car, which I'd parked around the curve in the road from number 67, our approach hidden from the Fiesta's occupants by the condensation of the car's windows. I headed straight for the house, the door lying slightly ajar where the visitor had neglected to pull it shut behind him; he wasn't planning on staying long.

We were just drawing abreast with the car when the rear door opened.

'I'm going in for a slash,' a voice said, and a youth stood up from the car, his hands already reaching for his fly. He stared at us stupidly for a minute, his eyes glazed, the opened door releasing a waft of cannabis smoke into the night air.

'The guards!' he shouted, struggling to get back into the car.

'Take him down,' I shouted to McCready, heading for the house. As I anticipated, before I had reached the door, the driver of the car had begun blaring the horn.

I pushed open the door and moved into the hallway, my gun drawn, though I had no expectation of using it; O'Connell didn't strike me as the type to pull a gun on a garda. Morrison wouldn't want that kind of heat, for a start.

'An Garda, on the floor!' I shouted.

In the kitchen two figures stood at a table on which sat a battery lantern. O'Connell looked up at me, a plastic bag in his hand. The younger man, who had only just arrived, looked around in panic. O'Connell pushed him to the ground, in effect blocking the doorway for a moment, then turned and ran.

I clambered over the young man, who lay prone, his hands pulled up in front of his face for protection. I had initially assumed that O'Connell was making a run for the back door, but he ran past it into the small room to the rear of the house. The door slammed. I ran at it, putting my weight against it. The door gave enough for me to see that O'Connell was standing legs apart, one trying to hold the door shut, while he stuffed the plastic bag down the toilet. I shoved again, though by now he had shifted his own position and was leaning against the back of the door. I heard the flush then shoved a third time, almost falling into the room as O'Connell stepped back, his hands now empty.

I shoved him against the wall, patting him down in the hope that he had secreted some of the drugs on himself, the flushing of the toilet a bluff, but his pockets were empty save for a wad of bank notes in his trouser pocket.

I pushed him ahead of me towards the kitchen, where McCready was pulling the other youth, now cuffed, to his feet. McCready held a small plastic bag of pills in his hand.

'I've never seen them before,' O'Connell said, before anyone spoke.

'He says you sold them to him,' McCready replied.

'He's a lying sack of shit. I never sold him nothing. He tried to sell them to me an' I said no.'

'And what were you dumping down the toilet?'

O'Connell looked at me, his smile lopsided. 'Took a piss, didn't I? Didn't know who you were breaking down the door.'

'Check the place out,' I said to McCready.

'What about the two in the car outside? They had a joint between them.'

'Take names and let them go with a warning,' I said. 'Be sure to phone their parents to collect them; they shouldn't be driving if there's drugs taken.'

I took O'Connell's details while McCready went through the house. Both actions were pointless; I already knew all I needed to about O'Connell, and I guessed from the cockiness of his demeanour that he had flushed away whatever drugs he might have had. That said, I also guessed that it must have been a fairly big score he'd had to dump, for he'd have had his evening's supplies with him.

Sure enough, a few minutes later McCready returned.

'Nothing, sir,' he said. 'The place is empty.'

O'Connell smirked, sitting down on the upturned milk crate he used for a seat.

'We'll never get uniforms out on a Sunday night. We'll bring out a team in the morning,' I said. 'The pumping station here is broken; everything that goes down the toilets around here gets flushed out onto a mound in the field running along the back of the next street across.'

McCready stared at me.

'*We* could look now, sir,' he said.

I considered it for a moment, then shook my head.

'We'll see nothing tonight,' I said. 'The morning will be time enough.'

O'Connell looked from one to the other of us as we spoke, his mouth slightly open, unformed words playing on his lips as he followed our discussion. He blinked slowly as he looked up at me, unable to quite believe his luck.

McCready tackled me once we had left the house.

'He'll be over there as soon as we leave, getting his stash back,' he said.

'Of course he will,' I agreed. 'His bag of drugs is currently sitting atop a pile of everything flushed out of thirty houses in this estate for the past six months. Do you fancy going in after them?'

McCready recoiled slightly.

'Exactly. What we *can* do, though, is wait in the field, let O'Connell go in there and get himself covered in shit getting back his stash, then arrest him with the drugs on him and take him into the station. Problem solved.'

McCready smiled broadly. 'I hadn't thought of that,' he said.

WE WAITED ALONG the edge of the field for less than twenty minutes. Once he was sure we had left, O'Connell crossed the broken-down yards behind the unoccupied houses and scaled the fence into the field beyond. The pumping station was a small red block at the field's far corner, though it had long since stopped working. Instead, a pipe around a foot wide broke through the earth six feet short of the station itself, spewing out a constant supply of effluent onto a growing mound. Despite the clear health hazard it presented, no one wanted to accept responsibility for it, for to do so would be to accept liability for its upkeep.

O'Connell approached it warily, clearly reluctant to take the final steps necessary for the retrieval of the drugs he had flushed. He pulled his top up over his mouth and, lifting a stick lying on the ground near him, began poking through the mound. He must have seen what he was looking for but couldn't quite reach it. Pulling his trouser legs up a little, he took a tentative step towards the mound, then a second. Leaning slightly forwards, he stretched to reach the bag. He straightened, took the stick and reached with it, twisting the stick as he fished for purchase on the bag. Finally, he leant a little too far and fell forward, having to use both hands, with only limited success, to prevent himself falling face-first onto the mound of effluent. Having decided he had already got himself dirty he took a final step forwards and lifted the bag.

For a second he seemed to struggle to understand why the bag was illuminated. Then he turned to where we stood, torches shining on him and his find.

'Weren't you ever told drugs would land you in a heap of shit?' I asked him.

Monday, 29 October

Chapter Sixteen

'I UNDERSTAND YOU allowed a suspect to sit in a cell for three hours last night covered in excrement.'

I had hardly made it onto Islandmore the following morning, when Superintendent Patterson arrived. The Commission had started early, having managed to get the new machinery delivered as a matter of priority. Millar was hopeful, he said, that they might have some luck in the search for Cleary by the end of the day.

The progress was slow and methodical. The digger operator scraped across the surface of the site where they were digging, lifting soil to a depth of four inches or so at a time. This soil was then deposited to his right-hand side, clear of the flagged spot the dog handler had marked two days previous. Jonas then sifted through the clay, looking for bone fragments, or anything which might indicate the presence of a corpse.

'He was found with enough drugs to supply the town for a week. We've charged him already; he's out on bail.'

'There'll be complaints,' Patterson continued. 'His lawyer has already been in touch with the local papers.'

'Do you think he'll get much sympathy? A dealer crawls through shit to get his stash and is caught in the process? Plus, who'd want to buy from him now, wondering if the goods they've just bought came via the U-bend?'

I could tell from the tone of his voice that Patterson was not that annoyed.

'It's hardly the result of the year, mind you.'

'But enough to convince Vincent Morrison that we're still watching him.'

'I don't think you leave him any room for doubt about that,' he muttered. Then he added irritably, 'What's happening with the son's case?' He nodded towards the dig site.

'We know Cleary was seen at Jimmy Callan's house on the evening of his death.'

'Who?'

'Callan was the father of—'

'Dominic Callan,' Patterson said. 'I remember. Is he their main suspect?'

'At the minute I thinks he's their only suspect. Cleary was at his house at 8 p.m. but died in the early hours. They still haven't recovered his phone or the contents of his wallet. Hendry tells me they're running a reconstruction this evening; I'll probably cut across and offer some help.'

Patterson nodded. 'Get this whole business cleared up ahead of the 2nd. The last thing we need is this all still boiling on when we get as far as that commemoration thing.'

'I'll do my best.'

ONCE THINGS WERE running smoothly with the dig, I excused myself, claiming I had paperwork to catch up on. In reality, I spent most of that morning with Joe McCready working our way through the list of names John Reddin had given me. Patterson had made it clear he didn't want me to follow up on the dead child, but I also knew that, with the two bridges down by the time the child was buried, whoever had brought her onto the island would have needed a boat. And, as Reddin had suggested, only net men and smugglers would have run boats at that point on the river. If one of them hadn't been the boat man, they might at least know who had been. I was acutely aware that the same logic applied to whoever had dispensed with Cleary's body on the island, too.

The ferryman, Seamus O'Hara, who lived on Coneyburrow Road on the way to Ballybofey, was not at home when we called, his house standing in darkness, the curtains still drawn. Tony Hennessey had died the year previous, so that eliminated him. Likewise Finbar Buckley, who'd died almost a decade earlier, despite Reddin's belief he was still alive.

Pete Cuthins was away for a few days staying with his family in Sligo, his neighbour told us when we called at his house on Gallows Lane. Alex Herron could not be contacted. We called at his home in Carrigans, but the house was empty. I made a note to call again; an empty milk bottle sat on the step, suggesting he had not gone far.

THE DIG WAS well progressed by the time I got back to Islandmore. I spotted Lennie Millar directing the group of men standing in the shallow hole the digger had scraped away. The machine remained at the edge of the hole.

Millar waved as I stepped down into the field.

'How's it going?'

'Slowly,' he said, taking the cigarette I offered him. 'We're taking it a few inches at a time at this stage; we think the body is just below us now.'

'Are you sure it's there?'

Millar dragged deeply on the cigarette, then flipped the butt away. 'I'd say so. We think there's a boulder over it, maybe to keep it buried, stop wild animals digging it up.'

'The same as the baby,' I observed.

'Indeed.'

'Lennie!' One of the men in the hole was clambering out, shouting to Millar. 'We've hit the stone.'

I followed Millar across to the hole. Around four feet down, four men stood. One of them had exposed the edge of a slab of rock, perhaps three feet long.

'Try prizing it out with the shovels,' Millar said, dropping down into the hole beside the men.

They lifted their spades and wedged them down the side of the rock, wriggling the blades in an attempt to jemmy their tips beneath it, allowing them to lift it upwards. Despite their best efforts, though, the rock remained steadfast in its place.

'Try the tip of the digger spade,' Millar called to the digger driver. 'Gently now.'

The large bucket rose up above us, the arm extending until it had cleared the rock. The driver lowered the bucket again, angling it so that the front edge scraped back along the floor of the hole. He drew it back inch by inch until it snagged on the edge of the rock. Once or twice he angled the bucket back and forth until he felt he had achieved a good hold, then he began to withdraw the arm.

The edge of the bucket caught a moment on the corner of the rock, then began to scrape up, breaking loose the strata of the rock's edge.

'Again,' Millar called. 'A little deeper.'

The driver lifted the bucket clear, then repeated the process. This time, the bucket found better purchase and, as he drew the arm back, the rock began to rise out of the earth onto its edge. Eventually, the stone was raised high enough that it tumbled to one side, exposing a cavity beneath it.

Declan Cleary's raggedy-clothed skeleton rested beneath, curled foetally, much as his son had been when we found him only a day earlier.

Chapter Seventeen

THE TEAM WORKED for several further hours, digging around the body. Earth had compacted around the legs and the right arm, so they began digging it back, gently, working always to preserve the dignity of the dead man's remains.

Millar had suggested quite early in the process that we should inform next of kin. I drove to Coneyburrow Road and collected Mary Collins and her husband and brought them to the site. Sean's body had not yet been returned to them for burial, and I could tell that, until her son was brought home to her, she would exist in her own personal limbo. She spoke little in the car, her hand at her mouth, her eyes vacant, focused on some point in the middle distance. I imagined such a time must have been a mix of emotions anyway, without the added pain of the loss of her son and the knowledge that neither father nor son had had a chance to meet – in this life, at least.

Mr Collins initially engaged in small talk, then moved to practical questions surrounding the dig, how the events would now unfurl, what they should or should not do.

'Lennie Millar will be best placed to tell you all that,' I said. 'He's more experienced in this than I am.'

Finally, the conversation stopped completely and we drove to Islandmore in silence, the only intrusion the rattle of the car's suspension as we crossed the temporary bridge onto the island.

The team had pitched a crime-scene tent above the spot where the body was found to protect it from the elements and to maintain privacy. Once it became clear that something had been found on the island, it would not be long until people would congregate on Park Road, opposite the island, to watch events.

John Mulronney, our local doctor, was called soon after to perform the absurd task of confirming death. I also called Father Brennan, who arrived and administered last rites, while Mary Collins and her husband stood at the edge of the makeshift grave, he hugging her while she silently wept and prayed.

The team who had uncovered the body stood, hands clasped, joining in the prayers, before in turn approaching Mrs Collins and offering their sympathies. While the remains could not be confirmed as Cleary's until DNA tests were conducted, the clothes hanging on the bones matched those which Cleary had been wearing on the day he vanished.

Not long after, the first of the press arrived, followed with astounding alacrity by local politicians of all shades, keen to use the media interest to promote their own agenda. One of the first to arrive was Miriam Powell. She had been our local TD during the latter boom years and had, in the last election, managed to survive the cull which had cost so many of her party colleagues their seats in the Dail.

She spoke for a moment about the new Ireland and how we had put the evils of the past behind us. She suggested that the recovery of the Disappeared was part of a wider Truth-and-Reconciliation process whereby we could move forward.

Patterson arrived as Miriam was finishing and delivered a few lines to the assembled press about the work of An Garda in supporting the Commission.

All this time the men who had recovered Cleary's body continued working quietly on recovering the corpse without further disintegration, with seemingly little awareness of the attention their work was receiving.

'So what happens now?' I asked Millar as we had a smoke just out of sight of the cameramen. I expected the usual activity of a crime scene, with forensics officers and SOCOs recording and photographing the scene, working hard to preserve the integrity of any evidence found. This was markedly different.

'We get the body freed up, the pathologist takes it and we go home. We'll do DNA comparisons and that in the lab. The remains will be held until final confirmation of identity. It normally takes a few months.'

'So you're done here then?'

'We'll be here a few more days,' he added. 'Just to complete the dig. We always have to dig a bit further around where the body is located to be sure we've got everything. With the best will in the world, it's not unusual afterwards to discover something we missed on the day the body was found. Once that's all done, we have to refill all the sites we've excavated.'

'I'm sure I'll see you before you finish up.'

Millar nodded, then stubbed out his smoke.

'It is shit thinking that people get away with this. But at the end of the day, all we can hope to do is bring some peace to those who've been left behind. That has to be enough, you know?'

He squinted at me as he spoke, though I suspected the words were as much for his own benefit as mine.

Chapter Eighteen

I MADE IT home just after six. Debbie had held back dinner so we could eat together. Penny finished first and went out to feed Frank while we cleaned up. I carried out a plate of leftovers from dinner for his plate.

Penny was sitting on the back step with Frank snuggled beside her, her arm around his neck, her hand playing with the skin beneath his long velvet ear.

'Everything okay, sweetie?' I asked.

She glanced up at me and smiled mildly, her hand scratching at Frank's skin.

'Frank is getting very slow,' she said.

'He's not the only one,' I said, lowering myself down beside her. 'He's getting old.'

She half-laughed at the comment, but I could tell her mind was on other things.

'They were talking in school today about *cillins*,' she said. 'They found one on Islandmore.'

'That's right.'

'Do you think those babies never got to heaven?'

'I don't believe that for a second.'

'Our teacher said that they were in limbo. That any baby that dies before being baptized goes to limbo. I told her she was wrong.'

'Did you now?'

'She sent me to the year head.'

'For telling her she was wrong?'

'For telling her she was talking shit.'

'Well, that would do it, right enough. You can't talk to teachers that way.'

'Even when they are?'

'Are what?'

'Talking shit.'

'Even then.'

She glanced sideways at me to gauge whether I was annoyed.

'I have to write a letter of apology. I don't want to.'

I considered her comment. 'I can understand why. But if you were personally rude to the woman you should say sorry. You don't have to apologize for what you believe, just how you expressed it.'

'It's just that, if she's right, then the baby you and Mum lost before me is trapped somewhere, in something people don't even know exists.'

'I think anyone who suggests the existence of limbo displays a very flawed understanding of God. It seems unlikely to me that the God I believe in would suffer to have children in particular separated from him for eternity.'

She smiled broadly. 'I must write that in the letter,' she said. 'Of course, it would help if I could really believe in God.'

With that she stood up and walked into the house before I could respond.

Penny had avoided any further discussion. Later I mentioned it to Debs, who seemed wholly unconcerned.

'Kids go through all kinds of things. She's just questioning what we've told her. Imagine, questioning authority! Where did she get that quality from? Apples don't fall far from trees, Ben.'

'So it's my fault?'

The ringing of the phone saved her having to answer.

'This is Letterkenny station, Inspector. We've got a call out about a public order incident in Islandview. The woman involved gave your name.'

BY THE TIME I got to her house, Christine Cashell's face was still flushed, her eyes red-rimmed and puffy with tears. The uniform who had lifted her told me that she had been much more agitated when he had arrived, screaming at the neighbours, and assaulting him when he attempted to restrain her.

'How did she assault you?'

He held out his arm; a thin red streak of blood revealed where Christine had scratched him as he tried to drag her from a neighbouring garden out into the street.

'That looks nasty,' I said, straight-faced. 'You might need medical attention.'

He stared at me, as if unsure whether I was joking or not.

'I'll maybe cut back to the station and get a plaster or something.'

'You do that. I'll take it from here.'

After he left I went back into the room and sat beside Christine. She had not spoken since my arrival, but the fact she had given my name to the officer suggested she had, at least, wanted me there.

'Where's . . .?'

'Andrew,' she said.

'That's right. Andrew? Is he here?'

She shook her head. 'He went to the pub with his brothers.'

'So what happened that you ended up assaulting an officer of the law?'

She looked at me, willing me to believe her. 'I heard Michael crying, in the monitor. He wouldn't stop. Then someone hit him. I heard them shouting. Heard the slap. It was horrible. It's like he's caught somewhere that I can't get to him and he needs me.'

I took her hand in mine.

'You know Michael's gone, don't you, Christine?'

She began to cry again, shuddering tears. Finally, she nodded.

'Why are you torturing yourself listening to a baby monitor?'

'I can't . . . I can't help it. I bought it; I never used one with my first and I started to panic when I was carrying Michael. I shouldn't have bought it. I should have waited till he was born. I tempted fate.'

'It's not your fault, Christine.'

'But this is all I have of Michael now. When he went, I plugged it in because I thought it would make me closer to him; this thing I'd got for him. Then I heard him crying. But no one believes me. Andrew wants me to turn it off, but that would be like saying I don't want my baby anymore. I can't do that.'

The monitor hissed quietly on the arm of the sofa, whispering through our conversation in a hush of static buzzing.

'What about tonight?'

'I heard something. I searched the house for Michael, but he wasn't there. I couldn't take the noise; I went outside. Andrew was away already. I could hear Michael crying, in my head; it wouldn't stop. There's someone in the show house across the way – a new woman. I went across to her, to ask her if she could hear it, too. She told me to leave her alone; she said I was insane. I lost it with her. I shouldn't have, but I couldn't control it. The crying wouldn't stop.'

'You need to get some help from the doctor, Christine. To help you through all this. You shouldn't be doing it on your own. Do you want me to call Andrew?'

'It's his first night out since the baby was born. He's trying his best, but I know he doesn't believe me. No one believes me.'

I wanted to tell her that I believed her, to offer her that comfort, but the words seemed to stick. Instead I stood up. 'Is there anyone else I can get for you before I . . .'

I stopped as the lights on the monitor, perched on the arm of the sofa, flickered into life. Quickly, the illumination strafed across the display, from one side to the other.

Christine noticed it too, for she sat up and pointed speech-lessly. I was moving back towards her when I heard it.

It was not so much a cry as a ghost of a cry, an echo without a source, its presence confirmed more by the flickering lights on the unit than by the tinny sound it produced. It was enough, certainly, to make me shiver, to cause me to rub the goose-bumps from my arm with the palm of my hand. The second cry, though, was differ-ent, growing in intensity to a strangled yelp of pain, then vanishing.

We heard the crackle of static, then the crying began again in earnest, a protracted wail punctuated with sobbing, building to a crescendo then subsiding into coughing sobs as if the child was wearying.

Christine turned to me, her face set defiantly, her eyes alive with a mixture of terror and elated vindication.

'Now do you believe me?'

The child roared for some minutes, its howls growing ever more anguished. Finally, when it seemed it would never stop, we heard a voice, muffled but deep enough to be an adult's. We could not make out what exactly was being said, but the tone left little room for misinterpretation. We heard a single abrupt smack, as the child whimpered. Then with an abrupt click the sound of the monitor stopped.

Chapter Nineteen

I walked the estate, hoping that the child we had heard might be somewhere in the vicinity, its crying audible, but all was quiet. The show house which Christine had mentioned was in darkness. So too was number 67, Peter O'Connell evidently plying his trade elsewhere.

I waited with Christine until Andrew Dunne returned from the pub. Christine had called him to tell him that, finally, she had someone who could corroborate the claims she had made and, in so doing, prove both to herself and to him that she wasn't mad.

I made it across to Strabane just before ten o'clock that evening to join Hendry on the reconstruction of Sean Cleary's final hours. Although Cleary was killed in the middle of the night, there seemed little point in leaving the reconstruction until then.

The weather was an improvement on the previous night, too. The sky was clear and starry, the air chilled and sharp. Uniforms stopped cars as they passed, offering leaflets with a picture of Sean Cleary on it. Taxi men in particular were being targeted. Cleary lived in Lifford, yet had been found in Strabane, despite not having his car with him. We also knew from Callan's neighbour that Cleary had arrived at his house in a cab; possibly he had used a cab at some stage later that evening, too.

Hendry was directing the other officers when I arrived, so I availed myself of the offer of a sausage roll and a mug of tea from a flask set up in the back of one of the police jeeps until he was ready to speak to me.

'Good of you to join us,' he said. 'I see you've got down to the important stuff first,' he added nodding at the cup I held.

'I like to get my priorities in order. What's happening?'

'The post-mortem was completed this morning. It confirms mostly what himself told us the last day; Cleary was shot with a silenced pistol at close range. The bullet shattered in the baffles and the pathologist recovered the pieces he could find, so we'll run ballistics; it'll be tricky, though, with the shattering.'

'Fair enough.'

'Time of death is probably between midnight and four in the morning, which doesn't help us wildly. He did find one thing which he was interested in. Cleary's fingers on his right hand were covered with paper fibres and smudges of ink. The pathologist has suggested newspaper fibres. The smudging of the ink suggested to him that someone pulled the paper from his grasp; the doc seemed to think it happened shortly before death.'

'It could mean he stopped at the chippie on his way to the play-ground and someone stole his fish supper.'

'It's all food with you, isn't it?' Hendry said. 'Milk and two sugars,' he added, gesturing towards the flask.

'We also got lucky on the bloody footprint Ryan suggested we would find. It could be the killer's. Small, mind you – a size 7 Adidas Ambition Powerbounce 2.0, apparently.'

'Short and snappy.'

'The name or the wearer?'

'Both by the sounds of it, if he wears a size 7. What's your theory?'

'I'm hoping some of the kids across the way will be able to help,' Hendry said, glancing across at the waste ground where we had seen the remains of the fire the day before.

In fact, we kept an eye on the old factory site throughout the evening. When I first arrived, three or four boys were lurking inside the wall, sticking to the shadows, watching the police operation with a mixture of disdain and fascination. As the evening progressed, though, the numbers grew, until by midnight there were over a dozen. They had tired quickly of watching the checkpoints and the lack of response they had got from the occasional insults they had shouted. Hendry had warned the uniforms not to react; he wanted them to settle, wanted to ensure there were as many of them there as possible. Only if they looked like they were leaving should someone approach them.

Eventually they drifted across to where we had seen the remains of the fire on Sunday morning. Sure enough, a few moments later we saw the first flickers of flames as they started burning some of the rubbish lying around. They were seated on the milk crates and, having perhaps been reluctant, initially, to start drinking alcohol on the street so close to a PSNI checkpoint, they soon grew braver and began passing round cans of beer. Their laughter grew as the night deepened.

'That seems to be the lot,' Hendry said, just after midnight. 'Shall we join them for a chat?'

The noise of the boys, and the light from the fire, made it easy for us to get close to them before one of them noticed us. Straight away three of them were on their feet. One in particular was slightly crouched as he stood, tensed as if to run if the need arose. He wore a puffy black jacket over a hooded top, and his trousers hung low on his hips, flapping loosely around his legs in the light breeze blowing across the factory yard.

'No panic, men,' Hendry said, lighting his torch and holding it aloft so they could at least see where the voice was coming from. 'We're only looking for your help.'

One boy who had turned to look at us as we approached groaned and theatrically turned his back on us again, muttering something to the others and gaining the approbation of their laughter in return.

The three boys who had stood up relaxed a little, though none of them sat down again.

'There was a murder across in the playground during the early hours of Sunday morning, men. Did any of you see anything?'

No one responded.

'Were any of you here on Saturday night into Sunday morning?'

Again nothing. I realized that several of the teenagers sitting around the fire were not boys at all, but teenaged girls. I recognized one of them as a young girl called Claire, a friend of Penny's. When she saw that I had recognized her she turned her head away quickly and muttered something to the boy in the puffed jacket who stood next to her. I tried to dismiss the thought that my own child might spend nights in such surroundings and company.

'Come on, fellas,' Hendry said. 'We're not looking for your blood.'

'What about you, girls?' I asked.

A few of the boys with their backs to us began to snigger, encouraging the girls to do likewise. The one to the other side of Claire smiled at me.

'Fuck off, Brit,' she said.

The circle exploded into laughter at this; all except Claire and the boy in the puffed jacket. He smirked a little, but remained on edge, wetting his lips briefly with the tip of his tongue. He was trying to play it cool, but the alcohol he had consumed caused him to exaggerate his actions. Still, it didn't mean he knew anything; he could have been carrying something; drugs, a knife maybe.

'He's not a Brit,' Hendry said. 'He's more Irish than you are, love. Do your parents know you're out?'

If anything was likely to clam them up, it was threatening them with their parents.

'We just need some help, folks,' I said. 'A man was killed in the playground two nights ago. We're just wondering if any of you saw anything. We know there were people here that night. Maybe you saw something?'

If I had imagined appealing to their sense of decency would prove any more fruitful, I was mistaken. Nervous laughter rippled around the group but none of them spoke.

Hendry took out his radio and clicked on it twice. We heard the static, then a voice said 'Sir?'

'We're across the street here,' Hendry said. 'I need someone with luminol, as soon as you can.'

'Sir?' the voice sounded bewildered, but Hendry cut off the radio quickly.

The youths feigned nonchalance, but it was clear that their interest had been piqued. As had mine; Hendry was clearly working a bluff, for there would be no one with luminol at a reconstruction.

'We have very good forensics people,' Hendry said. 'They've already told us that they found a footprint in the blood of the victim the other night, possibly from the killer; a trainer footprint. They were even able to tell us the make; Adidas Ambition Powerbounce.'

'2.0,' I added.

'Just so,' Hendry agreed. 'And the size; 7.'

He had the whole group's attention now. I could see a few of the girls scanning the ground, noting the make of each of the boys' shoes. I was trying my best to do the same, though aware that I wouldn't be able to tell one Adidas shoe from another.

'Now, blood stays on things for a long time. And just because you can't see it, doesn't mean it's not there. A quick squirt of luminol on each of your shoes, and we'll soon have all we need. So, who's first?'

I initially thought it was the heavy-set boy who ran, but in fact it was the youth in the puffed jacket and hooded top who had grabbed him and flung him towards the fire, before he began sprinting across the deserted remains of the factory floor towards the mounds of rubble at the far end.

Hendry was after him instantly, shouting into his radio for assistance as he did so.

The boy was running parallel to the roadway where the reconstruction was being held. As far as I could tell, there was only one entrance into the grounds, at the front gate, but I had not seen the bulk of them arriving that night, which meant they had entered the grounds from another spot.

Rather than follow Hendry I cut back out the front gates and followed the road alongside which the two of them were running. I rounded the corner in time to see the young man leaping from the roof of the post office and landing with a thud on the bonnet of one of the police cars parked in front of it. He rolled with the fall, landing on the ground, then picked himself up and began sprinting again.

I glanced up to see Hendry pull to a halt at the edge of the roof. For a second he seemed to be considering leaping as the boy had done, then instead he turned and began lowering himself over the edge, all the time gripping the roof. I left him there and took off after the boy.

I saw him cut left and begin running up the Melmount Road, the slight gradient of the street doing nothing to slow him but leaving me regretting I'd ever started smoking.

He glanced back and, for a second, lost his footing, sliding off the kerb and going over on his ankle. He lifted himself out of the gutter as quickly as he could and resumed his run, but his foot was bothering him and he kicked it out sideways a few times as he ran, as if trying to shake the injury he had incurred. I heard the siren behind me as a Land Rover joined our pursuit, presumably called by Hendry. It roared past me, its roof-mounted spotlight picking out the boy's figure as he widened the gap between us. To his left now was a school, and he stopped, trying to pull himself over the fence surrounding it, but his leg seemed to prevent him giving himself the thrust he needed to clear the top. By now the Land Rover had squealed to a halt and officers were beginning to jump out. The boy panicked and started running again, further up the road; then he dived over a low wall to his left and vanished from our sight.

When I drew level with the spot, I realized he had dropped down into a graveyard, across the street from the area's main church. Someone in the Land Rover was slowly sweeping the beam of the spotlight from side of side, running along the straight rows of the graves.

We moved into the graveyard, the PSNI officers splitting up and taking a row each. Further down the road I could see Hendry hobbling up towards us, finally having made it down from the roof of the post office.

I had not seen the boy as the spotlight made its broad sweep. At the far end of the final row, I noticed a small mechanical digger aside a mound of clay. Beside it, as the spotlight swept the grounds again, I caught a glimpse of the green baize that the gravediggers lay over an empty grave.

I slowed down a little to catch my breath, then called one of the uniformed PSNI officers. It was a young female officer who came across to me.

'Sir?'

'I need your torch. Come with me.'

We moved up through the row, trying not to step on any of the graves. I could hear the woman beside me singing a hushed tune to herself as we walked.

'Not a fan of graveyards,' she explained, as I glanced at her.

'I think you're in for a treat, then,' I said.

As we approached the freshly dug grave, I thought I could smell the acrid stench of burning rubber.

We reached the mound of soil and I motioned to the PSNI woman to direct the torch beam onto the baize covering the grave. Then I reached down and lifted the corner of the green cloth, pulling it back.

The woman gasped as her torch beam illuminated the startled expression staring back up at us. Six feet below, the young man stood in his socks, a fluorescent green trainer in one hand while his other held a flaming lighter against the sole, attempting to burn off the evidence of Sean Cleary's blood.

Hendry struggled across to us, holding his side.

'Where is he?' he managed, then glanced down at where the boy stood, patently unable to get himself back out again.

Hendry grunted, then winced and gripped his side again. 'Let the wee shite stay in there until the morning; we'll come back and get him then.'

Chapter Twenty

THE INTERVIEW ROOM felt decidedly stuffy after the freshness of the outdoors. Despite Hendry's misgivings, we had, after some pleading from the boy, handed him down a spade and instructed him to dig out footholds in the grave wall far enough up to give himself a boost and enable us to reach down and pull him the rest of the way.

After his initial panic at the thought of being left in a grave for the night, the boy had regained some of his hauteur once he'd warmed up in the station. He'd demanded a solicitor upon arrival and responded to every question since with 'No comment'. It lasted only until a forensics officer arrived at the door of the interview room with the boy's fluorescent green shoes in a clear-plastic evidence bag. The shoes had been taken from him before he was allowed up out of the grave, along with his name and age: Stephen Burke, 18. The forensics officer conferred a moment with Hendry who glanced at me and winked.

'Well, Stephen,' Hendry said, sitting opposite the boy again. 'The bad news is that we weren't able to get any evidence off this shoe.' Hendry held aloft the shoe with the scorch marks on the sole. 'Nothing usable.'

Burke tried hard not to smile. He ran his hand through the gelled tips of his hair. I noticed now, in the light of the station, that he'd had swirling Celtic designs shaved into his hair along the sides of his head.

'That may have been because you burnt it,' Hendry said. 'But more likely it's because *this* is the shoe which had Sean Cleary's blood all over it.' With that he held up the other, unburned shoe. 'Plus, we've got your fingerprints all over the victim's wallet.'

Burke glanced at his brief and licked his lips as he shifted in his seat.

'Which means I can place you at the scene of a murder, so we're done here. I'm arresting you for the murder of Sean Cleary . . .' Hendry began, turning towards the door.

Burke stood up quickly, backing away from the table. His solicitor had also stood, surprised at the speed with which Hendry was concluding the interview.

'I didn't kill no one,' Burke shouted. 'I didn't know he was dead. He looked drunk.'

'What?' Hendry stopped at the door of the room.

'He was just lying there; I thought he was drunk.'

'You'd best explain this to me,' Hendry said, making a performance out of reconsidering and taking his seat again.

'I was heading up to meet the lads and I saw him getting out of a taxi and going into the playground, but he never came back out. I thought maybe he was a queer, meeting someone in there. Then, when I was going home, I seen him lying on the bench, like he'd had a skinful. I went in to check on him and he was just lying there. I thought he was drunk. He was heavy breathing and that; just lying there. He wasn't dead.'

'And you didn't notice the pool of blood lying under the seat?'

'It was dark,' he said.

'Yet you were able to see him from the street,' I said.

The boy prevaricated. 'I'd had a skinful meself. I didn't notice. I saw the blood on me shoe the next day and couldn't remember how it got there. I thought I stood on something; a dead cat or something on the road, you know?'

'So, why did you go over to him?' I asked.

Burke squinted at me slightly, glanced across at his brief. 'I wanted to check he was all right.'

'So where's his phone and the contents of his wallet?'

Burke smiled, then laughed affably. 'Ah, come on,' he said, holding out his hands, palms upward.

'The contents of his wallet are missing, Stephen. Nor did he have a phone on him when we found him. Where are they?'

Burke glanced at his brief again and shrugged, as if we were abusing his sincerity.

'We can go back to the murder charge if that helps,' Hendry added.

'I believe we've dealt with that,' the solicitor managed, but Hendry was already moving on.

'We could, of course, also search your house. Your mother's house, I should say. Take it apart looking for stolen goods. And still go ahead with the murder rap, too.'

Burke coughed to clear his throat, shifting in his seat as he glanced from one of us to the other.

'I binned his cards. He only had twenty quid in his wallet. Not even – it was euro. I spent it.'

'What about the phone?'

Burke looked surprised. 'I never saw a phone.'

'Bullshit,' Hendry said.

'I swear. I never saw a phone. I was short some cash and I rolled a drunk for his wallet. I didn't know he was dead. I swear on me ma.'

'What about the taxi you say the man arrived in?' I said. 'What do you remember about that?'

Burke raised his chin a little, closing his eyes as if struggling to remember. 'It was a red Audi,' he said. 'Bright red; too flash for the driver.'

'Why?'

'He was an old guy, kind of baldy.'

Hendry nodded impatiently. 'I'm not hearing anything useful, Stephen,' he said. 'Nothing as compelling as the victim's blood on your shoes.'

'He had a southern plate,' Burke added, snapping his fingers and pointing at Hendry. '"WW" in it.'

'That's very specific,' Hendry said.

'I remember it because it wasn't "DL", you know? I was trying to work out what "WW" stood for, but I was too pissed to remember all the counties.'

Registration plates in the Republic contain both the year of the car's first registration and the initials of the county where it was registered. A new Donegal car will have a registration beginning '12 DL'. 'WW' meant the car had been bought in Wicklow. If it was a southern registration then it was probably a Donegal taxi company. It wouldn't be impossible to contact each and ask if they had a red Wicklow-registered Audi driving for them. Particularly considering the physical description Burke had given us of the driver. It would, at least, tell us where Sean Cleary had been before arriving at the playground.

Burke could see that he had bought himself some slack. He snapped his fingers again and fell backwards into his seat, flicking his hand towards us. 'That's it. He dropped him off. Can I go now?'

'We'll be needing a statement,' Hendry said. 'Then we'll have to decide what to charge you with.'

Tuesday, 30 October

Chapter Twenty-one

THE KIDS WERE up early the following morning. It was the last day at school before their Halloween break and they were having a non-uniform day in Penny's school. As a consequence, she spent forty minutes in the bathroom, trying on different outfits while Shane paced the floor outside, complaining that he needed to pee and refusing, on principle, the use of the en suite in our room.

When Penny finally appeared for breakfast, she was wearing the first outfit she had tried on, forty minutes previous.

'Can I go to the bonfire tomorrow night over in Strabane?' she asked, as she nibbled on a slice of toast.

'I wanted to go to Derry for the fireworks,' Shane complained.

'Tough,' Penny retorted. 'I asked first.'

'Tough for you,' he spat back impotently.

'I'm not fussed on the bonfire, sweetheart,' I said. 'There can be trouble there.'

'I'm not a baby,' Penny complained, then snapped as Shane stuck out his tongue triumphantly. 'Shane's sticking his tongue out at me,' she whined, undermining her previous statement.

'Don't stick your tongue out at people,' Debbie warned from the hall, where she was fixing her make-up.

Penny smirked at Shane. 'Can I, Mum?' she called. 'I'll be careful. All the girls are going.'

'I saw your friend, Claire, over in Strabane last night,' I said. 'She's keeping bad company. Stephen Burke?'

'Oh, him,' she said. 'He just tags along sometimes. He's a weirdo.'

'I'm surprised Claire's allowed over there on a school night.'

'You didn't say anything to her, did you?' Penny asked, appalled.

Before I could answer, Debbie stuck her head around the door frame. 'What do you think? Let her across for an hour or two, just.'

'Thanks, Mum,' Penny said, smiling, before I even had a chance to respond.

'That's not fair.' Shane let his spoon clatter to the floor as he stomped away from the table.

'We'll go to Derry first,' I said. 'That way everyone will be happy.'

If the compromise placated him, he didn't show it.

I WAS GLAD to get into the relative quiet of the station, and used the early start to follow up on what had happened in Christine Cashell's home. I'd taken the details of the monitor from Christine's machine the previous night and a quick Internet search provided me with a helpline number for the manufacturer.

'Hello. Thank you for calling; how can I help you?' The voice was English, upbeat.

It seemed too convoluted to explain the details of my enquiry, so instead I simply said, 'Yes. We have a problem with the monitor. We can hear a baby crying in it.'

There was silence on the other end, as the girl perhaps wondered if this was a prank call.

'Is that not what a baby monitor is meant to do, sir?' She managed to sound cheery, though a little suspicious.

'Of course. Yes, I'm sorry. I mean, we can hear someone else's baby in the monitor.'

'I see. And you're sure it's not your own baby, sir?'

'Definitely not.'

'I see,' she repeated. 'The most likely cause, then, is that one of your neighbours is using a monitor set at the same frequency as yours. That means that you might overhear their baby crying from time to time. And, of course, they'll overhear yours.'

'That explains it,' I said. 'Just as a matter of interest, how close by would they need to be for the monitor to pick it up.'

'Is it clear?'

'Fairly.'

'It would need to be close, then; a neighbouring house. No further than maybe a few hundred yards.'

'I see,' I said. 'Thank you very much.'

'Is there anything else I can help you with?' she asked, her voice lilting.

'No, thank you,' I said. 'You've been very helpful.'

I EXPLAINED THIS to Christine Cashell an hour later while her partner sat in the chair opposite, a little sullen and more than a little hung-over. He scraped at the stubble along his jawline as he spoke.

'So someone else around here is using a baby monitor like ours, Chrissie. See?'

She stared at him. If I had expected the revelation to bring her some comfort or relief I was to be disappointed.

'No one on our estate has a baby that young,' she said. 'No one else here has babies.'

'There must be some around here, Christine,' I said. 'The estate has a lot of young families in it; there's bound to be at least one baby in the estate.'

'But I be talking to the mothers in the shops and waiting at school; they'd have told me.'

I prevented myself from pointing out that they may not have done so, precisely because she had recently lost her own child. Still, the woman from the monitor company had said the house concerned would be a neighbouring property, and I doubted if Christine would have missed a pregnancy among one of her immediate neighbours.

'What about the woman whose house you were at last night? Would she have a child?'

Dunne shrugged. 'A lot of people live in and out of those unfinished houses. We don't know who half of them are. The one she's in was the show house for the estate, so it's probably well finished inside. Better than ours anyhow.'

'But the rest are incomplete?'

He nodded.

'Why would they choose to live in an unfinished house?'

Dunne rolled his eyes. 'They don't actually live there; they're using the address for benefits.'

For a number of years, the benefits system in the Republic had been markedly more generous than the system in the North. As a result, less scrupulous Northerners had 'moved', on paper, into properties in the south to exploit the fact that they could claim both in the North and in the Republic. Their child benefit would be paid in the North, while the south would top up the difference to bring it to Republic levels. That particular golden egg had cracked with the collapse of the economy and the subsequent bailout, though many of the registered addresses remained on the books. One impact of the scam was the disintegration of estates near the border where houses might be registered to a number of families without any of them actually living in them.

'So you don't know her name?'

Dunne shook his head. Christine looked at me and shook hers, too, once.

'I can always ask.'

'So what if she has a baby?' Dunne said. 'She's not breaking the law.'

'If she has one, we heard it being hit quite a smack last night. If she realizes that others can hear her, she might rein in her temper a little,' I explained, more for Christine's benefit than Dunne's.

THE HOUSE WAS unoccupied when I went across. I rang the bell a few times, then moved around to the side of the house and peered in the window. Inside was nicely finished; the ceilings were bordered with moulding and a small chandelier hung in the living room. The furniture in the room was perhaps a little large for the space, but even from where I stood it looked like good quality.

I moved around the rear of the house. The garden was no more than a plot of clay which the builder had not even prepared for seeding. Despite this, a few hardier tufts of grass and weeds had struggled through the lumps of hard-fill littering the ground. I glanced over the low fence bordering the garden at the outline of Islandmore in the distance, rising out of the river. In the stillness of the morning I became aware of the constant running of a motor and realized that the dig had resumed. Millar had said they would be back to dig further around the site of Cleary's burial, in case they had missed anything. I could not see the dig itself for it was on the opposite side of the island.

I moved back up towards the house, picking my way through the piles of clay. Standing up on tiptoe to see in through the window of the kitchen I missed the figure coming around the corner of the house.

'What the hell do you think you're doing?'

I turned to face a tall, forbidding woman, her features sharp, her hair tied back from her face. She looked in her late fifties. She carried two carrier bags emblazoned with the logo of the local supermarket.

I realized that she would not have known that I was a guard, as I was in plain-clothes rather than my uniform.

'I'm Garda Inspector Benedict Devlin,' I said. 'I believe you had an incident last night with one of your neighbours. I'm just following up.'

'The lunatic across the way? What about it? I told the young fella out last night I didn't want to do anything about it.'

'Miss Cashell's not mad. She lost a child recently and is having some difficulty in coming to terms with it.'

'What's her name?'

'Christine Cashell. She lost her baby.'

The woman stared down at the shopping she held, her manner softening. 'I'm sorry to hear that. I didn't know who she was.'

I was unsure how knowing who she was made a difference, but I was mollified by the woman's apparent understanding.

'She believes she can hear a baby crying in a neighbouring house. None of her other neighbours have children and she was wondering if it was coming from here; your child or grandchild maybe?'

'I don't have any children,' she answered sharply. 'She didn't hear anything coming from my house.'

'This is your house, Miss . . .?'

'Clark. Sheila Clark. I'm renting here for a few months; my own house is being repaired.'

'I see,' I said. 'But you haven't had a child in your house that Miss Cashell might have heard?'

'Despite being the one attacked last night, I get the feeling I'm being interrogated here,' Shelia Clark replied.

'I'm sorry it seems that way, Miss Clark. I'm just following up on things. I'll let you get on with your shopping. Would you like a hand in?'

'I can manage fine, thank you,' she replied tersely.

I went back round the side of the house to my car, waving across to where Christine Cashell stood nervously at her window.

As I sat in the car I noted the registration number on Clark's car. She may have claimed that she did not have a child in the house, but I had seen a box of baby milk through the translucent plastic of her shopping bag.

Chapter Twenty-two

I LOOKED FOR Joe McCready when I got to the station, but Burgess told me he'd called to say that he'd be late; his wife had a scan.

'I need you to do me a favour,' I said.

Burgess stared at me, not replying lest it encourage me to continue with my request. I did so anyway.

'I need to know who owns the houses in Islandview.'

'Every house?'

'Not the individual owners; I mean who owns the estate now.'

'Why?'

I shrugged. 'Someone is selling drugs out of one of the houses there; I want to know who's giving them the okay to use the property.'

He seemed to consider this for a moment, before finally nodding. 'I'll get on to it,' he said.

JOE MCCREADY DID not make it into the station until after ten-thirty.

'How did it go?' I asked as I poured us both a coffee in the station kitchen.

'Great. It's really great. Everything is okay, the heart was beating okay, the baby was moving, everything was . . . it was all good.'

He inhaled deeply and held the breath a moment, then let it slowly out, slumping his shoulders as he did so.

'You need to relax about it, Joe,' I said. 'It will all be fine. The hospital has never lost a father yet during a labour.'

Joe attempted a smile. 'It's not that. I'm . . . I'm nervous about being in there, during the birth. About watching Ellen in pain and not being able to do anything. What if I'm useless?'

'You will be,' I said. 'Your job is to take the flak from the midwives for leaving your own wife in this condition in the first place. You just have to stand there and take it.'

He smiled more warmly as I handed him his cup.

'We, on the other hand, have a taxi to track down today,' I began, then explained all that had transpired the day before.

Two coffees and seven phone calls later we located the taxi driver Burke had mentioned. The penultimate company I was planning to call knew who he was and gave me his home address in Castlefinn.

JEFF BRYANT FAIRLY much fitted Burke's description, despite the young boy being drunk when he saw him. Bryant stood just over 5'5" in his house slippers, his head smooth, his skin sallow. He wore thick glasses that magnified his already widened eyes and blinked constantly as we spoke to him.

He remembered Cleary when I showed him a picture. He had dropped him off in Strabane.

'You didn't think to contact us about it earlier?'

He blinked furiously, glancing from me to Joe McCready, who was circling his car.

'I didn't think it was important, like,' he said. He spoke with a Belfast accent, his vowels short and abrupt.

'This is a nice car,' McCready said.

'Thanks,' Bryant said, his blinking increasing.

'Your taxi plates are for a different registration, though,' McCready added.

'What?'

'The taxi licence on your car is for a different vehicle.'

Bryant laughed forcedly for a second. 'I changed car and never got round to changing it. I'll do it today.'

McCready took out his phone. 'I can do it for you,' he said. 'The number on your licence is your old car, is that right?'

Bryant licked his lips, running his hand across his smooth head. 'They might have a bit of difficulty tracing it. I can do it later.'

'It's no problem,' McCready continued. 'It's ringing now.'

'Wait, wait.' Bryant held up his hand in placation. McCready made a show of shutting his phone again.

'A mate of mine passed on his plates to me when he packed up the taxiing. I never got round to changing the number.'

'Which is why you didn't contact us, is that right?' I asked.

He nodded. 'I've not done anything wrong. I just didn't want the hassle.'

'We're looking into a murder. You may have been one of the last people to have spoken to the victim. You understand that?'

'I didn't speak to him,' Bryant added sullenly. 'He didn't say anything to me when I picked him up. He was on the phone, talking about something or other. He told me to take him to Beechmount Avenue in Strabane and that was it.'

Bryant cocked his head, his eyes half-closed as he struggled to remember something. 'No, that's not right,' he said, correcting himself. 'He wanted to go to Doherty's bar on the Derry Road, then changed his mind halfway through. It was like he was arranging to meet someone on the phone. He asked to be dropped opposite the old factory. That was it.'

'You didn't see anyone hanging around when you dropped him off?'

'Actually, there were a group of kids across the way, sitting around a fire or something, in the factory grounds.'

'We know. We've spoken with them.'

Bryant bristled slightly. 'Then you know I drove off and left him there.'

'No one suggested otherwise,' I said. 'I'm more interested in the start of the journey. Where did you pick Cleary up from?'

'Coneyburrow Road,' Bryant said. 'I'd been up at the garage getting diesel when the call came through and I took it because I was so close.'

'Cleary's own home,' McCready said to me.

'You don't remember what number, do you?'

'If I do, will we forget about my overlooking the change in details?'

'That depends,' I said. 'Give me the number first.' I knew Cleary's mother lived in 28.

Bryant went across to the car and opened the driver's door. A yellow Post-it pad was attached to the windscreen with a sucker. He flicked through the first two pages, which were covered with scribbled addresses, then tore them off and scrunched them up in his pocket. He rifled through the side pocket on the inside of the driver's door and pulled out a handful of balled-up Post-its. He unravelled each until he found the one he wanted.

'Lucky I don't clean it out every night. Number 142. I picked him up at 10.25 p.m.'

I made a note of the number myself. 'You've been very helpful, Mr Bryant,' I said. 'If you do remember anything else, please do get in contact.'

'I KNOW THAT number,' McCready said as we got into the car. 'I've been there before.'

We headed straight across to Coneyburrow while I called Jim Hendry to update him.

'Burke was lying, Jim. Sean Cleary definitely had a phone. The driver says Cleary was arranging to meet someone while he was in his taxi.'

'We'll try picking Burke up again. He was let out with a caution over the twenty euro. The DPP thought it wasn't worth the effort. The young fella lives in a hostel down town. His folks turfed him out of the house a year back apparently.'

'If we can get Cleary's phone we'll know who he was arranging to meet.'

'I'll get the number off his mother and try some of the mobile companies. We might be able to get his call listings without the phone itself. I'll be in touch if I hear anything.'

'On an unrelated topic, the bonfire up at the factory. Would you let your daughter go to it, if you were me?'

'If I were you, my daughter would be in a nunnery already,' Hendry quipped. 'Trust me, I'm the worst person you can ask for parenting advice. My own kids hardly speak to me anymore.'

'Seamus O'Hara,' McCready said suddenly from beside me. 'That's who lives in 142.'

As soon as he said the name I realized he was right. Seamus O'Hara, the ferryman Reddin had named when I visited him.

Chapter Twenty-three

O'HARA'S HOUSE STOOD on its own grounds of about half an acre, bordered on all sides by leylandii trees, which obscured it from the road. Only when we pulled into the driveway did we notice that the curtains were drawn across the windows, as they had been when we called the previous day.

As I approached the house, I could see thick-bodied flies flitting against the small pane of glass in the centre of the front door. I banged on the door a few times, then leaned down and, opening the letterbox, shouted, 'Mr O'Hara? It's the guards.'

There was no response, but I could see more flies flitting in the light shining through the door glass.

I stood back and, aiming my boot as high as I could, kicked the door. It shuddered in the frame but did not shift.

'Might be best if I try,' McCready said, stepping back then taking a run at it, shouldering the door open before tumbling into the hallway.

I moved past him, helping him to his feet. The hallway was dull save for the light from the doorway, the wallpaper old fashioned, the carpeting dark and worn. Ahead of us the kitchen door yawned open, the remnants of an evening meal still sitting on the worktop by the sink. The air in the hallway was damp and heavy with the musty smell of old books, and something sharper and more visceral, which confirmed our worst fears. Heavy bluebottles buzzed back and forth, alighting on the door frame.

To our immediate left was the living room. A number of large mahogany bookcases dominated the wall facing us as we entered, their shelves sagging a little beneath the weight of the books they had once borne, but which now lay scattered on the floor. An old TV lay on its side on the ground, still playing soundlessly. On the floor nearby, his hand stretched towards the TV, was Seamus O'Hara.

He was on his back, clad in his pyjamas, his housecoat hanging open. His belly bulged through a gap in his nightshirt and I noticed his skin had already developed a distinctive greenish tint. Small blowflies flitted from the body to the curtains.

'He's dead a few days, I'd guess,' I said, moving closer to the body. There was no need to check for signs of life; O'Hara's eyes were clouded and unfocused, his face and neck peppered with small black pellet wounds around which his blood had crusted.

'Shotgun pellets?' McCready commented.

I shrugged. 'Maybe.'

He had fallen in front of an old worn armchair positioned by the fireplace. Heaped ashes were piled in the hearth. O'Hara's pipe lay on the tiles nearby. A tumbler of whiskey sat near the leg of the chair, its contents shining amber in the dim light.

While McCready called the station to request SOCO and the pathologist, I moved through the rest of the house.

To the rear of the living room was a small office. The room was neat and clean; the only objects that appeared to be out of place were a newspaper lying open on the desk and a pair of scissors next to it.

I moved through into the kitchen. The rear door to the property stood ajar and the glass from one of its four small square window panes lay shattered on the floor.

'Anything?'

I shook my head, opening the door and glancing out.

'I'll check upstairs,' McCready said.

As he did so, I moved back into the living room. The TV had not been taken, but then its age would have hardly made it the most appealing prospect for a burglar. As I looked at the glass of whiskey I silently considered O'Hara's last night. Presumably he had left the glass there with the intention of lifting it in the morning, in the expectation that the morning would come for him. The room with its books but no photographs of family or children saddened me. It was as if the man's life was further diminished in death by the fact that no one had even noticed he was gone.

Chapter Twenty-four

A JUNIOR DOCTOR from the local health centre arrived within twenty minutes to confirm death. He blanched at the sight of the body and I assumed he'd had little experience in dealing with such ripe corpses. He conducted his checks with little conversation, confirmed death, and left again as hurriedly as he could.

Our forensics technician, Michael Doherty, arrived just before noon, toting his black sampling cases. He worked the scene while waiting for the State Pathologist, Joe Long, to arrive and examine the body. Patterson and I stood in the living room. McCready had already begun canvassing neighbours with a team of uniforms, but considering the isolated nature of the house, surrounded by the high tree-line, it was unlikely anyone would have seen anything of use to us.

'Fucking pathetic,' Patterson muttered.

He guessed from my expression that I was unsure what he meant, so he gestured around the room.

'This. All these books. What did the man have, like? He's dead how many days, and no one even noticed?'

'It's sad,' I agreed.

'So, a robbery, then?'

'Looks like it. The kitchen-door window was smashed to gain access to the house. Whoever they were, they came in here, trashed the place looking for something.'

'Didn't take the TV,' Patterson commented. 'Anything else obvious gone?'

I shook my head. 'No computer, no DVD player. A few old VHS tapes but no sign of a video player.'

'VHS? Jesus,' Patterson said to the SOCO dusting the hallway doorframe for prints, 'was he afraid to spend money or some-thing, eh?' Then, to me, he said, 'What about upstairs?'

'McCready checked it,' I admitted. 'I took a quick look around, but I'm not sure about anything missing.'

I followed Paterson up. O'Hara's bedroom was to the front of the property. The small bedside lamp was still turned on, the bed-clothes tossed back, though the bed was otherwise undisturbed. A tumbler of water sat on a bedside cabinet, its contents spilled slightly onto the wooden surface. The wardrobe facing the bed lay open a little. On top of the bed lay a paperback book.

I moved across to the window. It was pulled closed, but the handle was not fully turned to lock it shut. I looked across to the neighbour-ing houses, only just visible over the tops of the trees. I could see McCready standing at the doorway of one, talking with the occupant.

Patterson began opening the drawers of the bedside cabinet. One contained socks and underwear, the next pyjamas. He flicked through the contents of each.

'No money lying around,' he commented. 'Oh ho,' he added, pulling a magazine out from beneath the clothes in the middle drawer. 'O'Hara was one of them.'

I glanced at the cover; it was a gay pornographic magazine.

'That's why he never married,' Patterson added, flicking through the pages.

For my part, I found this was the most unpleasant part of our job. O'Hara had lived alone but even then had hidden the magazine beneath clothes in his drawer, presumably out of embarrassment. Through the necessary steps of investigation we learned things about victims that their own families would not know; every secret, every embarrassment laid bare.

I glanced back out of the window and saw Joe Long's car arrive outside, the uniform manning the cordon lifting the crime-scene tape to allow the car to pass under.

Doherty finished working around the remains to allow Long to examine the body, and moved out to the kitchen in the hope that those who had broken in might have left prints around the door.

We moved back down, Joe Long acknowledging us with a nod of his head as we came into the room again. He flitted away a fat-bodied fly that had lifted from the corpse.

The living room was untouched since our arrival. The books lay scattered across the floor, some still lying atop others, as if whoever had left them there had simply swept them from the shelves.

'What do you think they were looking for?'

'Could be cash,' Patterson said. 'Seems a bit deliberate, mind you. Nothing obvious is missing, unless there's something we're just not seeing.'

'The other option is that Sean Cleary did this.'

Patterson nodded. 'Revenge for his father? It's possible.'

'There was no mention of powder or blood on his hands, though,' I said.

'He could have been wearing gloves,' Patterson suggested. 'Contact the North and ask them to look again.'

'What about the weapon? If O'Hara was shot with a shotgun, Cleary would've needed to get rid of it somewhere.'

'Maybe he has,' Patterson said. 'We'll search the area if Dr Long here confirms shotgun.'

I moved back into the office area again, although, as with the other room, nothing was obviously amiss. The newspaper was open at a crossword. The page before it had been cut out, the edge rough with scissor cuts.

Joe Long stood up, pulling off his latex gloves.

'What's the damage, Joe? Shotgun?'

Long shrugged his shoulders. 'I don't know. There's definitely pellet dispersal, but the pellets aren't typical of shotguns. Get young Doherty out there to take samples. You can work the body then bag it and send it to Letterkenny General. I'll examine it there.'

WE SPENT THE remainder of the afternoon searching the house, checking the grounds and the outlying land near the house, and interviewing neighbours. Yet by five o'clock we were no closer to recovering the murder weapon or developing any clear leads on who had shot Seamus O'Hara.

There were, however, two significant items unearthed among the mess on the living-room floor. The first was a small carriage clock, lying under the piles of books. The casing at the back had opened and the battery had spilled onto the floor. It had stopped at three twenty-three. To check that the clock had been working before being knocked down, I pushed the battery back in long enough to see the red second hand twitch to life.

It had come to light because one of the forensics team had been sent in by Michael Doherty to dust down the books on the floor, lest O'Hara's assailant had removed their gloves to search through them. The books were aged, mostly pertaining to Donegal or environs. Many were fishing records and charts. It was during this process that I noticed that one of the larger volumes on the floor was an Ordnance Survey of Donegal. I picked it up from the top of the tottering pile where it had been set and began flicking through it, looking for the map of Islandmore. Sure enough, the page for that area had been removed. I believed I knew where I had last seen it: inside a plastic folder held by Lennie Millar.

'Anything interesting?' Doherty asked, coming into the room.

'I think we've found the source of the tip-off to the Commission for the Location of Victims' Remains.'

Doherty nodded. 'And I think we might have got lucky out here,' he said, gesturing that I should follow him.

He led me out to the kitchen where the broken glass from the floor lay.

'I found blood on the broken glass,' he said. 'I want to take it back and run it through the system. It could be the assailant smashed the window and cut himself in the process. We might hit a DNA match.'

'Good work. How soon will you know?'

'If it's someone on the system, tonight or tomorrow. I'll be in touch as soon as I know.'

Chapter Twenty-five

McCready AND I met with Harry Patterson that evening in the station. Burgess was still there when we arrived.

'I followed that information up for you, Inspector,' he said. 'I got the run-around all afternoon. There were a load of companies and investors involved; then the whole lot collapsed. The bank had to take the properties from the builder then auction them off. A company registered in London now owns the estate. I can't get a name on who runs it unless I file an official request through the UK police. Do you want me to?'

'No thanks,' I said. 'I think I know another way to find out. Thanks for checking for me.'

'Anytime you're ready, Inspector,' Patterson called from the doorway of the main office. I followed him in and sat down. This had been Olly Costello's office for all the years I had served under him. Patterson had chosen to make Letterkenny his headquarters, but had ensured that the office remained empty for his use when he was in Lifford.

The scene-of-crime team was continuing to work the house, he informed us, but had already provided a preliminary report on their initial findings. Forensics had come back on the weapon, Patterson having made it clear he considered this a priority.

'Not a shotgun, apparently,' Patterson said, reading through the report. 'The pellets were actually shrapnel-like pieces of bullet casing. He reckons it was a dodgy gun, probably fitted with a silencer.'

'The same as the one that killed Sean Cleary?'

'I've contacted the North for their ballistics report on the Cleary gun. But it seems likely.'

'Date of death?'

'Considering the state of the body, the pathologist thinks around two days.'

'Putting it at the same day as Sean Cleary, too.'

'So the question is, who died first? Did Cleary do O'Hara then have his own gun used against him in the playground?'

'The clock in O'Hara's living room was stopped at 3.23,' I said. 'Considering he'd been in bed and had the curtains pulled, I think we can assume it was a.m. rather than p.m.'

'So, what have we got so far?' Patterson asked, leaning back in his seat, his fingers steepled in their usual position on his belly.

'We know that Cleary's interview went out at 6 p.m. By eight o'clock that evening he was at Jimmy Callan's house. He left there within a few minutes, though we do know that they argued. He was collected from O'Hara's house at 10.25 p.m. We'll need to get someone back out to Bryant to double-check there were no details missed.'

'Like what?' Patterson asked.

'Like whether Sean Cleary looked like he'd just shot someone,' McCready commented, then remembered to whom he was talking. He apologized quietly and lowered his head.

'We know that at 10.25 p.m. Cleary was on his way to Strabane. He wanted to go to a pub on the Derry Road. Then, in the course of a phone call, he changed his destination to the playground on Beechmount. The kid in the factory grounds, Burke, spotted him there at 10.30 p.m. He was dead by 2 a.m.'

'What we really need to know is if O'Hara was dead before or after that,' Patterson said. 'Did he die as a result of Cleary's encounter with whoever he met in the playground, or was he already dead by then?'

'We also need to find Jimmy Callan. We know Sean Cleary was with him before he went to O'Hara. They both wind up dead and then Callan vanishes the following morning in a bit of a panic.'

'I'll put out an alert on his whereabouts,' Patterson said.

'The one problem with all this,' I said, 'is that the Commission can't prosecute anyone for the killing of Sean's father anyway. No matter what they find out there, nothing can come of it. Millar has made that abundantly clear in all the interviews he's given. Yet we have Sean Cleary and Seamus O'Hara both connected to the dig and both murdered. And the diggers being petrol bombed on the night of the killings. Why would someone try to block an investigation that can never go to court anyway?'

'What connected O'Hara with the father, Declan Cleary?' Patterson asked.

'Cleary disappeared in '76, by which time both bridges onto the island had gone. To get his body onto the island, whoever killed him would have needed a boat. Either O'Hara helped the killer bring Declan Cleary across, or, when he was out at the nets, he saw something he shouldn't have.'

'Why would he have helped take him across? He wasn't connected with any of the paramilitaries during the Troubles.'

'He was a smuggler back then. Chances are, if the money was high enough he'd have done it.'

'And regretted it now, if he was the one who contacted both Cleary's son and the Commission.'

'Find out what connected Cleary and Callan in '76, too. The rumour was Declan was killed for touting on Callan's young lad, Dominic. Why would Jimmy Callan have thought Declan Cleary had information on his son? Were Declan and Dominic friends? Do a bit of digging.'

'What about the Commission? We're not allowed to examine the Cleary killing,' McCready said.

'The original one, we're not. But this is the son's death we're looking at, not the father's. Or, more correctly, it's O'Hara's we're looking at,' I said.

'Leave the Commission to me,' Patterson said.

As we were leaving, Patterson stopped me. 'I heard you getting Burgess out there to run down info on Islandview?'

I began to offer an explanation but he waved it away.

'The DPP have been in touch. They're dropping the Peter O'Connell file. They say there are too many peripheral issues to make a prosecution likely. They're not taking it any further. Maybe give your vendetta with Morrison a rest for a while, until we get all this other stuff to bed, eh?'

Chapter Twenty-six

DESPITE PATTERSON'S SUGGESTION that I lay off Morrison, his comment had simply reminded me of the alternative way to identify the owners of Islandview. The company Burgess had identified was not local, yet Paul O'Connell had gotten a key from somewhere, as had Sheila Clark. Whoever was behind the company must live close by.

I knew where I would find O'Connell. Many of the fellas Vincent Morrison had running the drugs around the borderlands for him were also employed legitimately in some of Morrison's legal ventures, thus allowing him to pay them an apparently legal wage and therefore to provide legal assistance when they needed it. O'Connell was no exception. Appropriately enough, he was a stable boy for Morrison's horses.

Morrison's home sat on a ten-acre site just beyond Porthall. To reach his house I had to drive along a quarter-mile driveway bordered by fields through which his horses cantered. It was from one such horse that my own daughter, Penny, had fallen and injured her skull.

As I pulled up to the front of the house, a two-storey redbrick affair with faux columns standing either side of the doorway, I knew Morrison was in and that he would already be aware that I was there. I glanced up at his security camera as I made my way to the door. Unsurprisingly the door opened before I even had a chance to ring the bell.

Morrison himself was a slight man, a little shorter than I and significantly trimmer. He still sported his moustache, though his hair had thinned somewhat since the first time we met.

'Inspector Devlin; it's always a pleasure. How's your lovely daughter? Still well, I believe.'

Morrison's son was a classmate of Penny's and one of her friends. I had tried many times to weaken the friendship between them, until the depth of the young boy's concern for her in the aftermath of her accident forced me to accept the sincerity of the friendship.

'Fine thanks. How's John?'

'A teenager. But, what can you do, eh? Is this a business or personal call?'

'Always business, Mr Morrison,' I said. 'I wanted to talk to you about Peter O'Connell.'

'Surely Peter's parents might be more use to you. I'm just his employer.'

'I'm well aware of that.'

'He told me you let him crawl through shit the other night. That was nasty.'

'I didn't do anything; he choose to walk through shit to get back his stash. It tells me something about how much he fears his employer that he'd do that rather than have to tell him he'd flushed away his drugs without any sales.'

Morrison laughed lightly. 'I hadn't considered it from that angle, but now you mention it, that's true.' He seemed vaguely satisfied at the suggestion.

'I wanted to make him an offer, but I suspect you're probably the better person to talk to.'

Morrison began to protest again. 'As I said, his own father—'

'I want to know who owns the unfinished houses at Islandview. I know they're tied up in all kinds of legal stuff, but I need a name. If O'Connell has a key to one of the houses, you know who he got it from.'

'And what would Peter get from this?'

'We'll not press charges,' I said. It was a gamble, but I suspected that no one had gone so far as to inform O'Connell yet that the DPP wasn't pursuing a case anyway.

'That's an offer worth considering. You might need to let me put that to Peter himself. Obviously I know nothing about whatever arrangements he has going on at night, but I could appeal to his better nature in assisting the local gardai.'

'That would be very civic-minded of you,' I said. 'He can contact me through the station,' I added, going back to my car.

I had barely made it out of the driveway when my mobile rang. The caller's number was blocked.

'Devlin here,' I called into the hands-free on the sun visor.

'This is Peter O'Connell. You wanted to know about Islandview?'

'How did you get this number?'

'Mr Morrison gave it to me,' O'Connell said. I didn't want to guess how Vincent Morrison had managed to acquire my mobile number.

'He said you'd drop charges,' he continued.

'That's right,' I called. 'I need to know where you got the key to the house in Islandview.'

'The man who owns the estate. Niall Martin,' O'Connell said.

'Where does he live?' I asked.

'Wait a minute . . .' I heard muttering, a rub of static as O'Connell covered the phone with his hand, presumably asking Morrison. It was clear that, whatever arrangement had been made with Martin for access to the house, it was not O'Connell's doing.

'He lives in the big house, the mansion . . . the *manse*, on Liskey Road in the North,' he corrected himself, his words an echo of those I could hear Morrison speaking in the background.

'Thank your boss,' I began, but the connection had already been cut.

MY INTEREST IN Niall Martin was simply in finding out more about Sheila Clark. It was not only the initial lack of sympathy she had shown Christine Cashell which had annoyed me. More importantly, Christine and I had both heard someone hurting a crying child. Clark lived in close enough proximity and I was fairly sure she was lying about there not being a child in her house.

I called Letterkenny station and requested they send me down anything they had on either Niall Martin or Sheila Clark. It would be morning before it would be through, the desk sergeant told me. I decided to hold fire on visiting Martin until I knew a little more about him. Morning would be time enough.

Wednesday, 31 October

Chapter Twenty-seven

THE INFORMATION I had requested was waiting for me when I arrived at the station. There was almost nothing on Niall Martin, beyond a speeding fine in the early nineties. Sheila Clark was different, however. She was on record as having worked in Letterkenny General as a paediatric nurse. She was in her early sixties now, and so retired. As I scanned her details, though, something stood out. She had worked in St Canice's Mother-and-Baby Home for four years from 1974 to 1978, which meant that she had worked there at the same time as Declan Cleary.

The last listed address for her had been in the late 1990s, then she herself seemed to have disappeared.

I was finishing reading through the notes when Burgess loomed into view.

'The super wants you in Letterkenny. Forensics work on the O'Hara shooting is back.'

THE FORENSICS TECHNICIAN, Michael Doherty, was sitting outside Patterson's office, waiting to go in when I arrived.

'Anything of interest?' I asked, sitting next to him.

He stifled a yawn. 'Quite a bit,' he said. 'Enough to stop me getting to bed last night, at any rate.'

Patterson's door opened and, clicking his fingers, he beckoned us in, gesturing to a flask of coffee and a set of cups and saucers sitting on the table. He handed us copies of the postmortem report. I sat and read through the notes quickly.

'He was already dying,' I concluded, closing the report. Patterson reclined in his seat, watching me. 'The cancer would have killed him in weeks, apparently.'

'So it's not quite so bad, then,' Patterson muttered. 'If he was dying anyway.'

O'Hara had been suffering from terminal pancreatic cancer. The disease had spread to such an extent that he would have been in severe pain and would, in all likelihood, not have survived to the new year anyway.

'The cause of death was bleeding out from the multiple gunshot wounds. Depth of wounding suggests low caliber or, more likely, a silenced weapon.'

'Which fits in with our findings yesterday,' Doherty said. 'We got a match on the ballistics from the Sean Cleary shooting. It was the same gun.'

He opened the folder he had with him and laid out images of the broken window pane in the back door of O'Hara's house. 'I also found quite a bit around this door,' he began. 'The glass is lying inside the house, as we'd expect,' he pointed out. 'So the assailant struck it from outside.'

'Otherwise it would be a break-*out*,' Patterson joked. Doherty smiled thinly, then continued.

'As I mentioned yesterday,' he said, 'I found traces of blood on the broken glass. The bulk of it was small drops,' he said, pointing to a small circle of blood smeared to the right of the image.

'The smearing is caused by the impact between the object striking the glass and the glass itself. Now, I found fibres of leather on the glass's broken edges, suggesting the impact was made with a gloved hand. The smearing effect you can see suggests that the assailant already had drops of blood on his or her glove and, in punching the glass, caused smearing of the drops at the point of impact.'

'So they had blood on their hands before they broke in?'

'This is where it gets interesting,' Doherty said. 'For I found two different types of blood.'

'Two different assailants?'

He shook his head. 'One of the bloods, the one smeared on the glass, belongs to Seamus O'Hara.'

'He smashed his own window?' Patterson asked.

'The smears suggest that drops of his blood were on the glove when it struck the glass. At the edges of the broken pieces at the point of impact I also found small traces of Sean Cleary's blood. He gave his DNA samples in when the dig for his father started; as the only living blood relative, we'd have needed his samples to confirm any remains found were his father's.'

'What does that mean?'

'It suggests that the person who broke the window wore gloves with O'Hara's blood spotted on them,' I said.

'And Sean Cleary's blood, too,' Doherty added.

'Blowback?'

'Probably,' Doherty agreed. 'When the bullet struck either man, the ensuing mist of blood would coat the hand holding the gun, if it was close enough to the victim.'

'So the window was broken after O'Hara was shot,' Patterson said. 'Presumably to make it look like a break-in gone wrong.'

I nodded. 'So it would seem.'

'O'Hara must have known his killer,' Patterson continued. 'The front door was chained. There were no signs of forced entry. He let his killer in and closed the door behind him.'

'More than that,' I said. 'I think he expected them to come. If he was killed at 3.23 why was his bedside light on? Why the cross-word sitting on the bed?'

'Maybe he fell asleep while he was doing it.'

'Plus he had his teeth in,' Doherty added.

'What?'

'The State Pathologist commented on it yesterday. O'Hara was wearing false teeth.'

'The glass of water beside his bed,' I said. 'He put his teeth back in. Someone called to the door. He'd not have bothered doing that if he thought there were intruders.'

'Would you open your door to someone at 3.23 in the morning? Especially if you were a man of O'Hara's age?'

'Only if you were expecting someone to call.'

Patterson nodded. 'And if he was opening the door to someone at that time of the morning, after speaking with Sean Cleary, he probably knew why they were coming.'

'He wanted to die,' I concluded. 'Whatever he told Sean Cleary sent the young fella out to meet someone. Whoever it was he met killed him, then came and did the same to O'Hara.'

'So what did O'Hara know? What did he tell Cleary?'

Doherty began gathering together the images again. 'I can't help with that,' he said. 'Anything else comes up, I'll let you know.'

'Go back out to Bryant,' Patterson said to me. 'Take a statement from him, see if he recalls anything about the phone conversation Sean Cleary had in the back of his taxi. Maybe he overheard something.'

My phone began vibrating in my pocket. It was Lennie Millar. He was on Islandmore. He needed me across there urgently.

Chapter Twenty-eight

IT WAS CLEAR when I arrived that something had happened. The site where Cleary had been discovered had been widened and deepened, a mound of earth piled to one side. Near the edge of the pit a blue tarpaulin was spread, its edges weighed down with concrete blocks against the wind running off the river. On top of the tarpaulin I could see several mounds of bone.

'Inspector,' Millar said when I got out of the car. 'We've found more bodies. Of infants.'

I glanced past him at the small mounds.

'Are they part of the *cillin*?'

'We don't think so,' he said. 'We found the remains of two when we came back yesterday to finish excavating the Cleary site. Those two caused us to widen the search perimeter further; we've located six so far. All of them seem to be fairly recent; within the last fifty years.'

'Any signs of violence?'

Millar shook his head. 'Not like with the first.'

'Okay.' I could sense there was something else, something he had not told me.

'We'd expect white clothes or a box of some type if they were part of the *cillin*,' he said. 'As was the case with the body we found the other day, there are none here.'

I nodded.

'There is something more, though. They are all like the first one in another way, too,' he said. Moving across to one set of remains he lifted a skull and, bringing it back to me, held it up to the light.

The cheekbone was missing; the upper jaw, as if molten, seemed to drip down onto where the lower should have been.

'That's not animal damage, is it?'

Millar shook his head.

'It's the same condition as the first skull?'

He nodded.

'Are they all the same?'

'Six so far,' he said dryly. 'All with Goldenhar syndrome.'

Millar stared at me, and I suspected I knew what he was thinking.

'You can't investigate this,' he said. 'I contacted you because you're our liaison; but you know that, at the moment, legally, we can do nothing with this.'

'So I understand,' I said, remaining as non-committal as possible.

'That said,' he added, 'this is clearly not a victim-of-violence case, in the manner of one of the Disappeared. So I will contact our own lawyers again and see what the situation is regarding the deaths.'

'That's fair enough.'

Chapter Twenty-nine

As I DROVE off the island, I saw the houses of Islandview to my left. I had intended to call again with Christine Cashell and had wanted to follow up on Sheila Clark. Being so close to the estate I figured I could manage both. On the way in I called Joe McCready and asked him to call with Bryant, the taxi driver, to see if he had remembered anything about Sean Cleary's final journey.

I was momentarily surprised when Sadie Cashell, Christine's mother, answered the door when I arrived at her daughter's house.

'Sadie, it's good to see you.'

'I heard you'd been involved,' she replied. 'You may come in.'

I had not seen her since the death of her daughter, Angela. I had spoken to Christine soon after; she had told me that her father had left home and her mother had begun a secretarial course.

Certainly Sadie looked better than she would have had she remained with Johnny, her husband, a habitual drunkard and a career recidivist. Sadie was still heavy, her hair still thick and chestnut brown, though greying in places, but she seemed more self-assured.

'You've been helping our Christine,' she said, sitting on the sofa and gesturing for me to sit on the armchair opposite.

'I've not done much,' I said.

'You've taken her serious when others wouldn't,' Sadie remarked, looking at me sideways as she spoke. 'That means something.'

'How is she?'

She paused a moment before answering. 'She's all right. She's not here at the moment; she's taken the young fella to football.'

'Tony? What age is he now?'

'Ten,' Sadie said. 'He's a wee star. You want to see him; he's top of the class in reading. He won a medal in the Feis last year for reading a poem.'

She smiled as she spoke, her face flushed with the warmth of her pride and affection.

'Is he your only grandchild?' I asked, then immediately regretted the insensitivity of the question. 'Sorry, I didn't mean it like . . .'

She dismissed my apology. 'He's the only one. Christine did a great job with him. She moved out here to get him away from bad influences.'

I smiled and Sadie guessed at my reason.

'I don't mean me, you cheeky bastard,' she snapped good-humouredly. 'The other kids around Clipton Place. Christine reckoned he'd be nearing the age where they start getting up to no good in the evenings. She doesn't want that for him. She came here and sure look how that has turned out. The bloody toilets don't even flush anymore.'

'Is she still hearing the crying?'

Sadie shook her head, glancing involuntarily to where the baby monitor sat, its lights unblinking, the plug lying unconnected on the floor. 'It stopped. She sat all through the night, Andrew said, waiting to hear something. She seemed more heartbroken when she heard nothing than when she thought she heard a youngster.'

She looked across at me quickly, a thought forming itself on her lips. She paused, then asked, 'Do you think she's going mad?'

'No. The monitor company said she's probably overheard a local child,' I said.

'There are no local kids, Devlin. We all know that. Is she hearing things?'

I shook my head. 'I heard something, too. I think there was a child here, in one of the houses nearby. I'm looking into it. In fact, can you ask her to call me if she sees the lady across the street at that house again?'

Sadie nodded. 'But she's not losing it or anything?'

I shook my head. 'If she is, I'm losing it with her.'

Sadie slumped slightly where she sat, as if her shoulders had collapsed after holding too long a weight they were not able to bear.

'Thank you,' she said softly.

I stood up. 'Tell her I'll see her again,' I said.

Sadie glanced at me quickly and nodded but did not speak further, lest to do so allowed the tears forming in her eyes to be released. I could not tell if it was relief in the knowledge her daughter had been right, or guilt at having ever doubted it in the first place. I suspected, as a parent, it was a mixture of both.

I GOT INTO the car to leave and glanced across at Clark's house. It was in darkness, the driveway empty. She'd already caught me snooping around once; what harm would a second time do?

I knocked at the door, but without response. Finally I jogged back across to Christine's house.

Sadie seemed surprised to see me again so soon. 'Did you forget something?' she asked, holding the door open for me.

'Christine wouldn't have a spare set of keys lying around, would she?'

Sadie regarded me with suspicion. 'Why?'

'Best not know,' I said.

She prevaricated a moment, then padded into the kitchen and returned a moment later with a small bunch of keys. They were on a plastic key ring containing a picture of Christine's son, Tony.

'I'll drop them back in a moment,' I said.

I crossed over to Sheila Clark's house again and moved around to the rear of the property. Andrew Dunne had claimed his house keys could open the doors to other properties in the estate. One by one I tried each key in the lock of the back door. To my surprise the third key I tried opened it.

'Hello,' I called, stepping into the house. 'An Garda. We've reports of an intruder. Is there anyone home?'

Silence. The floor was tiled with cream ceramic, the edges bordered with brown tiles. As I moved into the kitchen, I could see that the house had been finished to the highest standards. The units were solid beech, the refrigerator a large American model. Christine Cashell's partner had mentioned this had been a show house. Clearly the sellers had pulled out all the stops; how galling then it must have been for those unlucky enough to buy to discover that, not only were the other houses in the estate not similarly finished, but the estate itself would never be completed.

The rest of the house was similarly styled. I glanced quickly into the living room, which I had already seen from outside the day I met Sheila Clark, and then on into the conservatory. There was no one around.

The rooms upstairs were all decorated, too, though they seemed uninhabited. It was only when I went into the back bedroom that I found what I had been looking for. In addition to a large double bed, a small travel cot sat in the corner. It was empty now, the child that had been in it long gone.

Sitting on the floor next to it was a baby monitor identical to Christine Cashell's.

Chapter Thirty

SHEILA CLARK HAD vanished, but I still had Niall Martin's address to follow up on her. As he lived in the North, I called Jim Hendry to see if he knew anything more about Martin than the scant details our records on him had provided. I started the conversation on the Cleary killing.

'Any luck on finding Jimmy Callan?'

'Not on our side. What's happening with the O'Hara killing?'

'We're fairly sure it was the same shooter as did Cleary. Certainly the same gun was used in both killings. And both died on the same night.'

'We got a request about checking Cleary for gun-powder residues on his hands,' Hendry said. 'He was all clear.'

'No massive surprise there. Jimmy Callan looks like the likely candidate. If we could find him.'

Hendry grunted agreement.

'I have something else to ask, too. Niall Martin, Liskey Road over on your side. Does the name mean anything?'

'His father, Alan, certainly does; he's a pharmacist,' he stopped. 'Sorry, not that, a *pharmaceuticalist*, if that's even a real word. The family is loaded. Why?'

'I wanted to get some details on a woman living over in a ghost estate here; I'm told Niall owns the houses.'

'Where?'

'Islandview,' I said. 'Why?'

'He could do. Martin likes to play the market. He's been buying up a lot of the half-finished housing estates left over from when the market collapsed. He owns places all around the show. Don't expect him to be too forthcoming, though, the same boy.'

HIS HOUSE WAS on the Liskey Road, nestled on an acre site on the edge of the river Kerry. The back garden afforded a view of the entire river, running towards Sion Mills, its position accentuated by a living room whose rear wall was sheet glass, offering the owner the daily comfort of an unrestricted measure of the extent of his wealth and success.

Martin himself was a stout man, in his late fifties. He wore a blazer over a pale blue shirt open at the collar. A thin gold chain bearing a crucifix hung tightly around his neck. His hair was thick, though almost entirely greyed. His skin was fresh, his complexion ruddy. He rubbed his hands together as he spoke, as if in expectation of an imminent business transaction.

'Sit,' he said, pointing towards the corner sofa, which looked out over the river.

'You have a very beautiful home, Mr Martin,' I said. 'Nicely finished.'

He nodded. 'What brings a guard over to this part of the world?' he asked, his smile flitting lightly.

'I wanted to ask about Islandview, the estate over on my side towards Carrigans.'

He feigned confusion for a moment.

'Vincent Morrison told me you owned it. Is that right?'

'Did he?'

'One of his drug dealers was selling out of an unfinished house.'

Martin shook his head. 'That's the problem with estates. You have no control over undesirable elements.'

'The dealer had a key to the property. He told me he got it from you.'

'A drug dealer told you this? And you believe him?'

'I'm also told you rent out addresses to people from over here looking to play the system and claim double benefits.'

'Was that information from a drug dealer too?'

'No, that was one of the unfortunate inhabitants who have to deal with the failed sewage system in the estate pumping their shit into a field at the rear of their houses.'

He worked hard to maintain his smile. 'This is fascinating,' he said. 'I'm glad you called.'

'Do you own the estate?'

'One of my companies does,' he said. 'That doesn't mean I have any knowledge of what happens there. We employ people to handle that kind of stuff for me.' He glanced at his watch. 'You'll have to excuse me, but I'm dealing with my father. He's quite unwell at the moment.'

'A woman named Sheila Clark is living in one of the houses in that estate, I suspect illegally. Though she also seems to have a key. Do you know her?'

Martin shifted in his seat. 'Never heard of her,' he said.

'She had been living in the show house on the estate, but seems to have gone.'

'And how would you know that she has gone?'

'I called this morning and the door was open. Fortunately nothing seems to have been taken.'

'That is fortunate. I must get the locks changed.'

'She was a paediatric nurse. In her late fifties, early sixties?'

He shook his head, as if considering this new piece of information. 'No,' he decided finally, pursing his lips. 'What has she done? Double benefits claiming?'

'Something like that,' I said. 'I need a permanent address for her. Perhaps you'd get that information for me.'

'I'll do my very best,' he said. 'Though, as a guard, there may be issues with whether you have a right to ask for this information over on this side.'

'I can get the PSNI to make the request for me if you want, Mr Martin,' I said. 'But it would be so much more amicable this way.'

He smiled coldly.

'Just out of interest,' I said. 'Why buy a ghost estate? Are you not just inheriting someone else's problems?'

He shrugged. 'The price was right,' he said. 'The market will recover some day.'

I stood and shook hands with him. His skin was soft and warm, not that of someone who engages in manual labour.

'I'd appreciate that address,' I said.

Chapter Thirty-one

Joe McCready called my mobile as I headed back to Lifford station.

'I've spoken with Bryant,' he said. 'He's remembered something else from that night. He said Cleary was holding a page from a newspaper when he was on the phone.'

'What?'

'He came out of O'Hara's with a sheet of newspaper in his hand.'

'A page? Not the whole paper?'

'A page,' McCready echoed. 'One page. He carried it out with him into the car and was looking at it as he spoke on the phone.'

I recalled that the post-mortem for Cleary had commented on ink and paper fibres on his hand. More importantly, I recalled the newspaper lying on O'Hara's study desk, the serrated edge where one page had been cut out, and the scissors still sitting on the desk. I suspected I knew from where Cleary had got the newspaper page.

'That's good work, Joe. I think I have an idea how to follow it up. I need you to do something else for me. Can you check up with

Letterkenny Hospital for children born during the seventies with Goldenhar syndrome? We'll need names and addresses.'

'Why?'

'The Commission dig on Islandview has unearthed more corpses with facial malformation consistent with the illness. They won't let us do forensics on them, but if the condition runs in families or that, we might be able to generate some leads.'

'Are we not meant to be steering clear of Commission-related stuff?'

'Apparently,' I said.

'Then why are we looking into this?'

'Someone buried seven children out on that island, at least one of whom was murdered. What's to say that all of them weren't killed? I don't really care what the law says. Someone needs to answer for that. Will you do it?'

He paused a second. 'Of course.'

O'HARA'S HOUSE HAD not been touched since the SOCO team had worked through it. Grey dustings of fingerprints were still visible on walls and door handles, and chalk circles remained on the carpet where fragments of the bullet which killed O'Hara had been found. The tumbler of whiskey remained beneath the sofa in the living room, never to be drunk. The smell in the house was a strange mixture of damp, blood and defecation that the closed doors and sealed windows had allowed to build and bloom. I opened wide the window in the living room, then moved into the study. Sure enough, the newspaper still lay open on the desk, the tear where a page had been removed obvious. It was a local free paper, comprising photographs and the occasional news report buried among all the advertisements for nightclubs and car dealerships, trying to convince us all that the party wasn't over and that we could still buy our way back out of the country's collective economic hangover.

I checked the date on the top of the next page: 15 May. O'Hara had held on to the paper for almost six months. The sheet which had been removed was pages 17 and 18. I knew the paper's office was in Ballybofey; it would not be difficult to get a copy of the paper.

TWENTY MINUTES LATER, the receptionist of the *Donegal Reporter* offices led me into a small room. On a desk sat a thick leather-bound ledger which held six months' worth of newspapers. I flicked through the various copies until I found the one dated 15 May. I opened it at page 17 and scanned the page quickly, looking for anything that might suggest why O'Hara would have given it to Cleary, but nothing stood out. The upper half of the page was an ad for a car-sales showroom in Letterkenny. The bottom half ran an advertorial for a double-glazing company.

I turned it over and glanced down page 18. The whole sheet consisted of old photographs. The banner line across the top ran 'This was the day that was . . .', beneath which were arranged twelve photographs taken on various 15 May dates during the previous half-century. A number were of groups of first communicants; one was of a church social-club meeting. The one which most interested me, however, was the second from the bottom in the left-hand column. It was a picture of a charity presentation. A tall, angular man in a suit stood smiling at the camera as he presented an oversized cheque to a younger woman. The hair style had changed, the face was more careworn now, but I recognized her as Sheila Clark. Four young men stood around the central pair, their hands clasped behind their backs. I read the caption that ran beneath the picture: 'Local businessman Alan Martin presents a donation of £10,000 to Shelia Clark, St Canice's. Also pictured are staff members Declan Cleary, Seamus O'Hara, Dominic Callan and Niall Martin. May, 1976.'

I studied the faces of the young men. Cleary smiled broadly, his head cocked slightly to one side. Callan stared directly at the camera, his expression stony. I wondered if either of them could have guessed that they would both meet violent deaths within six months of the picture being taken. I wondered why Alan Martin would make so big a donation to a mother-and-baby home in Donegal. And, most importantly, I wondered why Niall Martin had claimed not to know Sheila Clark when we spoke.

Chapter Thirty-two

DESPITE MY RELUCTANCE, we dropped Penny in Strabane for the bonfire, while we took Shane to Derry to watch the fireworks display. We had to start trusting her to behave like an adult, Debs reasoned. Eventually I acquiesced, but not before I'd warned Penny to avoid trouble, to stay well back from the fire and, in particular, not to be drinking.

'I don't drink, Dad,' she said. 'I'm not stupid.'

'I never suspected you of being stupid, Penny,' I said. 'But I've seen what happens at these things.'

'Why won't you trust me?'

'I do trust you,' I said. 'It's other people I don't trust. Don't let anyone . . .' I faltered as I struggled to complete the order.

'Don't let anyone what?'

'Do anything to you,' I managed, though it did not express what I had intended.

'Dad!' Penny shrieked. 'I'm going to the bonnie. That's all.'

AFTER WE'D WATCHED the fireworks in Derry, I dropped Debs and Shane back home and cut across to collect Penny again at ten, before things got too out-of-hand with the fire. I parked along Beechmount, not far from the playground where Sean Cleary had been found, and waited. Penny had said she would be standing at the main gates to the old factory site at ten on the dot. When she was still not there ten minutes later I went looking for her. Just as I entered the site I saw her coming towards me, her head down, her hood pulled up despite the wall of heat emanating from the fire.

Behind her I could see the skeleton of the bonfire through the thick flames which bloomed around it. Black circles of car tyres were being flung into its heart, each impact causing a shower of embers to flare from its top. The flickering of the flames and the movements of the crowds shifting around the site caused the shadows to play across Penny's face so I could not properly read her expression. She stumbled as she walked and I at first assumed the uneven ground had caused her to lose her footing. Then she did it a second time and put her hand out to steady herself.

I moved across to her. Her face was still in semi-darkness, though she seemed unusually flushed. She stumbled a third time and staggered against me.

'Are you okay?'

'I'm fine,' she mumbled.

'You're late,' I said. 'What kept you?'

Her response disappeared into a mumble.

'Have you been drinking?'

'Dad!' she shrieked and moved away from me quickly, stomping across to the car as if she were still an infant, her hands balled at her sides.

I opened the door and she climbed in without a further word, sitting in the back seat instead of up front beside me.

Once she was in I turned on the interior light and twisted in my seat.

'Now what's going on?'

She recoiled from me. In the shadow of her hood her face was slick with tears.

'Penny, what's happened?'

She angled her head slightly towards the light, even as she began shuddering, her tears beginning in earnest, slipping unbidden from a swollen black eye.

'Jesus Christ, what happened?'

'I want my mummy,' she sobbed.

'What happened?'

'I want Mummy!' she screamed. 'I want my mummy!'

I SPOKE TO her as soothingly as possible as I drove her back across the border, but I could not keep at bay my own fears. What had been done to her that was so bad she could not discuss it with me? Her clothes looked undisturbed, but she would not speak to me, would not explain how she had come to be injured.

Debs looked up when we came in, her expression freezing as she caught sight of Penny's face.

'What happened?'

I shrugged. 'She wouldn't tell me. She only wants to speak with you.'

Penny flopped on the sofa beside her and buried her head against her mother's neck, her body racked with sobs. Over the course of the next hour she explained to us what had happened.

HER FRIENDS HAD met her at the bonfire, as planned. A few of them, however, had arrived with blue carry-out bags of drink that one, Claire, had convinced her older brother to buy for them. They had sat around the smaller fire which had been used to light the torches for the main bonfire, and several of them, though not Penny herself, she stressed, had been drinking.

Sometime later a group of boys had come across to join them, including Stephen Burke, who had brought more drink with him. It had been good humoured at first, the boys teasing the girls about being under age, the girls pretending to be annoyed at their comments, but secretly delighted with the attention.

Bit by bit a few of them had begun to pair up, sitting together around the fire, sharing beer cans and cigarettes, huddled up despite the heat of both the small fire before them and the larger bonfire off to one side of them.

Claire, however, had begun to struggle. She had drunk too much too quickly, encouraged by the attentions of the older boy and buoyed up with pride at having secured the alcohol in the first place.

In turn, Stephen Burke had begun getting more adventurous in his attempts to get her to yield to him. While Claire had sat on his knee by the fire, he had attempted several times to put his hands inside her top, eventually succeeding. He must have noticed Penny watching him, for he said, 'You're the cop's daughter, aren't you?'

'He's a guard,' Penny managed, her mouth dry.

'He's a guard,' Burke repeated, mimicking her in a mincing voice. 'He's a prick,' he added suddenly.

'I think we should go, Claire,' Penny said, but her friend did not respond.

A few minutes later, Claire had fallen off his lap, landing in a drunken sprawl on the ground. Burke had sat where he was, laughing at her. Penny and her friend, Elaine, had helped Claire to her feet. It was clear that Claire was in no fit state to stay any longer; she was tripping over herself, her legs seemingly beyond her control. She felt sick, she said, and suddenly dashed towards the rear of the factory site, where the last remains of the building were intermittently illuminated by the flickering of the flames from the bonfire.

As Claire stumbled away from them, the two girls followed, but Burke stood and pushed them to one side, saying he would see she was all right. Penny, without the support of anyone else in the circle but Elaine, acquiesced, against her own better judgement. Still, over the next quarter of an hour, she looked constantly into the shadows, where she could see Claire, bent double, vomiting onto the factory rubble. Penny continued to watch, even when some of the boy's friends commented on her fascination with what was going on.

Finally, when she saw Burke heft Claire to her feet and pin her against the perimeter wall of the site, she got up and went across to them. As she got closer, even in the murk of the shadows, she could see that Claire was semi-conscious while the boy was opening the button on her trousers.

Penny had shouted at him as she approached, telling him to leave her alone. He had continued, his fumbling becoming more aggressive even as Claire slumped to the ground. Finally, in fury, the boy turned to face Penny.

'What do you want, you nosey bitch?' he spat. Then he added, 'Just like your da,' as he punched her in the face, knocking her to the ground.

'No one helped me get up again,' she said, her sobbing subsided now, but her tears still flowing freely.

'The little fucker,' I spat.

'Ben!'

'I'm going over to get him,' I said, grabbing the car keys.

Penny shrugged. 'Don't, Dad. Stop being such a cop.'

'I'm not being a cop, Penny, I'm being your father.'

'Claire will get into trouble, Dad. Her folks will kill her if they find out she's been drinking.'

'They'll be more concerned if they find out she's been sexually assaulted,' I said.

'Leave it for now, Ben,' Debs said.

I swallowed down my rage as I thought not of what the boy had done to Claire but that he had struck my daughter. As a father, I didn't want the boy arrested; I wanted to beat him senseless myself. I wanted to pummel his face for what he had done.

'He didn't try anything with you, did he?' I asked.

Penny shook her head, her eyes not quite reaching mine, as though embarrassed. 'He punched me, Dad.'

'How do you feel now?' Debs asked.

'Okay. A little shaky.'

Debbie angled Penny's head upwards, her face towards the light. 'Let me see your pupils,' she said.

'I told you I wasn't drinking, Mum,' Penny said.

'And I trust you,' Debs replied. 'But you had a brain injury and this boy hit you on the head. I want to be sure he hasn't damaged anything inside this beautiful little skull.'

Penny managed a smile and wiped her face with the sleeve of her jacket.

'I'm very proud of you, honey,' Debbie said.

'For not drinking?'

'For standing up for your friend when no one else did. Even if it meant you got yourself hurt.'

'She still had him pawing all over her. I should have gone over to her myself at the start.'

'You did just fine,' Debs said.

I heard something in the hallway and looked out to see Shane crouching on the stairway, listening to the conversation. As he stared at Penny's swollen face, his expression was drawn, his skin pale. When he noticed I was watching him, he stood and padded back up to his room without a word.

I went up the stairs, ostensibly to check on him, though also because I wanted to phone Jim Hendry. Penny had said she didn't want her friend to get in trouble, but I had no intention of allowing someone to punch my child with impunity.

As it transpired, Hendry was ahead of me. Claire had been lifted by an ambulance crew that had been on standby in case of any burn injuries suffered at the fire. Her parents had been contacted and the girl was already giving a statement to a female officer from the Public Protection Unit.

'It's Burke,' I said. 'Penny was with the girl. She tried to intervene and he punched her.'

'Jesus, is she all right?'

'She has a black eye. She's a little shaken, but she seems to be coming around.'

'It wouldn't have any implications on her . . . injury, you know, her brain thing.'

'We're going to take her to the doctor and get her checked out.'

'We'll be looking for Burke. I'll head down to the hostel where he stays myself and see if I can pick him up. If Penny feels up to it, a statement would be very useful.'

'As soon as she's at herself I'll bring her across,' I promised.

'Ben,' Hendry began. 'If I find Burke tonight, do you want to know about it before I bring him in?'

I was taken aback at the baldness of the question and, more so, by the time it took me to say, 'Thanks, Jim. Best not.'

Shane was standing in the doorway of his own bedroom when I came out of mine.

'Is Penny okay?'

I nodded. 'She'll be fine. She got hurt.'

'Did someone hit her?'

I nodded, not trusting myself to speak as I considered the pain and self-doubt that marked his expression.

'I didn't mean what I said about her,' he said, his tears already gathering.

'Forget about it, partner,' I said.

'I don't want anyone hurting her,' he blubbed.

'I know. Penny knows that, too.'

He was not to be convinced, though, turning angrily and going back to his bed. I could hear his mutters as I went back downstairs to where Penny and Debbie were still sitting together on the sofa.

Thursday, 1 November

Chapter Thirty-three

We sat in Accident and Emergency at Letterkenny General Hospital until 4 a.m. before Penny was seen. My parents had come up to watch Shane, allowing Debbie and me to take Penny in together. Once she had told us her story, she had settled somewhat. Still, considering her recent head injury it seemed prudent to get her checked following the blow to her face.

She grew sleepy while we sat, and despite our best efforts to keep her awake, she stretched out across the two chairs beside us and laid her head on Debbie's lap. I covered her with my coat and sat with her legs across my own knees.

Despite being mid-week, the ward was busy. Opposite us a young boy sat with his mother, his arm hanging limply in a sling. She explained to Debbie that he had fallen while getting out of the car and she thought he had broken his wrist. To her left sat a man in dress trousers and a white shirt. The front of the shirt was spotted with blood and he held a bloody wad of tissue to his mouth. He looked across at me and winked happily, his face breaking into a smile that revealed the gap where two teeth were missing and the split in the lip below where they should have been.

Around 1 a.m. the burns injuries started appearing. Most were teenage boys who had been handling fireworks. Some were minor scorches from mishandled sparklers, others more serious burns from firecrackers. One held his hand against his chest, the thick bandages wrapped around it unable to disguise the absence of several fingers. He was wheeled through immediately and no one else was called in for treatment for some time.

'Have you told Jim?' Debs asked me when Penny was asleep.

I nodded. 'Burke's known to them. We had him in over the Sean Cleary killing. He robbed the body.'

'Do you know where he lives?' she asked, not even trying to disguise the hope in her voice.

'He stays in a hostel in Strabane. His folks threw him out. Jim's going looking for him.'

'Maybe you should have found him before you told the North.'

I glanced at her to see if she was being serious. The set of her jaw left no room for confusion.

'He assaulted Claire. He'll do time for that.'

'He better,' Debs said, running her hand through Penny's hair.

'Would you rather I beat him up myself?'

'It wouldn't be the first time, Ben. This time you could do it for one of your own family instead of strangers.'

'I wanted to go across. Penny said . . .'

The discussion was cut short by our being called in to the triage room. After a further twenty-minute wait a locum doctor came in. He scolded us for allowing Penny to sleep, though by the time he did so she had woken anyway.

He shone a small pen-light into both of her eyes, using his thumb to hold open the lower lid on the swollen eye.

'Reactions look normal,' he said. 'What happened to her?'

'A boy struck her.'

'Maybe be more careful in the company she keeps.'

'She was protecting her friend from a sexual assault,' I said. 'I'd maybe mind my tone.'

'And you yours,' the locum said, putting away the light. 'She seems fine. Keep an eye on her; if she gets headaches or that, bring her back in.'

With that he turned and swept back the curtain of the unit in which we sat. The nurse who had been standing with us, smiled apologetically. 'It gets a little fractious, sometimes, when we're busy,' she offered by way of explanation.

I ATTENDED MASS for All Saints' Day later that morning. It was also the Requiem Mass for Sean Cleary, his remains having been released by the PSNI. Several times during the service, Father Brennan made reference to the macabre symmetry of Sean's life, which began just after his father's disappearance and ended just before the discovery of Declan's remains. He had no doubt, he said, that they had finally met in God's kingdom.

At the end of the service, before Sean Cleary's coffin was carried from the church, Brennan also announced his intention to bless the *cillin* on Islandview the following day, on the Feast of All Souls. He extended an invitation to any parishioners who may have had to bury children there, or who knew of brothers or sisters who rested beneath the island soil, to attend the service. He prefaced this with a short word about the whole idea of the *cillin* and the Catholic tradition of limbo. The rules had loosened, he said, so that, in the words of the Church, 'there was a very great hope' that those children who had been lost would be reunited with God. His own belief, he confessed, was much firmer with regards to the communion of God with such infants, and the special place they held by His throne.

As I scanned the congregation, I wondered if the seven infants found on the west of the island, alongside Declan Cleary, would be included in his blessing, so that they too might recover their rightful place among the consecrated dead.

On leaving the church, I approached Mary Collins and her husband and again offered my condolences on the loss of her son. She held my hand in both of hers as she thanked me, though she seemed so dazed I doubted she even knew who I was.

When I reached my car I noticed I had a new voicemail message on the phone. McCready had called; he had traced only a single name for a child born with Goldenhar syndrome in Donegal during the 1970s.

Chapter Thirty-four

'HIS NAME IS Christopher Hillen,' McCready explained as we drew up outside the address in Ballykeen an hour later. 'He was born in April 1976.'

The modest council house was part of a row of five. The entire estate consisted of such blocks, built as part of the social-housing schemes that had sprung up around the country in the eighties.

As we walked up the pathway to the house, the lace curtains at the front window twitched. Before we even had a chance to knock, a middle-aged woman opened the door.

'Mrs Hillen?' McCready asked.

'Yes,' she looked from McCready to me and back, her expression drawn. 'Is something wrong?' She was fine-featured, her hair thick and brown. She wore no make-up, her skin fresh save for some mild acne-scarring on her cheeks. She was not much older than fifty.

'No ma'am,' McCready said. 'I'm Sergeant McCready; this is Inspector Devlin. We wanted to talk to you about Christopher.'

'What's Christopher done?' she asked, standing more erect, her tone suddenly defensive.

'Nothing ma'am,' I said. 'We're looking for some help, to be honest. Is your husband home?'

'My husband?'

'Christopher.'

She smiled warmly. 'You're a right charmer, too, aren't you? Christopher's my son.'

'This is Christopher Hillen? Born April 1976? He's your son?'

'Get away with you,' she smiled. 'He's my son. I was only a kid myself when I had him. You may come in.' She stepped back, laughing to herself as we passed.

She was little more than 5'5", standing as she did barefooted. She wore a loose grey tracksuit, her hair pulled back and twisted around a biro pen, which held the bun in place.

The hallway was narrow and dark, the staircase to our left-hand side separated from us by a flimsy sheet-wood banister. The kitchen was cramped, the only space for sitting two bar-stools either side of a breakfast bar. The ceiling retained its original wood panelling.

'I'm just having tea, do you want a cup?'

'Lovely,' I said. 'Milk and one sugar, please.'

'Just milk for me, thanks.'

'No wonder you're so sweet,' she said to me, gesturing for us to sit while she made the tea in two mugs and handed them to us. 'What can I do for you, then?'

'We wanted to ask about your son's illness.'

'Oculo-auriculo-vertebral spectrum,' she said, rolling the 'r's. 'What about it?'

Joe looked at me uncertainly, then said, 'We thought he had Goldenhar syndrome.'

'It's the same thing,' she said. 'Different name.'

'Can you tell us something about it, Mrs Hillen?' I asked.

'Jane,' she said. 'There's not much to tell. When Christopher was born he had bones missing on one side of his face. He had some hearing difficulty in one ear and his speech was a little slow. He got some help when he was a child, quite a bit more when he grew up. That's it. He was very lucky.'

'Lucky how?'

'He has a relatively mild version of it. He had no other defects, heart or kidneys or that. Some babies who develop it don't even live to birth.'

We heard a rattle at the door as a key turned in the lock and, a moment later, a man I assumed to be Christopher clomped down the hall. He was a little stooped, though that may have been due to the bags of shopping he was carrying.

'Hello,' he said. Even having seen the skeletons on Islandmore, I was a little taken aback by his face. On the left-hand side his cheekbone seemed to be entirely missing, with the consequence that his skin had puckered into a gap several inches above his mouth. His upper lip was pulled back, his lower eyelids drooping. He wore his hair long, but I could see that his right ear was smaller than the other, the tan plastic of a hearing aid visible above it.

'Christopher, son,' Jane said. 'These men are here to talk about your condition. Do you want to tell them anything about it?'

'It's shit,' he said. 'I can't get a girlfriend for a start.'

'Which is why he's still living with his mother at the age of 35,' Jane added, laughing.

Despite his facial abnormality, Christopher's speech was fairly clear, if a little sibilant in places.

'I expected . . .'

'Worse?' Jane asked.

'To be honest, yes,' I said. 'No offence.'

The man shrugged as he began sorting through the bags.

'I told you we were lucky. Our health insurance covered the essential surgery when he was younger, but what he needs now is cosmetic work and they'll not cover that. We'll have to pay for it ourselves but it costs a bomb. We'll get there, even if it takes a while.'

'What causes it?' McCready asked. He had barely spoken since Christopher had arrived and I noticed the tea in front of him remained untouched.

'No one knows. It's purely random, doesn't run in families or that. It just happens.'

'You're very accepting of it,' I said. 'It's remarkable.'

'What choice have I? He's my son, what am I going to do? I've had thirty-five years with it, you know?'

I nodded.

'So, what does this have to do with the guards?' Jane asked.

'We've found the remains of several children with Goldenhar syndrome,' I said. 'One of them, we think, may have been murdered. I had hoped to identify them. I thought maybe you might have known other families with children similar to Christopher, maybe from when he was younger?'

She shook her head. 'Me and him have been on our own since the day he was born. No help, no support, just the two of us.'

'What about support groups? Your family?'

Jane glanced at Christopher as he put groceries into one of the kitchen units.

'Son, would you run to the shop for me again? I forgot to get sweetener?'

'What?' he said, exasperated. 'You're not dieting.'

'I'll need to start again,' she said. 'Be a love.'

Muttering to himself, he laid down the two cans he held and headed back out again.

'Do youse want anything?' he said to McCready and me as he passed.

'No thanks, Christopher,' I said.

'I'm fine,' McCready managed. 'Thanks.'

When he had gone, Jane leaned back on the counter. 'My family have had nothing to do with me since before he was born. I got pregnant when I was 15. My first boyfriend. He was a real rat, too, but what could you do? I was a shy wee'un – not that you'd think it now. Spotty, like. The first fella that showed any interest in me, well I couldn't believe it. It was only afterwards that I realized he was only showing interest in me cause he thought I'd be desperate for it. Never spoke to me again.'

She stared at us openly, as if looking for some reaction, some judgment.

'What you'd love to tell your fifteen-year-old self, if you could, eh?'

'What happened?'

'My old man flipped. What would the priest say? What would the neighbours think? The usual shit. They put me in care. After I had Christopher, when they heard what he looked like, they wanted nothing to do with him.'

'I'm sorry to have brought all this up for you,' I said.

'He came to the home when Christopher was born and told me they'd let me come back. He said he'd buy me a bike if I left Christopher behind. Let them give him away. I'd always been at him to get me a Chopper.'

I laughed, remembering my own Chopper.

'I know,' she said. 'A Chopper, for Christ's sake!'

'What home were you in?'

'St Canice's. They stuck me in there to get rid of me. Then the people in charge must have called him when Christopher was born. It was the only time he visited during the whole time there. Him and his fucking bike.'

'What did you do?' McCready asked, his voice dry. He shrugged. 'Well, obviously, I know what you did, but . . . were you not tempted?'

'Of course I was,' she replied incredulously. 'I was a wain myself, not stupid. But I went into the room where they kept the babies, in the home, and looked at him lying in his cot. No one wanted him, no one would ever have adopted him looking the way he did. He'd have been alone in the world. I thought it would have been a shitty thing to do, to leave him like that. I knew how it felt to not be wanted.'

The room had quietened around us and she faltered as she finished speaking, her tongue clicking dryly in her mouth.

'So here we are.'

'Any regrets?' I asked.

'Are you kidding? Loads,' she said, laughing. 'But, as I say, here we are. So is that any help?'

'None,' I admitted. 'We have no leads on who the children are. I had half-hoped you might have known some families who had children similar to Christopher.'

'There are no children similar to Christopher,' she said. 'Leastways, I've never met any.'

WE HAD RETURNED to our car and McCready was starting up the engine when she ran down from the door to speak to us.

'Look,' she said, after some hesitation. 'I don't want to get anyone into trouble, but I think I might know about one of the babies on the island.'

'The way things are going, Miss Hillen,' I said, 'The only person likely to get into trouble over the dig on the island is me.'

She laughed uncertainly. 'There was another girl who was with me in St Canice's. Her name was Margot Kennedy. She had her baby about a month after Christopher was born. I met her in Strabane once, a few years after, and asked how the baby was doing. She said it had been born dead. It hadn't been right. She'd looked at Christopher when she said it. "He looked even worse than him," she'd said.'

'I appreciate you telling us, Miss Hillen,' I said. 'I understand your reluctance.'

'I don't want her getting into trouble. The baby died in the home, you know. I guess at that time they might not have had a choice but to bury it on the island. Just, don't tell her it was me who gave her name. Especially if . . . you know.'

'The child we found was a girl, Miss Hillen,' I said. 'You have nothing to worry about.'

Chapter Thirty-five

I PHONED THROUGH to the station while McCready drove and asked Burgess to run Margot Kennedy through the system for me. We were passing the turn-off for Raphoe when he called back.

'I have the details on that woman. Her name's Hughes now; she lives on the other side of Ballybofey.'

He ran through the details before adding. 'Your informant was wrong, by the way. Margot Kennedy's child didn't die.'

'What? How do you know?'

'Max Kennedy was given a PPS number when he was a year old. She must have put him up for adoption, though, for his name now is Max McGrath. He still has the same social-security number, and a passport, driving license and everything.'

'Where does he live?'

'Donegal town. 64 Shandon Park.'

I reported all this to McCready after I hung up. 'We'll visit Margot Hughes first. If we need to, it's just a short run onto Donegal town.'

'Putting the child up for adoption isn't illegal,' McCready said. 'We'd have no reason for following up on her son.'

'But why would she have told Jane Hillen the child had died?'

'Maybe she was ashamed,' McCready said. 'Maybe she felt she couldn't keep it with a disability and was shamed by the fact that Hillen had.'

It seemed a plausible reason.

Hughes's house was set back from the road on the way out of Ballybofey. To the rear of the property a large garden stretched down towards a low fence, above which could be viewed the expanse of the Blue Stack Mountains.

Margot Hughes sat nervously in a wide armchair in her living room while I introduced myself. Her husband had been out working on a car in the garage when we had arrived, his boiler suit pulled down off his trunk and tied around his waist, despite the cold, his T-shirt smeared with engine oil.

He had demanded to know why we wanted to speak to his wife and had followed us into the living room when she finally answered the door. He perched on the arm of the sofa, glaring from her to us.

'So what's going on?'

'We need to speak with your wife about St Canice's,' I said.

'Where?' His accent was Northern, Newry perhaps. He was clearly not a local, which explained why he didn't recognize the name.

'It was a hospital,' Margot Hughes replied timidly. 'A children's hospital when I was an infant. I was never in it, though,' she added quickly, looking at me momentarily.

McCready sat forward in his seat. 'We were told you had been—'

'A friend of a patient there,' I added quickly.

Mr Hughes stared at me with open suspicion.

'I'm afraid we have some bad news about her. We wanted to ask you a few questions.'

McCready finally realized what was happening.

'Is that a DS out there?' he asked the husband. 'What year?'

'Sixty-five,' Hughes replied. 'Why?'

'I used to drive a 2CV,' McCready said. 'I always wanted a DS.'

'Don't,' the man replied, a little less gruffly. 'They drink petrol.'

'It would be worth it for the drive, though,' McCready said, smiling. 'Can I see it?'

Hughes glanced from his wife to me one last time, seemingly satisfied that the reason for our visit was as innocuous as we had claimed.

'I'm rebuilding it,' Hughes said. 'I got the body in a scrap yard and I've been buying up the parts off eBay. It's a bit of a labour of love.'

'I'm sure it is,' McCready said, standing as Hughes stood.

'Thank you,' Margot Hughes said quietly after her husband had shut the front door.

'He doesn't know about the baby?'

She shook her head, her eyes already filling. 'I met him when I was in my late-twenties. I'd been in St Canice's over a decade before that. There was never a reason to tell him.'

'He doesn't strike me as the type who would take such news well,' I remarked.

'He's a good man,' Margot Hughes replied quickly. 'He just likes to know what's going on. Who gave you my name?'

'I can't say, Mrs Hughes. I'm sorry to bring this all back up for you. We've been digging on Islandview and have uncovered the remains of infants. We believe they were buried there as part of a *cillin*.'

She nodded.

'We were told that—'

Her tears began freely now. 'My son is there, if that's what you want to ask.'

'I'm sorry, Mrs Hughes,' I said. 'I didn't mean to upset you.'

She shook away the offer of a handkerchief and instead wiped at her tears with the sleeve of her jumper.

'They told me they would bury him for me. They said he couldn't be buried in a church. They told me there was a *cillin* in Lifford. I never knew where it was exactly.'

'Your son was one of a number we recovered with some physical injuries to the face.'

She nodded. 'He was born disabled. He never breathed, not once. I remember waiting to hear him cry after they ripped him out of me; I was so young it almost broke my pelvis. They worked with him as best they could, but I could tell it wasn't right from their reactions when they saw him. He never cried. They didn't even let me hold him. I asked to see him and they held him out to me. His face looked like it had collapsed. His eyes were closed, his little mouth pursed. They let me kiss him once. Even through the blood I could see his hair was the most beautiful gold. "He's still warm," I said. I thought maybe he was still alive, but the doctor said it was because he'd been inside me. I knew, though, from his colour. He was grey.'

She did not shudder or sob as she spoke, though the tears coursed freely down her cheeks.

'But he was dead, is that right?'

She nodded. 'Why?'

'Someone claimed a PPS number for your son when he was a year old,' I said. 'That wasn't you?'

She shook her head, horrified. 'Of course not. Is my son alive?' she asked, her face alight with both hope and terror.

'I don't know, Mrs Hughes,' I said. 'I'm sorry.'

As I watched the conflicting emotions play in her expression, I felt that, in implying that her son may still be alive, I had caused her much greater hurt than I had in reminding her of his death.

'I want to know if my son is alive,' she said.

'Honestly, I—'

'I understand you can't tell me his name,' she said, leaning towards me suddenly, her hands reaching for mine. 'But if you know where he is, can you give him the choice to find out about me. Only . . .'

Her eyes shifted towards the door whence we could hear the voices of her husband and McCready approaching.

'I'll do my best,' I said.

The door opened and Hughes came in. When he saw the tears on his wife's face he immediately straightened.

'What the hell's this all about?'

'We recovered the body of a friend of your wife's,' I said, standing myself now. 'We wanted to inform her.'

He held my stare, his back erect. 'Are you all right, love?' he asked finally.

'I'm sorry if I upset you, Mrs Hughes,' I said. 'If I do have any further news, I'll be in touch.'

Chapter Thirty-six

'HE'S A PIECE of work,' McCready said as we left. 'Though he knows his way around a car. Handy with his hands.'

'He strikes me as the type who might be a bit too handy with his fists at times, too,' I said. 'As for her, either she's an incredibly convincing liar, or she knows nothing about her child still being alive.'

'So what do you think?'

'Maybe the home lied about the child dying to make it easier for her, you know. Taking the baby from her and that.'

'It seems a bit callous, telling her the child was dead.'

'Let's head for Donegal town.'

'Why?'

'If Max McGrath looks anything like Christopher Hillen, we'll know for sure.'

'Do we have to?' McCready said.

'St Canice's is at the centre of all of this. Declan Cleary was buried with those seven youngsters. Whoever carried out the recent killings must be connected with it in some way. I think the attack on the Commission's diggers was to stop them finding these children. We need to find out what happened to them.'

HE DIDN'T SPEAK as we drove through Barnes Gap on the way to Donegal, though I could tell he had something on his mind. His skin had paled and he chewed at a rag-nail while he drove.

'It's not going to happen,' I said.

'What?' he glanced across at me, distracted from his own thoughts.

'Your child won't have Goldenhar syndrome.'

'How do you know?' he said petulantly, then quickly apologized.

'It's rare; you heard her yourself.'

'Not that rare if we've found seven cases of it here.'

'I understand your fear,' I said. 'Every parent has it. But it won't happen.'

'You can't say that. No one can say it won't happen. What are you meant to do if it does?'

'You adapt. You deal with it. You'll always love your child, no matter what.'

He nodded, but I knew my words could do little to pierce through the darkness of his thoughts. 'Seeing another kid with it is the last thing I need,' he said.

He lapsed into silence again, continuing to bite at the side of his thumb as he drove on to Donegal town. But one aspect of the conversation played on in my mind.

As we passed the petrol station on the outskirts of Donegal town I asked McCready to pull over so I could get a packet of cigarettes. While I was out of the car, I took the opportunity to phone the pathologist, Joe Long.

'What can I do for you, Inspector?'

'I was wondering about the children on Islandmore,' I explained. 'If you'd done the post-mortems yet?'

He paused a moment, considering his response. 'I understand this is part of the Disappeared dig. I will have to report back to the Commission. I can't share any information with you, Ben.'

'I'm sorry,' I said. 'I shouldn't have asked.'

'Is there anything in particular you'd like to discuss?' he added quickly. 'Any aspect of the children, or their appearance?'

It took me a moment to realize that he was offering me an alternative way in.

'They all appeared to have Goldenhar syndrome,' I said.

'That's correct,' Long replied. 'And . . .'

'Would that have killed them?'

'The evidence to date suggests natural causes of death. That's what I will be reporting to the Commission, certainly.'

He waited and I knew I wasn't asking the right question. I returned again to my conversation with Joe McCready in the car.

'Is Goldenhar syndrome rare?' I asked.

'Extremely, Inspector,' he said. 'One birth in maybe 125,000.'

'Yet all the bodies date from the same period.'

'Indeed they do.'

'Is it normal to have that level of incidence in such a small geographical area?' I asked.

'Now, that,' Long replied, 'is exactly the type of question I'd be asking.'

'So what causes it?'

'No one knows for sure. But with seven infants displaying the same symptoms, I'd want to examine it further.'

'In what way?'

'I report only to the Commission on this,' he replied. 'So I've contacted them to ask permission to send away bone fragments for analysis. Lennie Millar is to get back to me to let me know what the legal position is. If I get the all-clear, I'd hope to have the results in a day or two.'

'And might I get an indication of the results you'll be reporting to the Commission.'

'That might be doable,' Long said, laughing. 'Though of course you can't use any of it,' he added. 'If this was uncovered during a dig for the Disappeared, it won't be admissible in court anyway.'

'So everyone keeps reminding me,' I said.

Chapter Thirty-seven

MAX MCGRATH WAS not there when we called. Indeed, though it was his registered address, he had not lived there for five years, apparently, since taking up a teaching post in Dublin. This all was explained to us by his mother, a small, greying, wispy-haired woman, her upper spine bent so that she had to stoop and look up at us sideways.

'Is something wrong? Is Max in trouble?'

'No Mrs McGrath,' I said. 'We're sorry for bothering you. We're in the middle of an investigation and Max's name came up.'

'What are you investigating that involves Max?' she asked, horrified.

'Nothing important, ma'am,' I said. 'We're trying to follow up on children who may have had a similar ailment to Max, who were born at the same time as him.'

The woman twisted her head sharply, regarding me full on. 'What ailment?'

I was a little wrong-footed, unsure how best to refer to the disfigurement that Margot Hughes had described.

'Oculo-triculer-vertebre spectrum,' I said, knowing as I spoke that I was saying it wrong.

'What are you talking about?' Mrs McGrath said angrily. 'There's nothing wrong with Max.'

'Does your son not have a facial disfigurement?'

'You people need to do your homework,' she snapped. 'Max is perfectly healthy.'

'Can we see a picture of him, Mrs McGrath?' I asked.

She led us into the front room. A graduation picture hung on the wall. Mrs McGrath, looking considerably younger, and a heavy, grey-haired elderly man stood either side of a lithe young man wearing his graduation gown, a rolled scroll clasped in his hand. He smiled broadly, his face perfectly normal, his hair thick and black.

'HE'S OBVIOUSLY NOT Max Kennedy,' McCready said, as Mrs McGrath made tea. 'Burgess is an idiot.'

'He's pig-ignorant at times, but he's not stupid,' I said. 'He said the child was given a PPS number when he was a year old.'

The old woman returned, carrying a tray on which two cups and saucers, alongside a plate of biscuits, sat atop a lace doily.

'I can't apologize enough, Mrs McGrath,' I began.

She waved away the apology impatiently.

'Why did you think Max was sick?' she asked. 'He's never been ill, beyond the odd cold.'

'We were told . . .' I began. 'I'm sorry for asking this, but we were told Max had been born in St Canice's. Is that the case or have we completely the wrong person?'

She paused momentarily, then nodded. I stood and took the tray from her and she lowered herself onto the seat opposite me.

'You adopted him?'

'My Harry was quite a bit older than me, God rest him,' she said. 'We couldn't have children of our own. We'd tried for years. When we found out what was wrong, it was too late. The adoption agencies all refused us; we were too old, they said.'

I nodded, pouring the tea and offering her a cup. She took it without comment.

'Anyway, we were told that St Canice's was always desperate for people to take the children born there. And we were desperate for a child. It was all above board. We filled in all the forms, everything was legal,' she added, glancing across at McCready worriedly.

'I'm sure it was, ma'am,' he said. 'You were very good providing a home for Max.'

'We kept his Christian name,' she said, mollified by McCready's comment.

'Would you have Max's birth certificate, Mrs McGrath?' I asked. 'Just so we know he is the child we've been told about. If so, it's clearly our mistake.'

'It should be upstairs,' she said, putting down the untouched cup of tea and rising. She walked so softly we could barely hear her steps on the stairs above us.

'So, what do you think? Clerical error in St Canice's?'

'Maybe,' I said.

Mrs McGrath reappeared a moment later, her hands shaking as she unfolded the document.

'His name was Kennedy,' she said, handing me the sheet.

I glanced through the details. He had been born in September 1976. His mother's name was listed as Margot Kennedy. It was as I reached the bottom of the sheet that I saw a further name I recognized. The birth had been registered by Sheila Clark.

'Sheila Clark?' I said. 'Did you have any dealings with her?'

The old woman nodded. 'She was the woman who arranged everything for us. She was young herself. It must have been her first placement. She arranged all the affairs, though. It was her we paid.'

'Paid?' McCready asked.

She nodded, blinking several times, as if the light from the window beyond was irritating her. 'We paid 5,000 punts to the home, as a donation.'

Chapter Thirty-eight

JOE MCCREADY DROPPED me off at the station and I sent him to follow up on Sheila Clark, to see if he could dig up anything further about her on the system. For my own part, I wanted to see Niall Martin again.

There were a number of cars sitting in the driveway outside Martin's house when I arrived. To one side, an ambulance was parked with its engine running, the rear doors ajar. I glanced in as I approached the front door, but the vehicle was empty.

A harried young woman, who I assumed to be the housekeeper, answered the door when I knocked.

'Is Mr Martin here?' I asked, smiling.

She glanced beyond me to the marked Gardai car. 'Which Mr Martin?' she asked. Her accent was eastern European, which surprised me a little. The Martins must be paying well, for most of those who had come to the country in search of the Celtic Tiger had long since departed.

'Either, I suppose,' I said. 'My name is Inspector Devlin.'

I was working on the assumption that she would not be totally aware of the vagaries of judicial jurisdiction. After a moment's prevarication, she proved me right.

'You'd better come in. Alan is unwell. The doctor is with him; you'll have to wait.'

'What happened to him?'

The girl bit her lower lip nervously. 'We think it's his heart,' she said.

'I'm sorry to hear that. I'll wait for his son.'

I stood at the sheet-glass wall at the rear of the room, looking down to where the river below split into two streams at the old linen mill which dominated the bank opposite.

I could hear raised voices from a room off to the left, but the tone was of concern rather than anger. Finally the voices became clearer. Two paramedics appeared down the hallway, wheeling a stretcher on which lay a man I recognized from the picture in the paper. He was, of course, older, frailer, his features sharper, accentuated by the fact that he was lying flat. His pyjama shirt was open, cables taped to his chest running to a monitor which a doctor wheeled alongside.

Niall Martin followed behind. He glanced across at me and, upon realising who I was, failed to conceal his irritation. I could understand why and felt awkward at being there.

He raised his hand, telling me to wait, then headed out to the driveway with his father and the medical team. A few minutes later he returned, his face flushed. As he spoke he tugged his coat from the row of hooks on the wall of the hallway.

'This isn't a good time,' he said. 'You were told that my father was sick?'

'I'm sorry to hear about it, Mr Martin. I hope he's okay.'

'He's patently not okay,' Martin snapped. 'What do you want? I'm going to the hospital.'

'I wanted you to look at something for me, sir,' I said, pulling out the newspaper page I had taken from the *Donegal Reporter* offices.

'Can't this wait?'

'I'm afraid not, sir,' I said. 'Would you take a quick look? It won't take a moment.'

'Are you being deliberately obtuse?' Martin asked as he approached, pulling on his coat, glancing at the picture. 'It's my father, so what?'

'Is that you, too, sir?' I asked, pointing to where he stood.

'Yes,' he said exasperatedly, glancing again. 'Are you done now?'

'The woman standing with your father is Sheila Clark,' I said, following him to the front door.

'And?'

'That's the woman you allowed to use your house in Island-view, Mr Martin. The woman you claimed not to know, when I asked you. Yet here you are pictured with her.'

'Thirty-five years ago,' Martin replied angrily. 'How the fuck am I meant to remember everyone I worked with thirty-five years ago?'

'I'm sure you remember the other three men here,' I said. 'They're all dead now. Indeed, one of them died just a few days ago.'

'Seamus O'Hara is dead?'

'You hadn't heard?'

He shook his head. 'We've had other things on our minds over here with my father's ill health.'

'O'Hara was a smuggler. What was his involvement with St Canice's?'

'He was an orderly; worked part time. Like the rest of us, really. I didn't really know him.'

'You said you didn't know Miss Clark, either,' I said. 'The same person who killed O'Hara also killed Declan Cleary's son.'

'And I'm responsible for that too, am I?' he snapped. 'I've had enough of this.'

He snatched his keys from the table in the living room and strode towards the front door. He stopped as the housekeeper appeared from the kitchen doorway.

'If this man arrives here again, don't let him in. He's a guard. He has no authority here. Do you understand?'

'Yes,' she whispered.

'You never got me that address,' I said.

'We don't have it. I checked yesterday. Obviously I've been busy since. Don't come back to my house again or I'll call the actual police and have you hauled back across the border.'

With that, he walked out to his car, leaving the front door ajar. He reversed sharply across the driveway and drove out, following the ambulance which had just left, and spraying gravel against my car.

I looked apologetically at the young woman.

'You should leave,' she said.

Chapter Thirty-nine

PAUL BLACK, ONE of our part-timers, was manning a checkpoint on the border as I crossed back into the south again. He was one of a number of uniforms tasked with finding Jimmy Callan. He looked bored, absentmindedly waving cars through with little more than a cursory glance at the registration plate of each as it passed. He seemed more concerned with the activities of three young fellas working on the bridge. Two of them carried a steel ladder between them, the third struggling with a bundle of sandwich boards he was attempting to hold clamped under his arm. I could see from the one he was flourishing in his free hand that the boards carried posters featuring the image of Dominic Callan. The picture was grainy; Callan looked blurred, his features indistinct. He had worn his hair long, his upper lip shaded – though, at this distance, I couldn't tell if it was a moustache or simply a shadow.

I rolled down the window as I drew alongside Black.

'All quiet?'

'Apart from those three bozos,' he said, nodding towards the trio as one mounted the ladder to attach the posters to the lamp-post nearest us. 'They arrived an hour ago and realized they'd no bloody string to tie up the pictures,' Black commented. 'Amateurs.'

'No sign of Callan?'

Black shook his head. 'Nothing, sir,' he said. 'I'm checking everything that comes through, too.'

'So I saw,' I commented. 'I need you to look out for a second person, too. Her name's Sheila Clark. There's her registration number.' I passed him the details I had recorded the night I met her.

'What do I do if she comes across?'

'Find out where she's headed, without drawing too much attention to it. Then let me know.'

'Yes, sir,' Black said.

'And keep up the good work, Paul.'

I pulled in at the service station a few hundred yards up the road and sat in the car to have a smoke. Sheila Clark had been involved in something dodgy when she had been in St Canice's; the McGraths had paid 5,000 punts for their child. The mother-and-baby homes had been glad to find people willing to adopt the children born there; I had never heard of them charging for doing so. Presumably Clark had been involved in some kind of illegal-adoption scam, then. More importantly, she was, potentially, still involved all these years later. It would certainly explain why she had denied the presence of a child at the house in Islandview. Niall Martin's involvement, though, was less clear. Was he simply giving her a safe house to use? Was he in partnership with her?

The radio buzzed with static and Burgess's voice echoed tinnily through the speakers.

'DI Devlin?'

'The very same,' I said, taking a last drag of my smoke before folding the cigarette on the ashtray.

'Superintendent Patterson is looking for you,' he said. 'James Callan has been spotted in Raphoe. A uniform managed to follow him to a cafe in the village. The super says you're to get out there and wait for back-up.'

RAPHOE WAS A small village about eight miles past Lifford. It didn't take long to locate the cafe in question; it was the only one in the village square and was actually a sit-in deli counter in the village supermarket. The uniform who had called in the sighting was standing on the pavement outside. I recognized him as Sean Cahill. He was middle-aged, having stayed with the traffic corps for over two decades, seemingly without wish of advancement.

'I was doing a speed trap on the road into Raphoe and he passed,' he explained, his arms resting on the sill of my open window.

'Did he make a run for it when he saw you?'

Cahill shook his head. 'Damn the bit of him. Headed into the local market for groceries. I packed up the speed check and followed him over. He's in there eating his dinner. He's not trying too hard to stay hidden.'

'Maybe he feels he doesn't need to,' I commented, undoing my seat belt and opening the car door. 'Let's go and ask him why.'

Cahill glanced in at where Callan sat with his back to the door, hunched over his table. 'Shouldn't we wait for back-up?'

As if aware of our presence, Callan twisted in his seat. He was a heavy-built man, his face ruddy, his hair white and unkempt. He wore a v-neck pullover over a white shirt, the sleeves pulled up to reveal the thick tattoo that coloured his forearm. He raised a mug of tea in salute.

'Apparently not,' I said.

I pushed open the door and headed in. Callan was the only person in the deli apart from the waitress behind the counter, who looked up from her magazine with ill-disguised boredom when I passed.

'James Callan?' I asked.

He nodded. 'I've been expecting you before now.'

'I'd like you to come with me to Lifford station.'

'Let me finish my dinner first? Do you want tea? Ask the fat man who was doing the hairdryer, too. I thought he was going to stand out there all day.'

Cahill stood at the door uncertainly, flicking his attention from Callan and myself to the road outside, clearly hoping that back-up would arrive sooner rather than later.

'You're wanted in connection with the murder of Sean Cleary,' I said.

Callan nodded. 'I thought I might.'

'And Seamus O'Hara,' I added.

Callan laughed lightly. 'Are you planning on clearing all the crime in Lifford on the back of me?'

'You need to come with me, Mr Callan.'

'Will you get this man tea, love?' Callan called the waitress, then lifted a half-eaten slice of toast from his plate and smeared it through a slick of egg yolk.

'You don't seem unduly worried about any of this,' I said.

'That's because I didn't do it,' Callan replied.

'Then why did you do a runner the morning of the killing?' I asked, pulling out a chair opposite him and sitting. Patterson would have a team on the way anyhow.

'Because I knew I'd get the blame for it no matter what,' he said.

'Running just makes you look guilty.'

'Sitting where I was would have done the same,' Callan replied, his mouth full.

The girl appeared from behind the counter with a small teapot and a mug. As I poured the tea, some spilled from the loose-fitting lid.

'So someone killed Seamus O'Hara?' Callan said. 'When?'

It was such a bald attempt to deny knowledge of the killing that I was almost inclined to take it as genuine. 'The same night Sean Cleary was killed. And with the same gun.'

'Which is why you think I did both?'

'That and the fact you were spotted having a row with Sean Cleary on the evening of his death.'

'That fucker next door told you, right?' Callan shook his head as he lifted a napkin and wiped his mouth clean. 'I did have a row with the young fella. He came looking to pin his da's death on me. I had nothing to do with it and told him that. He didn't believe it. It got a bit heated.'

'What about Declan Cleary? Was he killed in revenge for your son's death?'

Callan shook his head. 'I was inside when it happened. The Brits wouldn't even let me out for Dominic's funeral. I told Cleary that.'

'He ended up at Seamus O'Hara's house. Did you send him there?

Callan shook his head again as he slurped from his tea. 'He knew about O'Hara already. O'Hara had called him and told him that he had helped bring the body across. He was the ferryman, you know, bringing the dead across the river to the island. He told Cleary his da was done for Dominic. I told Cleary that that was shit. Or if it was true, it had nothing to do with me.'

'You knew nothing about it?' I asked incredulously.

'I didn't say that. I said it had nothing to do with me.'

'But he was killed in revenge for your son's death?'

'If you say so.'

'And you know who did it.'

'Again, if you say I do.'

'So where were you later on the evening Sean Cleary and Seamus O'Hara were killed?'

'In the house, with no alibi. The one next door might have heard me moving about, but I couldn't count on it.'

'So you ran?'

'I was inside for fifteen years after Dominic died,' Callan said. 'I never got to his funeral, never got to his grave. I swore when I got out that I'd not miss an anniversary again. I wanted to be able to go to his grave tomorrow.'

'What about this demonstration tomorrow? Are you speaking at that, too?'

'There's no room for the likes of me at that. That's a day for hawks; young lads fancying they could be something big.'

'And you're not a hawk?'

'My young fella's lying in a grave in Strabane these thirty-five years. I should be a granda now. Instead I'm not even a husband. Dominic wanted to be like me. What the fuck did I know? Everyone signed up when I joined – it was what you did. We thought it would be a bit of craic, like the riots. Then we thought we were somebodies, walking around with a gun in your belt like someone off *Chips* or something. That's all it was – feeling big for a change, after years of being made to feel like shite. For all the good it did. I went inside and Dominic thought he'd be following my footsteps – as if I ever knew where I was going in the first place. Now he's in the ground, I'm on me own, the Brits are still here and the Shinners are in government. The English want out cos we're costing them a fucking mint, the south doesn't want us cos they can't even handle the twenty-six counties they do have. What fucking good would it do anyone, me talking tomorrow?'

He stared at me, his mouth hanging a little open, his lips wet with spit. I drained my tea then placed the empty mug on the table.

'Fair enough,' I said.

He lowered his head slightly. 'This thing tomorrow means nothing to me. They're using it to try to stir up something. As if another 3,000 dead would change things.'

'I have to take you in, Mr Callan,' I said, standing.

'I know,' he said softly. 'I'm done here.'

As he was standing, Patterson and three armed-response gardai swept into the shop.

'On the floor with your hands flat,' one of them shouted, moving towards us, his weapon angled towards the floor and shifting back and forth between us.

Callan's shoulders slumped as he reached out his hand to the table to steady himself as he began lowering to the floor.

'He's unarmed,' I said. 'We're coming out.'

The guard who had shouted lowered his weapon a little further, but stepped lightly back from us.

'You are unarmed aren't you?' I muttered to Callan.

He smiled quickly. 'For your sake, you better hope so.'

Chapter Forty

'You were told to wait for back-up,' Patterson snapped, as we stood on the pavement watching Callan being helped into the back of the garda car.

'He wanted to talk,' I said. 'This way was simpler.'

'It could have gone to shit,' Patterson said. 'It was stupid.'

'I don't think he did Sean Cleary or Seamus O'Hara,' I said. 'He doesn't have an alibi, but there's no evidence to tie him to the scene, is there?'

'That means nothing. He'd know how to be clean, the same man.'

'He says he didn't do Declan Cleary either.'

'Sure, he was innocent the whole way through the Troubles.'

'He was inside when Declan Cleary was done. I'd say he knows who did it, all right, but he claims he didn't order it.'

'I got another complaint about you this afternoon,' Patterson said. 'Quite the portfolio you're developing. Niall Martin claiming you were harassing his family illegally over the border.'

'I asked him to help me out with an address. He's illegally renting out houses in Islandview.'

'The ghost estate.'

I nodded. 'A woman was staying there with a child. She used to work in St Canice's. I think she may be involved in illegal adoptions. She appeared in a picture with Martin and his father, plus Dominic Callan, Declan Cleary and Seamus O'Hara, taken in St Canice's a few weeks before Cleary was killed. I believe Seamus O'Hara gave Sean Cleary the picture on the night he died.'

'And you know all this despite being told to steer clear of the original Cleary case by Lennie Millar?'

'The children found on the island all showed symptoms of Goldenhar syndrome. We followed it back and traced someone who adopted a child from the home.'

'We? Sergeant McCready was involved, too?'

I ignored the question. 'I believe that Clark used the birth certificate of one of the dead children recovered from the island to create an identity for another child that she then sold for adoption.'

'Why would she do that? Create a new identity?'

'Presumably the children she was using were not Irish.'

'And you know this because . . .?'

'We spoke to a women who lost a child with Goldenhar syndrome at birth. Consequently I visited a woman who had adopted the same child, except he was very much alive and very much able-bodied.'

'Do you deliberately ignore every instruction given to you? You were told by Millar that you couldn't investigate this. I told you that you couldn't investigate it.'

'It all connects, Harry. Somehow.'

'So what? We can't prosecute any case which involves evidence found in the dig. It's a waste of time, Inspector. And a waste of garda resources.'

'Those children deserve their story to be heard. Joe Long has requested that the Commission give him permission to examine the bodies more forensically. He believes there is something more to it, too.'

'Go home,' Patterson said.

'What about Jimmy Callan?'

'He'll be processed in Letterkenny. I'll have a chat with him myself this evening, once he's lawyered up. The North will be looking to have him extradited across.'

'He wants to attend his son's grave tomorrow.'

'Well, I do hope our murder investigation doesn't get in the way of his plans,' Patterson responded.

I PUT OFF making the call until after we'd eaten dinner and I'd helped Debs wash up. I went out back and sat beneath our cherry tree to have a smoke. Finally I called Mrs Hughes.

'Yes?' The voice was timid when it answered.

'It's Benedict Devlin, Mrs Hughes. My colleague and I called with you earlier.'

'Have you found him?' The question was urgent, whispered.

'I'm afraid not, Mrs Hughes,' I said. 'I'm sorry to have brought all this up for you today. I checked out the possible lead I had, but the person in question is not your child.'

'What about the PPS number?'

'It seems to have been a clerical error,' I said. 'I just thought you would want to know.'

The line fell silent for a moment. Finally I heard the snuffling of her breath against the receiver.

'I suppose it makes things easier,' she said at last. 'With everything here.'

'I am sorry, ma'am.'

'Do you know where he is? My son?'

'I believe you were right when you said he was buried on Island-more,' I said. 'The pathologist is working on the bodies recovered from the grave there at the moment.'

She did not respond, so I added, 'The local priest is conducting a service there tomorrow, to consecrate the ground where the infants lie. It's at 11 a.m., I understand, if you wanted to come.'

'I'd . . . I'd like to,' she said. 'It's just . . . with . . .'

'I understand completely, Mrs Hughes. I just thought you might like to know.'

There was silence again on the line.

'Mrs Hughes, I am sorry,' I said.

'He was my only chance to be a mother,' she said suddenly. 'I never had any after that. It's as if God punished me.'

'I'm sure that's not the case, Mrs Hughes,' I said. 'Perhaps your son was too good for this world.'

'Have you children, Mr Devlin?'

'Two, ma'am.'

'Mmmm,' she said, as if agreeing with something I had not said. 'Thank you for letting me know.'

She hung up before I could respond.

Friday, 2 November

Chapter Forty-one

A LOW MIST hung over the fields around our home as I left for work the following morning, the tops of the trees bordering our property cresting the mist's upper edges.

I checked in at the station, half-expecting to have heard something from Patterson regarding the questioning of Callan, but there were no messages. I signed out a squad car and headed across to Islandmore after 10 a.m. to attend the blessing of the *cillin*.

When I arrived the only person at the site was Lennie Millar. He was standing in the field where Cleary had been recovered. A number of mounds of earth, spoil from the various holes the team had excavated, spotted the site, some piled almost six feet high.

'Good to see you, Inspector,' Millar said when I parked and got out.

'Ben, please. How're things?'

'Fine,' he said, refusing my offer of a cigarette with a shake of his head. 'The post-mortem on Declan Cleary is done. He died of two gunshot wounds to the skull. Now we're just waiting for final DNA confirmation that the remains were his.'

'I'm sure you'll be glad to be done here.'

He glanced around him. 'It's not a bad spot. If I had to be buried somewhere, this would do better than most graveyards I've seen.'

'That's not quite what I meant.'

'I know.' He smiled. 'We're finished now. I didn't want the diggers running here today, with the blessing and that going on, but they'll be out on Monday to push all the spoil back into the excavated holes, and that'll be that.' He paused before continuing. 'The State Pathologist has been in touch looking to carry out further tests on the children found here.'

I nodded.

'You don't seem surprised,' he said.

'The children all suffered with the same syndrome,' I said. 'Yet it's rare. It seems a little odd to have such a high incidence of localized cases.'

Millar grunted. 'I'm glad to see you've been deepening your knowledge of Goldenhar.'

'There's nothing stopping me finding out about the syndrome, after all.'

Millar appraised me warily. 'You do know that I would like these deaths investigated as much as you would, don't you?'

I nodded, though obviously with not enough enthusiasm.

'I'm not happy to think that someone killed a child and dumped her on that island any more than you are. But my role is to recover the bodies of the Disappeared. That is all I can do, whether I like it or not. I've put pressure on our own people to allow this through so that it can be investigated. I'm going to give the go-ahead for the tests on the infants anyway, regardless of what they say, but I have to warn you, the issue here, Inspector, is whether you could ever prosecute anyone for the killing. The wording of the act which created our commission has never been tested.'

'I understand that,' I said.

'Then why do I feel judged?'

'I'm not judging you,' I said. 'I just find it impossible not to investigate something like this. I can't think that someone got away with killing a child. I know your position means you are restricted in what you can do.'

'I think what would be more galling would be to discover who did this, get them to court and for them to walk. No one would have answered for the killings and instead it would be public knowledge that the guards were bending the rules of the Commission for the Location of Victims' Remains. No one benefits from that outcome – neither you, me, nor the children we found.'

Our conversation was cut short by the arrival of Father Brennan.

'Men,' he called, as he locked the car. 'Just the three of us, is it?'

'For now, Father,' Millar called. 'They'll be more here. It's a good thing you're doing today. People will come.'

As Millar moved to step away from me I put my hand on his arm and offered my free hand. 'I'm sorry if you feel I've judged you. I understand your position.'

'And I yours,' Millar replied, shaking my hand. 'More than you think.'

Behind us we heard the slamming of car doors as the first of the congregation began to arrive for the ceremony. The bridge which had been erected for the Cleary dig had been left in place to allow the traffic onto the island. What would happen afterwards was not so clear, whether the island would become isolated once more or, having been received into the community's collective conscience, remain connected again to the mainland, no longer in limbo.

BRENNAN STOOD AT the edge of the shoreline in his vestments. He held in one hand his prayer book. The other clasped a small silver rod for distributing holy water, while one of the local women stood beside him, holding the small container that held the water.

I watched the crowd while he went through the ceremony. Over a hundred people had come onto the island, almost exclusively middle-aged men and women. Many wept silently as Father Brennan spoke, their expressions a mixture of mourning and relief that their pain was finally acknowledged. A few of the women clasped small toys, aged teddy bears or dolls, talismans that had sustained them through decades of being told that their children were lost not only in this life but in the next.

At the back of the crowd, holding a small blue bear in her hands, her face glistening with tears, I saw Mrs Hughes. Her husband was not with her. However, beyond her, across the shore on the Republic side, I saw someone else I recognized. Christine Cashell stood at the edge of the water, at the outer boundary of Islandview Estate. Andrew Dunne stood with her, his arms around her as she watched, following the prayers which must have echoed across to her.

When she saw me, she raised her hand in silent salute.

Chapter Forty-two

JIMMY CALLAN WAS sitting on the bed in his cell when I came in, reading a paper which one of the guards must have given him. He looked drawn, his face silvered with stubble, his eyes bleary. Patterson himself had interviewed him through the night, attempting without success to get him to confess to Seamus O'Hara's killing. He was now being held pending proceedings by the PSNI to have him brought across to the North.

He watched me come into the cell without comment, then turned his attention again to the paper.

'They want you across in the North in connection with Cleary.'

'The father or the son?'

'The son.'

'I'd nothing to do with it.'

'What about the father's killing?'

He shook his head. 'I'd nothing to do with that, either.'

'That being the case, you've nothing to fear in going across.'

Callan snorted dismissively, though did not raise his head.

'I was thinking, though. We have to hold you until the North gets all their extradition stuff in gear.'

'Which they won't. Even with a European arrest warrant, you can't hand me over if they only want to hold me as part of an investigation. They'd need to charge me. And they've got fuck all.'

'That's very impressive, Mr Callan. You should move into a career in law.'

'It's not my first time in this situation. So what else have you got?'

'You could go across voluntarily and hand yourself in for questioning. If you're clear, they'll have to let you out again.'

'And I'd do this because . . .?' he said, looking up at me now.

'Today is your son's anniversary,' I said. 'Despite your better efforts, here you are in a jail cell again. We'll have to hold you until bail is set. You'll not be out today. Unless you agree to head across.'

Callan did not speak but his jaw flexed instinctively, as if he were chewing on a piece of gristle.

'I know the inspector in charge of the Sean Cleary investigation. I could take you across to the PSNI, hand you over to them. In the graveyard. After you've had a chance to pay your respects.'

'What if they decide to lift me before I've had a chance to get to the grave?'

'They won't,' I said. 'I guarantee it.'

Callan lowered his gaze, staring into the middle distance as he considered the offer. He glanced at the paper on the bed once more, then folded it shut.

'Fuck it,' he said. 'Why not?'

'IF THIS GOES to shit, I'm holding you personally responsible,' Patterson said. 'You shouldn't have offered that without checking with me.'

'Have we anything to connect him to O'Hara?'

Patterson accepted the point with a slight shake of the head.

'He's sitting in there, our responsibility. Hand him over to the North and let him be their problem.'

'What's the angle?' Patterson asked. 'There's always an angle with you.'

I could not admit that, having spent the morning in the company of so many grieving parents – men and women who had waited years to publicly express their loss – I had felt sorry for Callan. Though his son's death had seemingly been the starting point for all else that had happened, we had nothing to connect him to the killing of Seamus O'Hara. In truth, Callan looked beaten now; a man who had given his life to a cause, only to find himself left behind.

McCREADY AND I sat up front while Callan sat cuffed in the back of the squad car. By the time I had contacted Hendry and made the arrangements, it was approaching 3 p.m. The PSNI would lift Callan at 3.30, allowing him fifteen minutes at his son's grave. I had no doubt they would be in the graveyard long before that, in case he tried to run, but Hendry had agreed to allow him time at the grave without interruption. As we left the station, I warned McCready to avoid Lifford Bridge, where the anniversary commemoration would be ongoing, and instead head further on to Clady and cross at the bridge there.

As we drove, though, McCready's wife called him on his mobile. While he spoke to her on the Bluetooth receiver he had clipped to the sun visor, I turned and checked on Callan. It was only as I turned my attention back to the road we were taking that I realized McCready had driven through the roundabout and had joined the queue of traffic waiting to get across Lifford Bridge, which was temporarily closed while the Memorial Service for Callan was conducted.

'Reverse and we'll head back through Clady and cross over there,' I said to McCready, but too late. The traffic behind us had already backed up, the car immediately to our rear parked almost against our bumper, hemming us in. A single car in front separated us from the crowd that had gathered on the bridge.

'Lie down on the seat,' I said to Callan, removing my jacket and passing it to him. 'Cover yourself with that.' The last thing we needed was for any of the protestors to see Dominic Callan's father handcuffed in a garda car fifty yards from the crowd.

Paul Black, one of the gardai who were policing the demonstration on our side of the bridge, came across to us.

'Can you head to the back of the queue and get people to back up?' I said to Black. 'We need to get out of here sharpish.'

Black looked uncertainly at the bundle on the back seat. 'I'll see what I can do, sir,' he said, and set off up the road, looking for a gap in the traffic wide enough to allow all the cars behind us to reverse enough for us to manoeuvre out.

While we waited, we could hear the voice of the speaker on the bridge reverberate through the PA system which had been set up. Those who listened numbered less than fifty, but they had taken up positions in the centre of the road on the bridge, each holding placards bearing pictures of the dead man. Some were obviously relatives or friends, their faces puffy with weeping. Others, though, stood erect, their expressions defiant. A handful closest to us wore military paraphernalia, their hoods pulled up, their eyes covered by darkened glasses. They stood to attention, their hands clasped behind their backs. Despite their attempts to disguise their features, it was clear that some of them were barely out of their teens; certainly not old enough to have been alive when Dominic Callan was shot.

Even through the windows of the car we could hear the dull resonance of the speaker's voice. 'Dominic sacrificed his life for the cause. How would he feel now, seeing the blatant betrayal of that cause, of what his death achieved. Our politicians have failed us, have failed the cause. They call us traitors, yet they are the ones who have become agents of British justice. Dominic Callan's death has been belittled by their actions, his sacrifice invalidated by their capitulation to the continued presence of foreign soldiers on our streets.'

The group standing closest to us cheered, raising their placards in the air. I was struck by the simmering aggression of the group, palpable even where we sat. Several of the younger men who had seen the garda car turned and directed their shouting towards us. I glanced over my shoulder and realized that Jimmy Callan had sat up to watch the crowd.

Simultaneously one of the older protesters must have spotted Callan. He nudged the man next to him and pointed towards us.

'Get down,' McCready snapped at Callan, but it was too late. A small faction of the protestors was beginning to move towards us. I glanced in the rear-view mirror, in the hope that Black had created room enough for us to manoeuvre out, but the cars behind us had not shifted.

'Get moving,' I snapped at McCready.

He attempted to reverse but the car immediately behind us was too close. Before I could stop him, he pressed the horn, which served only to attract the attention of the group standing on the bridge fifty yards from us. Several more joined the protestors approaching us.

In the middle-distance to our rear, reflected in the interior mirror, I saw Paul Black instructing one vehicle at a time to begin backing up to create space for us to move, but nowhere near quickly enough.

The lead figure of the group had reached us by now and was staring in over our shoulders where Callan lay still across the back seat. He hammered on the bonnet of the car.

McCready shifted forwards suddenly, striking the man side on with the car, though at such a slow speed that it did little more than shift him back a foot or two before he moved in again. We could hear him trying the handle while the other men surrounded us.

Black came running down towards us, shouting, while three other uniformed guards had finally managed to come across and were trying to hold the men back from the car long enough for us to complete the U-turn.

McCready shifted forwards again, clipping the bumper of the car in front. He reversed sharply, then, circling the wheel, shot forward so quickly we mounted the traffic island in the centre of the road, knocking over the illuminated road sign. Then he floored the accelerator, even as the crowd to our rear surged forwards again, banging the back windscreen with fists and placards.

'Good work,' I said to him, craning over my shoulder at the receding figures of the protestors. I radioed through to the station to request support for Black and the other men on the border. I had a feeling they would need it.

'I never thought I'd be happy to see the PSNI,' Callan said from the back. 'But Jesus, just hand me over.'

THE HOLD-UP ON the bridge meant that by the time we got to the graveyard the PSNI were already waiting for us. Jim Hendry stood at the entrance; behind him two cars with armed officers sat, exhaust fumes fogging in the air behind them.

'I knew they'd screw me over,' Callan said. 'So much for your promises.'

We drew alongside Hendry, who looked at his watch elaborately.

'I didn't realize we were working on Lifford time,' he said.

'We had an incident on the bridge,' I explained.

'I heard. The people on our side were delighted; it's normally us that gets it when these things blow up; it was the guards' turn today.'

'I promised Mr Callan that he'd get some time alone at his son's graveside,' I said.

Hendry stared in at Callan.

'Mr Callan,' he said, nodding solemnly.

Callan scowled but did not speak.

'We'll be here, watching,' Hendry said. 'Fifteen minutes, and no hassle. Understood.'

If Callan's expression softened at all, it was so slight as to be imperceptible. He did not look at Hendry but merely nodded to show his agreement.

We drove him into the cemetery and dropped him at the grave. Hendry followed us up and stood with us while we waited.

'Any luck on Burke?'

He shook his head. 'We've checked the hostel and have been with his mum. He's gone underground. Presumably he's staying with one of his mates. How's Penny?'

'She's okay. Any word on the girl, Claire?'

Hendry nodded. 'She's given her statement and was examined by the doc. The good news is he didn't actually succeed in what he was trying to do; Penny possibly saved the girl from being raped.'

I nodded, my sympathy for the girl's ordeal mixed with the pride I felt in my daughter.

'A chip off the old block, obviously,' Hendry added. 'Speaking of which, Mr Callan's obsequies seems to be concluded.'

Callan was walking down towards us, his head bowed. As he approached he held out his hands for Hendry to cuff him.

'Really?' Hendry said.

Callan scoffed. 'What's this? Good cop, good cop? That's a new one.'

Hendry looked at me and smiled. 'He's not a good cop,' he said to Callan. 'He's a walking disaster. I only hang around with him to see what he'll do next.'

Chapter Forty-three

PATTERSON WAS WAITING for us when we returned to Lifford. He'd had to come down to help settle the fracas on the bridge, an end finally achieved through the quiet diplomacy of local community workers rather than an armed-response unit and the garda superintendent.

'What the hell happened?' he snapped as soon as we walked in. Burgess sat at his desk, studiously ignoring the whole thing. Or appearing to, at least.

'We took a wrong turn,' I said.

'Do you think? Who was driving?'

McCready stepped forward and began to speak.

'It was my fault, Harry,' I interjected. 'I sent us the wrong way. Joe handled it well and got us out of there before it got ugly.'

'It *got* ugly,' Patterson stated. 'I warned you not to mess it up.'

'I'm sorry,' I said. 'We got him across eventually. The PSNI have him in custody.'

Perhaps he had been expecting more of an argument and my contrition had taken the wind from his sails. Grudgingly he allowed the topic to drop, though not before saying, 'If anything comes back on this, you'll be held to account for it.'

I nodded. 'I understand.'

THE SKY WAS darkening by the time I got home, the bank of clouds rising to the east heavy with rain. Debbie was putting out dinner while Penny set the table. The bruise around her eye had fully purpled now, the skin reflecting the lights of the room in a livid sheen.

'How're my girls?' I asked, kissing Penny lightly on the head.

'Hey, Dad.'

'Where's Shane?'

Debbie pointed towards the back room with the potato masher.

Shane was lying on the floor in the back room, watching TV. A group of high-school kids were singing about wanting to be famous while their teacher nodded along in agreement that this was a worthy ambition.

'Are we still on for the flicks tonight, wee man?'

'Yep,' he said.

'It's at eight, isn't it?'

'Yep,' he repeated, his eyes following the young girl on the screen as she danced across the tops of the desks, kicking off the books with youthful abandon.

'Any word on the young fella from the North?' Debs asked.

It took me a moment to work out to whom she was referring. It was only when she nodded towards where Penny stood that I realized.

'The PSNI are still looking for him,' I said. 'Jim Hendry will let me know when they find him. He'll do his best.'

She nodded, but did nothing to conceal her scepticism.

Just after seven my mobile rang.

'Inspector Devlin? Letterkenny station here. We've had reports of a disturbance on Gallows Lane. One injured. You're to go out.'

'Can some of the uniforms not do it?'

'They're all on duty on the bridge. There was an incident there earlier today,' he replied dryly.

Gallows Lane was so named because, several hundred years ago, when Lifford was still the seat of judicial power for Donegal, criminals were led to the top of the lane and hung from one of the three huge chestnut trees which had stood there. Their corpses might remain hanging for days as a reminder of the particular type of summary justice which operated in the area.

I drove almost to the top of the lane before I found the source of the disturbance. A crowd had gathered on the roadway, encircling a figure lying prone on the ground in front of a car. The car's engine was off and the doors open, though a teenage girl sat in the front passenger seat. I assumed, as I approached, that the car had struck someone crossing the road. Even when I pushed through the gathered crowd and saw, properly for the first time, the person lying on the roadway, I maintained that assumption.

Stephen Burke lay curled on the ground. His face was badly bloodied, one of his eyes swollen shut, the other bloodshot. Blood seeped from his nose, which was obviously broken.

I knelt beside him, careful not to move him.

'Stephen? Can you hear me?'

He nodded. His clothes smelt strongly of body odour, as if they had not been changed in days. The crotch and upper legs of his trousers were dark with damp where he had voided his bladder.

'You need to call an ambulance,' someone said.

I glanced round at the group. 'Who was the driver?'

A young lad, no more than eighteen stepped forward. 'Me. He was just lying there.'

'What happened?'

'What I just said. We came up here for a bit of, a bit of peace, like,' he said, nodding to where the young girl sat in the car. 'I was driving up the lane and he was lying there like that. I stopped and checked on him, then called you.'

'What speed were you doing?'

'I didn't hit him,' the young fella said. 'He was like that when I stopped. I swear.'

Burke's injuries did not look to have been inflicted by a car.

'Can you stand, Stephen?' I asked.

Burke shook his head and muttered something.

'What?' I asked.

'I pissed myself,' he hissed. I realized that he was reluctant to stand in front of the crowd.

'What happened to you?'

He muttered again.

'I can't hear you.'

'Nothing. I'm all right.'

'He needs an ambulance,' someone repeated.

'I'll get something sorted,' I said, standing up and moving back to my car, out of ear-shot of the group. I took out my phone, but it wasn't to call an ambulance.

'Devlin,' Hendry said. 'You haven't caused another riot have you?'

'I've found Burke,' I whispered.

'Okay,' Hendry replied uncertainly.

'He's on my side. Is there a warrant out on him?'

'Not yet. We need to question him first. The girl he assaulted was 16 years old and drunk; she remembers nothing. Plus he did nothing that left any evidence. We're working on Penny's assault.'

'And?'

Hendry hesitated a second. 'We can do something if we pick him up here, but I'm not sure the PPS will go to all the hassle of an extradition order for a charge that will probably result in a caution. He wouldn't volunteer to come across and answer our questions, I take it?'

I shook my head, then realized Hendry couldn't see me. 'Unlikely.'

'How did you find him?'

'Lying in the middle of Gallows Lane. Much the worse for wear.'

'Okay,' he repeated. 'Sure, release him at the bridge and we'll wait to pick him up as he comes across.'

'He's not really in a fit state to walk across, to be honest.'

Hendry whistled softly down the line. 'I see.'

'I haven't done anything to him. But he needs medical attention. If I call an ambulance for him here, he'll be taken to Letterkenny. We can't arrest him over here unless there's a warrant out for him.'

'I'll meet you on the bridge.'

I MANAGED, WITH the assistance of some of those assembled, to help Burke to his feet. He swayed a little, initially. I explained that the ambulances were on other calls and I would take him to hospital myself. Burke looked at me suspiciously through his one good eye, but said nothing.

I manoeuvred him into the back of my car and told him to lie on the seat if he felt dizzy. Instead he sat up, shifting his way across the seat until he was sitting behind the passenger seat, with a view of me. I realized that he thought he was being set up, that I was taking him somewhere to take revenge for his attack on Penny. I did nothing to reassure him on that count.

'So who did this to you?' I asked, once we got moving.

'I don't know,' he muttered. I glanced in the rear-view and saw that he was watching me, gauging the authenticity of my question and perhaps wondering if I had, in fact, arranged the beating myself.

'No idea?'

He shook his head, wincing as he did so.

'You must have pissed someone off,' I said.

'You can let me out here,' Burke said. 'I'll walk on across to Strabane.'

I shook my head. 'I'd be failing in my duty of care, Mr Burke, if I didn't see you handed over to the emergency services in the North.'

We travelled in silence for the duration of the journey, until I drove onto the bridge, having been waved through the garda checkpoint. I heard the change in the sound of the tar beneath the car wheels as we passed into the half-mile stretch that, though officially in the North, sat between our checkpoint at one end of the bridge and the PSNI one further along the road towards Strabane. A single PSNI car was parked on the bridge, Jim Hendry standing beside it, staring down at the river beneath.

'I'm sorry about your daughter,' Burke said, as I slowed the car to a stop. 'I'd been drinking and that.'

'Don't,' I said. 'Don't try to excuse it.'

'Fuck you, then,' he said, spitting a globule of bloody saliva onto my seat, narrowly missing my shoulder.

The door beside Burke opened and Jim Hendry reached in and roughly pulled him from the car.

'You do look a state, Stephen,' Hendry said. 'Let me get you seen to.'

With that he frogmarched him to his own squad car and helped him into the back seat with a shove.

'He was like that when I found him,' I said.

'I'm sure,' Hendry said, his eyes wrinkling against the glare of the streetlamps above. 'I'll let you know when he's ready to talk.'

WHEN I MADE it back to the house Shane was sitting on the bottom step of the stairs. He waited for me to come in, then stood and stared at me accusingly without speaking.

It took me a second to realize the cause of his anger.

'The cinema. Shit,' I said. 'I'm so sorry, Shane; something came up.'

He stared at me a moment longer, then turned and ran up the stairs to his room. I turned to where Debbie stood in the doorway to the living room.

'He cried for twenty minutes,' she said. 'You promised him, Ben.'

I followed him up to his room. He had already turned out the light and was lying in bed, the duvet pulled up over his head, so that I could not see him.

'Shane, I'm really sorry,' I said. 'I know I promised we'd go together but something unexpected happened that I couldn't leave.'

'You left me instead,' he said, the duvet dulling his words, though doing nothing to blunt the sharpness of his tone.

'I had to deal with something.'

The shape on the bed shifted and an opening developed. Shane poked his head out. His face was slick with tears.

'You always put work before us.'

'That's not true, Shane,' I said. 'Besides, this wasn't work. This had to do with family.'

'How?' he demanded.

'It was the boy who hit Penny.'

If I had thought the mention of his sister's name might placate him, I was sorely misguided. Instead he scrammed under his duvet.

'I knew you put her first,' he spat, then tugged the duvet up over his head again, his body shaking as he cried.

I rubbed his back through the bedclothes, but he shrank from my touch.

'Leave me alone!' he shouted, the words muffled.

Eventually, when it became clear that he would not be comforted, I stood up.

'We'll go tomorrow night,' I said. 'I promise you, we'll go tomorrow night.'

The duvet flung back and Shane stared at me angrily. 'No we won't,' he said.

Saturday, 3 November

Chapter Forty-four

THOUGH BURKE WAS brought to Strabane PSNI station before 10 p.m., his solicitor didn't arrive until after midnight. Hendry phoned me when they were gearing up to start questioning. He had refused to allow me to sit in on the interview, for obvious reasons, the charge being that Burke had assaulted my child. However, he had given the go-ahead for me to watch the interview via a video link in the adjacent room.

Debbie's anger at my letting down Shane had been lessened significantly by the knowledge that I had done so in order to get Burke across to the PSNI. When I told her the state in which I had found the boy, she had opened her mouth to ask something, then evidently had thought better of it and remained silent.

'Make sure he doesn't get away with what he did,' she had warned me as I left, as if I might have some influence over how the PSNI would prosecute the case.

Burke slumped in the chair of the interview room. He wore an old blue boiler suit usually given to those whose clothes have been removed for forensic examination. In Burke's case, I assumed it was because Hendry had taken pity on the boy and had allowed him to change out of his soiled trousers. One of his eyes was still badly swollen, the other carried a fresh purple bruise beneath it. The bridge of his nose had been stitched, as had his lip, which was puffy and red.

The lawyer who sat next to him was a middle-aged man, rheumy eyed and obviously irritated at being called into the station at midnight. Burke had contacted his parents first, apparently, to ask for their solicitor but his mother, aware of the incident being investigated by Hendry, had refused to help the boy.

'Do you understand why we'd like you to make a statement?' Hendry asked. 'You've been identified as the perpetrator of a sexual assault on one teenage girl and the physical assault of a second. Coupled with the charges still hanging over you with the theft of money from the victim of a murder, you're facing jail time.'

'These are two separate issues,' the lawyer muttered. 'Let's stick with the assault.'

Hendry nodded. 'We have a witness who saw you plying her friend with drink, then attempt to have sex with the teenager while she was incapable of giving consent. That's tantamount to rape.'

'But isn't actually rape,' the lawyer said. 'And if the alleged victim was so drunk as to not be able to give consent, her evidence against Mr Burke must likewise be compromised and therefore unreliable.'

'The evidence of her friend, her sober friend, who saw what happened and who was left with a black eye by Mr Burke is, however, extremely reliable.'

The lawyer stifled a yawn. 'I do think we're missing a bigger issue here, namely how Mr Burke came to be in custody in the first place. He claims he was in Donegal and—'

'Where he had gone to escape charges following the assault,' Hendry countered.

'Inspector,' the lawyer said. 'Someone assaulted Mr Burke. Then a guard – the father, indeed, of one of the alleged victims – handed him over to the PSNI despite there being no warrant outstanding for his arrest in the Republic. That's rendition, is it not?'

'That's a separate issue,' Hendry corrected. 'And one which we will investigate with full vigour. But it shouldn't distract from the fact that Mr Burke assaulted two girls, one sexually. On top of all that has happened to date, we will be asking the PPS to push for a custodial sentence. There's no way around that.'

'It'll never get to court after the way he was brought across to the North.'

'The guard in question felt that Mr Burke would receive treatment quicker in Strabane than Letterkenny, which is much further away from Lifford. His bringing Mr Burke across was in your client's best interests. I don't believe the PPS will have a problem with that.'

Burke glanced at his lawyer to see what he might offer, but nothing was forthcoming. 'I can get you the phone,' Burke said suddenly.

'What?'

'The phone. Off the dead guy. I know where it is. I'll get it for you, if you drop the charges.'

'You're joking, aren't you?' Hendry said incredulously. The lawyer, on the other hand, was suddenly interested, perhaps sensing a way to wrap things up more quickly than he had expected.

'I'd like a moment with Mr Burke,' he said.

HENDRY CAME OUT of the room directly to where I was sitting. He grimaced when he saw me.

'What do you think?' he said.

'He's bluffing. The phone is long gone.'

'Maybe,' he agreed. 'But just for sake of argument, let's say he does have it. It could lead us to Sean Cleary's killer. And Seamus O'Hara's.'

'He tried to rape someone. He punched my daughter in the face.'

'I understand that, Ben,' Hendry said. 'But you know as well as I do that the PPS will probably pass on this anyway. The way he was found, the claims about his being smuggled across to the North; I know we had no choice, but it will muddy the waters.'

'You can't let him skate on the assault, Jim,' I said. 'He already walked on robbing Cleary.'

'But if he helps us get Cleary's killer, Ben, you know it makes sense; drop the smaller stuff to prosecute the bigger.'

He raised a hand of placation in advance of my inevitable argument. 'I'm not suggesting that what happened to Penny was small, but this is a murder case he could help break. You said yourself that if we had Sean Cleary's phone, we'd have the person he arranged to meet.'

'Track the phone.'

'We haven't been able to,' Hendry said. 'And we can't trace the calls. He must have had automatic network roaming on, because the phone seems to have kept shifting between different mobile providers north and south of the border. We've got records from his home network, but there are gaps all over the place.'

Burke's ability to act with impunity infuriated me. I thought, once more, of Sean Cleary's anger on learning his father's death would not be investigated, even if his body were recovered.

'I've no choice, Ben. If it wasn't about Penny you'd agree with me on it.'

Fifteen minutes later, Burke left in a police car to locate the stolen phone. Hendry waited with me in the station canteen for his return.

'We'll be letting Jimmy Callan out today,' he said as he tipped a third sachet of sugar into his coffee cup.

'Nothing on him?'

He shook his head. 'No evidence tying him to the scene, no evidence of his involvement except for the row he had with Cleary earlier that night, and your taxi man proved that Cleary was alive and well after that.'

'So what next?'

'We wait for Burke and this phone and see what it reveals.'

We sat in silence. Presumably Hendry could sense that I was angry at Burke's release, but he made no apology. He would admit to punching Penny and would be cautioned for it. The sexual-assault charges would be quietly dropped.

Eventually Hendry spoke. 'So was Burke really like that when you found him?'

'Are you asking did I smack him around a bit?'

Hendry raised his hands again. 'You don't have to tell me. I'm not judging you. If he'd done that to my wee girl, he'd have more than pissed his pants, trust me.'

'I didn't touch him,' I muttered. Had I known at the time how things would pan out, I'm not sure I'd have made the same decision.

BURKE AND THE lawyer arrived back soon after with the phone. He had removed the SIM card, which he had had to retrieve from the waste basket in the room of his hostel. The phone itself he had sold to a friend, who was convinced to return it only by the presence of three police officers on his doorstep at 3 a.m.

Wearing his gloves, Hendry reassembled the phone and card and powered it up. He scrolled through the calls list in the memory. There had been one or two calls to the phone on the day after Cleary's death, presumably before those who knew him had learned of his killing. There were, however, three calls on the night of his murder. The first was a call received. It was a Donegal number. So too was the second number, though this was a call dialled. I phoned through to Letterkenny and had them run both numbers for me. The desk sergeant did not even need to check the second number; 'That's a taxi firm, isn't it?' he said.

Sure enough, it was the number for the taxi firm for which Bryant drove. The first number, unsurprisingly, was Seamus O'Hara's. He must have called Cleary, which explained why he had been at O'Hara's house. Cleary had then called a taxi which had taken him to town, while he rang the third number. By the time Letterkenny had given me the details of those two calls, Jim Hendry had identified the owner of the third number; Niall Martin.

Chapter Forty-five

MARTIN'S HOUSEKEEPER OPENED the door on the fifth knock. The sky was lightening, the stars fading at the imminent approach of dawn. A single gash of red bled along the horizon to the east. Early morning traffic trundled along the road outside, mostly larger freight lorries making deliveries.

The woman wore a dressing gown, which she clenched closed at her chest with one hand while the other hand rested on the door, barring our entrance.

'We'd like to speak to Niall Martin,' Hendry said. 'Is he here?'

Martin appeared behind the woman, wearing a pair of striped pyjamas bottoms beneath a white T-shirt. He was comparatively lean for his age, though he was beginning to soften around the trunk and the flabby outline of his belly and chest was clear under the tautness of the T-shirt.

'What's going on? Is it my father?'

His glance shifted from Hendry to me, then seemed to harden as he recognized me.

'What are you doing here?'

'You two know each other?' Hendry asked. 'That saves introductions. We'd like to come in, Mr Martin.'

'He has no jurisdiction over here,' Martin said from behind the young woman. She stayed where she stood but had turned her head to face him. Her outstretched arm still barring the entrance, it looked like she was protecting him.

'He's here on work placement,' Hendry said. 'He's just observing. I have some questions I'd like answered, sir. It seems wiser that we do it here than in Strabane station.'

Hendry waited a beat while Martin considered his choices. Finally he nodded lightly and the woman lowered her arm and stepped back.

'Let me put something on,' he said, disappearing into a room down the corridor from the main sitting area. The young woman followed him into the same room.

Hendry arched his eyebrows. 'Who's she?'

'I thought she was the housekeeper.'

'She clearly provides the full service.'

The room was gloomy. Martin had not turned on the main light and only the growing luminescence of the sky beyond the large plate-glass window provided some illumination. The objects in the room seemed to have lost their definition, as if their edges were blurred.

Martin came out of the room alone, closing the door behind him. He had put on a light dressing gown and a pair of bedroom slippers, though he had been gone for longer than it would have taken him to do only that. I guessed he was giving instructions to his companion. For now, she remained in their room.

'So what's amiss that calls the sleepers of this house so early in the morning? Is this about that woman again?'

'Sheila Clark?' I shook my head. 'No. Though I'd still like that address.'

'And I told you I don't have it,' Martin countered.

'We're investigating the murder of Sean Cleary a few nights ago,' Hendry said. 'He was found shot in a playground in Strabane.'

Martin nodded his head, smiling bemusedly, as if unsure how this appertained to him.

'I heard about that. That's right.'

'Your phone number was the last one he dialled before he was killed,' Hendry said. 'Would you be able to explain why?'

Martin composed himself. I suspected he was considering his options; there was no point lying about it, because we had his number. Furthermore, there was no point claiming it had been a wrong number, for we knew the call had lasted almost five minutes.

'He called me about his father,' Martin said.

'What about him?'

'I worked with his father around the time he died.'

'When your father donated money to St Canice's?' I added.

He nodded. 'My father offered them a lot of financial support, that kind of thing. He had been adopted himself and felt a bit of an affinity to the place,' he explained. 'In turn they employed me and a few mates for the summer.'

'So what did Cleary want to know?'

'He wanted to know why his father died. I told him that, as far as I knew, his father had been suspected of informing on that lad who was shot on the river.'

'And how is your father now?' I asked. 'I trust he's okay.'

'He's not recovered consciousness yet,' Martin replied, his smile faded. 'The hospital are doing all they can.'

'I'm sorry to hear that,' Hendry said. 'Did you meet Sean Cleary that night?'

'Of course not,' Martin replied. 'He phoned and we discussed his father. That was it.'

'Did you leave the house that evening at all?'

Martin tilted his head to the side, considering the question.

'No, I don't think I did.'

'Can anyone verify that you were at home that evening?'

'I'm sure they can,' Martin replied. 'Am I a suspect?'

'We know that Sean Cleary phoned someone and arranged to meet them.'

'And you know the content of the call because . . .?'

'He was in a taxi when he made the call,' Hendry said. 'The taxi man overheard the arrangement being agreed.'

'I see.'

'The problem is that we have Sean Cleary's phone and the only call he made or received after calling for a taxi was to you.'

'He did ask to meet, now that you mention it,' Martin said. 'I told him there was no point. I didn't know anything. Besides I couldn't leave my father here alone.'

'Your father is your alibi?' I asked.

'Well, if you put it like that, then yes, he is.'

'Your unconscious father?'

'I only have the one, unfortunately.'

'What about your housekeeper?' Hendry asked. 'She wouldn't be able to confirm whether you were here?'

'You could ask her,' Martin said, smiling as if at a private joke. He went back to the room and knocked softly before opening the door. 'Maria. Are you decent?' he said. 'The police would like a word.'

The young woman came out of the room sheepishly. She had dressed, despite the fact that it was not yet dawn. She wore skinny jeans which clung to her lower calves, accentuating their shape. Above them she wore a heavy woollen jumper. Her hair was scraped back into a pony tail, her face still a little bleary from sleep.

'We're investigating the murder of a man in Strabane several nights ago. Mr Martin tells us that he was at home for the duration of the evening of the 28th. Is that correct?'

She glanced from Hendry to myself nervously, then turned to look at Martin, who nodded encouragingly. She turned to Hendry again and licked her lips quickly with the tip of her tongue. 'Yes,' she said, her accent sharpening the word. 'He stayed here with me all night.'

'With you?' Hendry said. 'You slept together all night. Or with you, meaning in this house.'

'Yes,' she replied again. 'The first, I mean.'

'Mr Martin couldn't have left and come back again?'

She shook her head. 'He did not leave,' she said.

Hendry nodded. 'Thank you, Miss . . .?'

'Votchek,' she said.

Hendry turned to Martin. 'We'll have to have forensics do a sweep of your house and clothing,' he said. 'Just to be sure. Perhaps you'll submit for gunpowder-residue tests on your hands, too. And we'll need to impound your car for forensics.'

'The car won't be much use to you, I'm afraid.'

'Why?' Hendry asked suspiciously.

'All the visits to my father, the car was beginning to stink of hospital. I had it valeted the other day to get rid of the smell.'

'We'll check it anyway, sir,' Hendry said. 'I'd appreciate it if you'd get dressed and come into the station to make a statement.'

'Maria has just told you I was here all night,' Martin protested. 'This is ridiculous.'

Hendry nodded. 'You were, as best we know, the last person to speak to Cleary before he died. You might remember something which would help us catch his killer.'

Martin smiled archly. 'I see,' he said.

Chapter Forty-six

I WENT HOME to get washed before going back to the station. Shane barely spoke to me over his breakfast. Debbie, on the other hand, compensated for his silence when I told her that Burke was being released with a caution.

'Was letting down one of the children in an evening not enough?'

'What?'

'Penny trusted that you would do the right thing,' she said. 'What if she sees that young fella walking about again? How's she meant to feel, knowing he got away with it?'

'He got a caution,' I said.

'For all that's worth!'

'What would you rather I'd done? Beat him up a bit more myself? He'd already been given a kicking.'

'It wouldn't be the first time you'd used your fists on someone,' she retorted. 'It was okay when you did it for Caroline Williams, but apparently not when it's for your own daughter.'

Caroline had been my old partner in the guards. Her abusive husband had been on the wrong end of my anger after he had driven her to attempt suicide.

'He's little more than a child himself. Trust me, the state he was left in, he'd had enough.'

Shane slunk off his seat and padded up the stairs. I followed him out to the hall. 'Are we still on for the flicks tonight, wee man?' I asked.

'I'm not a wee man,' he said.

'You are to me.' I climbed the stairs and sat on the step next to him, patting the carpet beside me to encourage him to sit, too. After some reluctance, he did.

'I am so sorry about last night, Shane,' I said. 'Something came up and I had to deal with it. But I shouldn't have put that before you. I promise you we will go the pictures tonight.'

'What if something else comes up tonight?'

'I'll ignore it,' I said. 'Scout's honour.'

'Were you a scout?' he asked.

'No,' I admitted. 'But I won't let you down again. Buddies?' I held out my hand to him.

He turned from me, but did not move away. 'Buddies,' he agreed finally, though he did not go so far as to shake on it.

I was clearing up some of the outstanding paperwork on my desk in the station when the pathologist, Joe Long, phoned.

'The Commission gave me the go-ahead on the bones,' he said without any introduction.

'So I believe,' I said. 'Good morning.'

He grunted a return greeting. 'It's just as well, actually,' he said. 'The results came in this morning. I'd have had some explaining to do if they'd said no.'

'What's the story?'

'Retinoids, apparently,' Long said.

'Excuse me?'

'Vitamin A,' he said. 'That what's caused the disfigurements.'

'How?'

'Increased levels of vitamin A in pregnant women can lead to birth defects or, depending on the levels, death of the unborn child. The most commonly reported defects include facial malformation, hydrocephaly, heart defects and problems with ears and eyes. It can also lead to mental-health issues with the adults using them, again depending on the levels of retinoids.'

I knew little science but I recognized the term 'retinoids' at least.

'I think Debbie uses retinoid cream,' I said.

'She probably does, though whether she'll appreciate you telling people is another matter. Most women will use some type of vitamin A cream; it's very good for the skin, especially as you get a little older.'

'So how come our children weren't affected?'

Long breathed in slowly, as if considering how best to explain it to me. 'Retinoids are used extensively in skin creams. There is, however, a type of cream called isotretinoin. It has very high retinoid levels; it was used in America to treat acne, under the brand name Accutane. They discovered that it caused birth defects in the children of pregnant women who had used it. It's still available, as far as I know, though they now won't prescribe it to pregnant women or those thinking of getting pregnant.'

'Do you think that's what happened to the Islandmore babies?'

'I think it's very possible. The bone analysis of the infants showed high levels of vitamin A. All of them.'

'Have you told the Commission yet?'

'I just spoke to Millar. He knew right away that I'd ordered the tests before he gave the go-ahead, but he was okay about it. He's going back to his own people now for legal advice on how to proceed.'

'This clearly means the children can't be classed as "victims of violence", mind you. I'd say they'll have to let us investigate.'

'Investigate what, Ben? Even if it was something to do with retinoids that led to those birth defects, there's no malice involved. There's no intent to kill. The Accutane findings didn't show up for years, long after these bodies were buried.'

'Where are you most likely to find a high proportion of acne sufferers?'

'Among teenagers – schools and so on.'

'And where would you have found high proportions of pregnant teenagers in the mid-seventies?'

'A mother-and-baby home?'

'A mother-and-baby home,' I agreed.

McCready arrived about half an hour later. I was online, reading up on the Accutane debacle. The images on the screen when he entered the office made McCready blanche; an ultrasound of a foetus with obvious facial abnormalities.

'Some light morning reading,' he commented, hanging his coat over the back of his chair. He eyes were red-rimmed with tiredness, his face pallid and pinched, the lack of colour accentuated by the stubble enshadowing his jawline.

'You look rough. Bad night?'

'Ellen can't sleep,' he said. 'She feels it's only fair that I should join her in this.' As he spoke, his attention was constantly drawn back to the image.

I scrolled down the screen to a text section.

'How's she feeling?'

'Fed up. She wants the whole thing to be over, you know. Just get the baby out and make sure everything is okay. Intact, like.'

I nodded. 'I need you to do something for me,' I said.

'I'd rather not if it involves deformed babies, to be honest, sir.'

'Only peripherally,' I said. 'You can do the easy part. I want you to run a background check on Alan Martin's company. In particular, I want to see if they developed or were developing a topical skin cream for acne during the seventies.'

'Okay,' he said, though I could tell he was wondering why.

'Joe Long thinks the infants on the island may have been born with abnormalities because their mothers were using cream high in vitamin A.'

His eyes widened. 'Ellen uses vitamin A cream at night.'

'I've been through this with him about Debbie. Skin cream is fine – it's specifically a kind of acne cream, isotretinoin,' I read the name from the notebook in front of me.

'I'll get to it, sir.'

It was obvious that all the cases connected to St Canice's. I recalled being vaguely aware of the place when I was child, but it had closed down soon after. Most of those I knew to be connected with the place were dead. Those who were still alive, such as Niall Martin, would not be forthcoming. In the end, I went back to the one person who I knew would help.

Chapter Forty-seven

OLLY COSTELLO SAT perched at the edge of his armchair, a wheeled table positioned in front of him. On it was a plate with a piece of fish, a small scoop of mashed potato and a mush of indeterminate vegetables. To the plate's left was a small robin-egg blue bowl containing something that appeared to be neither creamed rice, nor custard, but a substance somewhere between the two. He scraped the knife determinedly across the plate, cutting off a small piece of the battered fish, then worked to spear it with his fork. That achieved, he raised it with shaking hand to his mouth, then began the whole process over again.

'Meals on wheels,' he explained, chewing slowly. He shifted the food around his mouth, then, raising his fingers, picked something from his lips and laid it at the side of the plate.

'Kate says I'm getting too old to look after myself. She wants to put me in a home.'

'You're still too young for that,' I said, though without much conviction.

He nodded. 'Two visits in a week. What can I do for you?'

'I wanted to ask about St Canice's Mother-and-Baby Home,' I said.

'Is this still about Declan Cleary? Or poor Seamus O'Hara?' he asked, blessing himself.

'It's not quite Cleary that I'm interested in. What do you know about the home?'

'It was one of those places that just . . . were there. Every county had one.'

'Is anyone connected with running it still about?'

He shook his head. 'The last person I knew of was a young woman, Shana, Suzanne something, maybe.'

'Sheila? Sheila Clark?'

He repeated the name, as if testing out the sound of it.

'That sounds about right. She was a real looker in her time.'

I took out the picture of the group that O'Hara had given Cleary. 'Is that her?'

He took the picture from me and held it in his shaking hand.

'That's right,' he said. 'She managed the place till it closed.'

'When was that?'

'Late seventies,' he said. 'It was your man there.' He pointed to the page.

'Who?' I asked, moving beside him to see who he was pointing at. 'The tall man?'

'Aye. The drugs-company boy. What's his name?'

'Alan Martin?'

'Aye. He bought the place out. The state was glad to be rid of it. He shut it down within a few months. The whole place was razed to the ground. He was trying to sell it off for development, but kept getting turned down because he had no roots in the county.'

'Where was it?'

'Drumaghill Road. I think they finally built on the site a few years ago. I don't know if he still owned the land by then, of course. It'd have been worth a lot more than it was when he bought it. Not anymore, of course.'

'Did you know him? What was he like?'

He considered the question for a moment before answering. 'Rich,' he replied, scooping up a spoonful of the dessert, the spoon clenched in his fist in the manner Shane used to hold his when he was a baby.

As I WAS lighting my cigarette after I got back into the car, my mobile rang, causing me to start and drop my cigarette onto my lap. I brushed it off quickly, rubbing out the red embers from my trousers.

'McCready here, sir.'

'Yes, Joe,' I managed, clamping the phone between my cheek and shoulder while I stamped out the smouldering butt lying on the car floor.

'I've done a bit of searching on Martin's company. He made his money in topically applied analgesics, apparently.'

'In words I understand, Joe.'

'Painkilling creams and gels – stuff you rub on your back or that if you put it out. He developed something during the sixties that treated burns victims, some kind of cream that treated the burn and killed pain at the same time. It made him a fortune.'

'Anything to do with retinoids?'

'That didn't, but the company was put up for sale in the mid-seventies. There were rumours that Martin was developing a skin-care range, too, though it never materialized. He sold the company off in 1976.'

'What about the son?'

'He does nothing by the looks of it. He runs his father's investments, that's about it. Alan Martin invested in various building developments following the last boom. He seems to have done the same again during the recent bubble, before it burst.'

'What about at the minute?'

'There are a number of different companies involved here, sir, that invested in a number of the housing developments about three years ago. The company involved in Islandview was actually in the name of Maria Votchek. It collapsed at the start of 2009, bringing down the developments it had bankrolled and bankrupting Votchek and the builders who she had supported.'

'Maria Votchek? She lives with Martin.'

'Well, she was the name on the initial investment company which brought the developer down. The builder kept going, using up his own money on the promise of more from the investment company. By the time he found out they'd screwed him over, he'd run his own business into the ground, but the houses were nearing completion.'

'Then Niall Martin's company bought up the unfinished estates,' I said.

'That's right. For a fraction of the price it would have cost had the initial investor seen the project through. The banks sold off the estates at rock-bottom price to Martin because he couldn't do anything with them and no one else wanted them.'

'So why buy them? The amount he'd make from renting out to people doing the double on benefits would hardly make it worth his while, considering the money his father must have got for the company in the first place.'

'Well, I was chatting with someone in the fraud division in Harcourt Street. What Martin is doing isn't actually illegal, but it's very smart.'

'Why?'

'The government is going to announce a fund to finish off the ghost estates around the country, for county councils to complete the roads, street lighting and the like. Martin will get the infrastructure of the estates finished for free; he completes the houses while labour is cheap and everyone's desperate for work, and then he sells when the market starts to recover.'

'*If* the market recovers,' I muttered. Even if it stagnated for another few years, Martin would still be on a winner eventually.

'Good work, Joe,' I said. 'I'll speak to Patterson and see where we go from here.'

'Martin isn't breaking the law, sir,' he said.

'I don't really give a shit what he does with his money,' I said. 'But the children on Islandmore are a different matter.'

Chapter Forty-eight

IT WAS ALMOST five by the time Patterson was free, having been in a meeting all afternoon. He was readying himself to leave for the day, buttoning up his overcoat while I stood in his office and relayed the information we had uncovered.

'I hear all *this*,' he said, mimicking talking with his hand next to his ear, 'but I don't hear what, exactly, Martin has done to rile you. He's a clever bastard with the housing scam, but you say it's not illegal. The company that went bust is not his.'

'I'd bet Maria Votchek is his housekeeper. Or the person I assumed to be his housekeeper. I suspect she's actually his girlfriend.'

'His girlfriend? Really? Is he fifteen?'

'Partner, then,' I said. 'She's an eastern European. How many of them came over here with the money to start investing in housing developments? She's obviously a front company for Martin's own money.'

'Maybe, but you'll not prove it. Even if you do, no one will care. Have you not seen what's going on in the country, Devlin?

The banks have screwed the lot of us and they gave them bonuses for it. Do you really think anyone is going to chase up someone making a few quid on ghost estates? The people who live there will be happy just to see them finished.'

'Martin is leasing out houses to benefit-fraudsters. He's letting people use his houses to claim on both sides of the border.'

'We have one murder on this side of the border. Seamus O'Hara. Have you done anything to find out who killed him?'

'This is all connected, Harry. If we can get who killed Sean Cleary we have O'Hara's killer, too.'

'You're still not telling me how you plan to do this.'

'I want a search carried out for Sheila Clark.'

'Who?'

'She worked with Cleary Senior,' I explained. 'She's connected with the killing.'

This was, to the best of my knowledge, not strictly true. I was counting on Patterson's eagerness to get home to discourage him from pushing it any further.

'And where should we be looking? Border checkpoints?'

'Martin let her live in a show house on Islandview estate,' I said. 'I think he's still covering for her. I'd like to have all the estates he owns searched for her car. Unoccupied houses, probably show houses that are already finished but not sold.'

'Is this a benefit-fraud thing again, or is she actually connected in some way with this?'

'I think she's at the centre of it. Or at least knows who is.'

He lifted his bag and flicked off the monitor of the computer on his desk.

'You can have three cars do drive-arounds. Get a list of the estates to Burgess, to send through to here when you're ready.'

'Thanks, Harry.'

He nodded. 'The Chief Super in Strabane tells me your girl was involved in something on Halloween night. Is she okay?'

I was a little taken aback by the question.

'She's fine, thanks, Harry. She got punched in the face.'

'So I believe. By someone who you then presented to the PSNI badly beaten.'

'That's right.'

'Any idea what happened him? Who gave him the kicking?'

'None, Harry. Nor do I care.'

'You didn't do your usual on him, did you?' he asked.

'It's hardly my usual,' I said.

'That's not the answer I wanted to hear,' Patterson said.

McCREADY GATHERED UP a list of all the estates, both ghost and finished, owned by Martin's company and gave them to Burgess to send through to Letterkenny, along with the car-registration details I had taken the day I met Clark in Islandview. There were twelve estates in all, few enough that I could probably have gone around them myself were two of them not as far away as Gweedore, well over an hour's drive from Lifford. I had promised Shane that I would take him to the cinema and it was a promise which I knew I had no choice but to make good upon.

The film we saw concerned a villain who wanted to prove his greatness by shrinking and stealing the moon. Over the course of the movie, through adopting three children as part of his plan, he learned the error of his ways. I could have told him as much anyway – the real villains do not need such elaborate plans; they brought a whole country to its knees armed with nothing more advanced than ledger books and gentleman's agreements thrashed out on golf links.

BY THE TIME we arrived home, Penny and Debs had come back from a shopping trip to Derry. Penny went upstairs to try on her latest purchases while Shane wandered up to his room looking for a book. Less than a minute later, the two of them stood on the landing shouting at each other about some incursion one had made on the other's territory. The argument ended with Shane's roar, 'I hate your guts,' its final punctuation the slamming of his bedroom door.

Debs looked at me and smiled bemusedly. 'You didn't think one trip to the cinema would change anything, did you?'

Chapter Forty-nine

I HAD MANAGED the first mouthful from the cup of tea when Paul Black called.

'It's Garda Black, sir,' he whispered.

'Where are you, Paul?' I asked, straining to hear him.

'In the car.'

'Why are you whispering?'

'I . . .' he coughed lightly and when he spoke again did so with a little more volume, though still *sotto voce*. 'I was sent out to look for that woman you wanted: Clark. I think I've found her.'

'Where?'

'She was coming along the N13 from Derry to Letterkenny. She took a right at the roundabout on the dual carriageway and is making her way towards Lifford now on the N14.'

'Has she spotted you?'

'Well, I'm driving a marked car, sir, and I'm right behind her, so I'd say she probably has.'

'Is there anyone else in the car with her?'

There was silence for a few seconds. 'There doesn't seem to be, sir,' Black said.

'She may have an infant in the car with her,' I called. 'Don't push her too far. The last thing we need is her going off the road. I'm on my way.'

IF CLARK AND Black were heading on the N14 towards Lifford they would be travelling towards me, so I guessed that it would take only five minutes or so before I would have sight of them. My plan was to block the road ahead of Clark and, if Black stayed behind her, hem her in between the two cars.

Once in the car, I made radio contact with Black again to let him know I was on my way. I had only completed doing so when the radio buzzed into life and his voice echoed through the speakers. 'She's cut off, sir. At Carrickadawson, onto the R236. She's heading towards Raphoe on the back road.'

I turned onto the R236 myself at the next junction and accelerated. On the road ahead I saw two cars round the bend coming towards me, the latter a garda car. I pulled my own car across the centre of the road and, getting out, turned on my torch and began circling it to tell Clark to slow down.

Initially I thought she was going to try to ram through my block, but I saw her begin to slow and draw almost to a stop. Suddenly she twisted the steering wheel and accelerated into a U-turn. Black tried too late to manoeuvre his car across the road behind her and she managed to slip past him, then sped up and headed back along the road. Black completed a U-turn and followed while I jumped back into my own car and set off in pursuit.

Clark sped in the direction of the N14, the main Lifford– Letterkenny road, the furtive red winks of her brake lights as she took each corner just visible beyond the flashing blue lights of Black's car.

I radioed through to Black's car.

'Keep on her, Paul,' I shouted. 'I'm behind you.'

'She's a fast driver for her age,' Black called back through the buzzing of the connection. 'I expected *Driving Miss Daisy*.'

'Just don't push her off the road. There might be a baby with her.'

I was able to pick up speed myself and, fairly soon, was right behind Black, my own flashers turned on. Clark braked ahead of us as she reached the junction with the N14. She stalled a second, as if deciding which way to turn; left towards Letterkenny, or right towards Lifford. Either way her options were limited. She was still some ten miles from the border and at least five miles from Letterkenny. I hoped she would turn left, for, a mile further along the main road, she would reach the roundabout at Corkey which fed onto a dual carriageway. Two lanes would make pulling her over significantly easier.

In the event, this was the direction she took. She pulled out onto the road quickly, her passage marked by the low resonance of an articulated lorry's horn. The vehicle in question had been headed towards Lifford and she had crossed onto its path coming out of the junction. The lorry skidded and stalled, partially blocking the road, while Black and I sat waiting for him to move again so that we might catch up with Clark.

The driver stared out at us, outraged at Clark's driving, not realizing he was blocking us in. I leaned out of the window as he rolled his own down.

'Move your fucking lorry!' I shouted.

He raised his middle finger in quick salute, then turned the key in the ignition, the hydraulics hissing as the lorry moved past the junction and afforded us a gap to clear.

I pulled around Black, who had stalled, and set off down the road in pursuit again.

Clark had created a fair degree of distance between us. I spotted a set of tail lights ahead of me and was initially heartened when they brightened as the driver slowed to pull in. As I drew closer, I realized that the car in question was not Clark's at all and sped past, waving my acknowledgement to the driver for stopping.

A moment later I spotted her. She was struggling to pass a tractor which was trundling along the road, its rear wagon too wide to allow her to safely get around it. Beyond her I could see the glare of the streetlamps on the roundabout. If she passed the tractor now she would be on it before she had a chance to stop.

Sure enough, she pulled sharply out and passed the vehicle, her car wavering on the road as if she had realized too late the closeness of the roundabout. She sped out towards the centre of the roundabout, as a car approaching from her left struck the rear of her car, spinning it around on itself before it mounted the central reservation and came to a halt against the lamp-post at the roundabout's edge.

I hit the sirens and pulled out past the tractor, coming to a halt in the centre of the road. If the baby was in the car, especially in the back seat, it would have borne the brunt of the impact.

I felt sick as I climbed onto the reservation and tried to open the rear door of Clark's car. The impact had concertinaed the bodywork on one side, effectively sealing the door. A baby seat hung off the seat belt on the back seat. I smashed the window and leaned in, frantically looking for the child.

Clark sat in the front seat, her face bloody, her nose broken from impacting on the steering wheel, which was slick with blood.

Pulling open the driver's door, I leaned in and, gripping her shoulders, shook her.

'Where's the baby?' I screamed.

She looked at me stupidly, as if attempting to process the events of the previous few moments.

I slapped her hard across the face, shaking her again. The driver of the other car had struggled out and was behind me.

'What are you doing?' he said. 'Help her.'

'Where's the baby?' I shouted again, struggling to remain in control.

'What happened?' she managed.

'She needs a doctor,' the other driver shouted as I stepped away from her and took out my mobile to call for an ambulance.

'She'll need more than that,' I said.

Chapter Fifty

I MET PATTERSON at Letterkenny station, while Black accompanied Clark to the hospital.

'There *is* a child,' I said. 'She had a baby seat in the car.'

'We're lucky the kid itself wasn't there, the way this went down,' Patterson said.

'I want to search for the infant.'

Patterson stared at me. 'You said you wanted this woman because she was connected with the O'Hara killing. Babies didn't come into it. Especially not ones that some grieving mother heard in a baby monitor.'

'If we can catch Clark on illegal adoptions, we can push her to bargain. It would give us something to encourage her to talk. But we need to have the child.'

Patterson considered it.

'Plus, if I'm right, there's an infant in a house somewhere at the minute with no one looking after it. That's not something that's going to end well unless we find it soon.'

He shrugged reluctant agreement. 'So what do you want to do?'

'The estates we searched looking for her. I'm betting that the child is in one of the completed houses, the show houses. If we start with the ones nearest where she was picked up and work our way out . . .'

I worked through the list of Martin's estates which Burgess had compiled earlier. Black had picked up Sheila Clark on the Derry road to Letterkenny, though that didn't necessarily mean she was heading to Letterkenny itself; she could have just as easily been going to Lifford, taking a left at the roundabout where she ended up crashing. In that region, from Lifford to Letterkenny, there were four possible estates.

I sent one squad car to check the smaller of the three; an estate of fifteen houses at Drumbarnet off the Derry road. The second estate was at Drumleene, not far from Lifford itself. The third estate was Islandview, though I suspected that Clark would have been unlikely to return there. And I knew that Christine Cashell would have alerted me if Clark had been in the area, particularly with a child. The final estate was one I wanted to check myself, at Drumoghill, the site of St Canice's Mother-and-Baby Home.

THE ESTATE LAY about a mile off the main road to Letterkenny, a cul-de-sac located in the middle of farmland, bordered on one side by two large metal feed barns. The fields behind the estate were meadow land and heavy-bodied cattle were grazing near the back fences of the rear houses.

It was much better-finished than Islandview. All the external work on the houses was completed, though a few remained unpainted. The roads had had one layer of tar at some stage, though it had weathered badly and was potholed near the kerbstones, which sat too high above the road surface. As I drove I had to steer around the raised ironwork of man-hole covers and gratings.

Sure enough, as I made my way through the estate, I saw a billboard announcing the reduction in prices of the final few remaining homes. The poster was badly weathered, but it did announce the presence of a show house.

I parked up and called at the first occupied house. The man who answered was in his thirties, a little heavy built, with a crying child in his arms.

'I'm sorry to bother you,' I said. 'I'm looking for the show house.'

He stared at me, then pointedly looked at the child crying in his arms, which had, I suspected, been asleep until I rang the doorbell.

'It's eleven o'clock at night,' he said.

'We've reports of a break-in,' I said. 'I'm sorry for bothering you so late. And for waking your child. I have two of my own, so I know what it's like.'

The comment mollified him. 'It's across there,' he said, pointing over to a large house on the corner, the upper windows illuminated by the landing light.

Thanking him, I headed across the street. The house was unoccupied, the doors locked. I moved around the outer windows on the ground floor, hoping that I might see something inside. The furnishing was markedly similar to that in the house in Islandview, as was the decor. There was, however, no sign of an infant.

I was considering trying to break in when a woman hailed me from a house next door to the one I had originally called at.

'She's gone out,' she said.

'Excuse me?'

'The one living in there. She went out a few hours ago.'

'Sheila Clark?'

The woman bridled a little. 'Is that her name?' she asked disdainfully.

'Did you notice if she had a child with her, Mrs . . .?'

'Keeney,' the woman said. 'No, not tonight. She normally does, but she went out by herself tonight.'

'Normally does what?'

'Have a child with her. She left this evening about eight. Another car arrived before nine, with a couple in it. They sat for almost an hour, then left again.'

'You're very observant, Mrs Keeney,' I said.

She turned and pointed to a small blue Neighbourhood Watch sticker on her front window.

'We've had problems with undesirables in the area – youngsters hanging around the unfinished houses. We all keep a close eye on the houses in the area.'

'That's what we like to hear, ma'am,' I said. 'What can you tell me about this house?'

'Just as I said. A couple arrived in a Northern car and sat for an hour. They left and shortly afterwards someone else arrived and took the child with her.'

'Her? But not Sheila Clark?' I knew it could not have been Clark; she had been in the hospital since the accident.

'No. I didn't see her car, I'm afraid. But I saw her coming out of the house with the child. She must have parked down the street a little; my fence restricts my view.'

'I see,' I said. I imagined Mrs Kenney spent a lot of time watching the neighbourhood and not always for altruistic reasons. 'Has anyone been back since?'

She shook her head. 'Only you.'

'I'll take a look around and see if anything looks . . . untoward.'

I crossed the street and rang the doorbell, though, as I expected, there was no answer. I moved around to the rear of the house and tried the back door. It was locked. Jim Hendry would have made short work of picking the lock; unfortunately, it was not a skill I had developed. Instead I lifted a rock from the flowerbed to my left and cracked it smartly against the small pane of glass in the door. It shattered, falling in onto the tiled floor of the utility room. Reaching in, I unlocked the door and stepped inside.

'Garda,' I shouted, entering the utility room, which contained a set of kitchen units and appliances. Like the house in Island-view, the interior decor was expensive and showed little sign of use. Ahead of me, in the kitchen, I could see a mug sitting on the worktop beside a kettle; it was lukewarm when I touched it. An empty milk carton sat next to them. Perhaps Clark had left the house to get milk.

I moved into the living room and flicked on the light.

'Hello,' I shouted again.

I moved through the house quickly, checking the ground-floor rooms first, though they were all empty. I took the stairs two at a time and began checking the rooms above. The first was a bath-room. The second was the main bedroom. A shape lay slumped on the floor at the foot of the bed. Turning on the light, I realized it was an overnight bag, half-packed and misshapen.

The next room, as with the one in Islandview, contained a cot, the blankets bunched up at its foot, the mattress still bearing the imprint of the child that had slept on it.

Having confirmed that the other rooms were empty and that the child had indeed been taken from the house, I went back into the first bedroom and opened the overnight bag. It contained a selection of pale-blue baby suits and vests. A medical record book lay beneath them; I recognized the orange cover, having had one for each of our own children, in which to record each developmental assessment, each vaccination or hospital visit. I opened the book and flicked through it. The child to which it referred had already received his first set of injections. Inside the plastic flap at the back of the book, a document had been folded and placed for safe keeping. I removed it.

Unfolding it, I could see it was a birth certificate. It took me a second to locate the name of the child listed on the page, but as I did, I felt sick. The name of the child was Michael Cashell.

Christine was named as the mother, the father was marked simply as 'Unknown'. The birth had been registered by Sheila Clark.

Chapter Fifty-one

SIX HOURS AFTER her crash, Sheila Clark sat in the interview room in Lifford, her solicitor beside her. She'd been examined in hospital and, following stitching to the bridge of her nose, had been released into our custody. The skin beneath her eyes had already begun to darken with the bruises that would develop as a result of her nose injury. The effect of this, coupled with her tousled demeanour, had left her with a wild appearance at odds with the measured, clipped tone of her speech.

Harry Patterson sat next to me as I introduced each of the people in the room for the benefit of the twin recorders set up to tape the interview.

Having confirmed her name, I explained to Clark why she had been brought in to the station.

'Where's the child?'

'What child?'

'I know you had a child in the house on Islandview.'

'And this is a reason for questioning because . . .?' her solicitor asked.

I ignored him and continued. 'Your neighbour heard a child there. I heard a child there. You claimed you didn't have one, yet you had baby milk the day I met you. I found a baby monitor in the house.'

'Am I missing something?' her brief said. 'What has any of this got to do with the guards?'

'Are you offering children for illegal adoption?'

She raised her chin slightly. 'No,' she said.

'So if I told you that we have spoken to someone who claims to have paid you for a child, you would deny this?'

She nodded, though she did not speak, perhaps trying to work out who might have told us this.

'Do you deny that you were using the identities of infants who had died for children you were offering for adoption?'

Again a nod. I said as much into the microphone of the recorder.

'Why do you have this?' I asked, passing the birth certificate for Michael Cashell across the desk.

She glanced down at it, but did not lift it. Her shoulders sagged, though she fought to remain composed.

'That belongs to a child I was watching for a friend.'

I smiled. 'We both know that's not true. You should recall that I know Miss Cashell. I know her infant died. Why have you registered the birth?'

'I help out with administrative work in the hospital,' she said.

'Why have you this certificate?'

'I must have lifted it by mistake.'

Her brief sat forward. 'I believe Miss Clark has explained this issue.'

'Where is the child that was in the house at Drumaghill now?'

'My friend collected him. He's perfectly safe with his mother and father.'

I reached into my coat pocket and, flattening out the picture from St Canice's, laid it on the table.

'Do you recognize these people?'

The shift in focus seemed to disconcert her, for she looked worriedly to the man beside her, as if to ask whether the new topic was one we had a right to raise.

'What's the relevance of this now?' he asked.

I ignored the question and addressed Clark. 'Do you recognize the people in it?'

Clark nodded, even as she remained silent.

'That's you, obviously. And that's Seamus O'Hara. And Declan Cleary. And Dominic Callan. They're all dead now. And, of course, the Martins.'

'If you knew who they are, why did you ask?' she said, her tongue dabbing at her lips as if she was thirsty.

'We've found seven children on Islandmore,' I said.

'Sorry,' her solicitor said. 'Just to be clear on this, are we talking about a child in a house, seven children on an island, or a photograph from thirty years ago?'

'They're all connected, though, aren't they Miss Clark?'

'I don't know what you're talking about,' she said. 'I was helping a friend look after their child. You have no right to harass me like this.'

'Why are you doing this? The adoptions. I know that you were paid 5,000 punts by a woman named Hughes in 1976 for a child who was given the identity of one who had died.'

'I arranged adoptions during that period,' she said. 'I don't deny that. Do you know how many people want to offer children a home but can't get onto adoption lists?'

'So you bypass the paperwork?'

'Occasionally, the bureaucracy, yes,' she corrected me.

'And make a packet on the side.'

She laughed forcedly. 'I made nothing on it. The costs cover bringing the child into the country.'

'And the birth certificates? You register the births of stillborn infants?'

'The poor souls who died; I use their names to let other children live. Organ donors do it all the time. It's only a name.'

'It's more than that,' I said. 'It's the child's identity, the only connection grieving parents have with the child they've lost.'

'Grief is the inevitable cost of having loved.'

'What?' I said incredulously.

'I've done nothing but help children find parents who would otherwise not have had any.'

'And that's all you did in St Canice's?'

'Those girls didn't want the children they had; we found other parents for them.'

'And what of the children on Islandmore?'

She swallowed back whatever she was going to say and considered her response.

'It was not our fault that the Church prevented those poor souls from being buried in holy ground.'

'There is a *cillin* on that island,' the solicitor said. 'It's been on the news this week.'

'Really?' I said. 'That's very useful, thank you.'

'I mourned for every child that died in that home,' Clark said. 'I still do.'

'Even the ones you killed?' I added.

She flushed with anger. 'I never hurt a child.'

'Apart from the seven who were born with parts of their faces missing.'

She shifted sharply back in her seat. 'Those children were born that way. That was God's will.'

'That was vitamin A, actually,' I said. 'We know that the children have high doses of retinoids in their bones. Was Alan Martin using a skin drug on the girls in that home? An acne drug?'

'The Martins donated a lot of medicines to the home for free; medicines, nappies, things we wouldn't have had otherwise. They are good people. Those girls received care that the state would never have given; their own families had thrown most of them out.'

'He was testing an acne drug, wasn't he?'

'I don't recall that,' Clark said. 'You'd need to ask him yourself.'

'When those children started being born with abnormalities it wasn't long before you or he realized that it might be connected to the drugs their mothers had been given. I think you got rid of those children, buried them on the *cillin*, and brought in other children to use their identities so that the paper-trail continued and no one would know. I believe you continue with the illegal adoptions still.'

'You're wrong. Those children died in birth.'

'Not all of them. One of them was murdered. A girl. When we found her remains there were a series of fractures around her neck and throat. She was strangled. Someone killed her.'

Clark opened her mouth to speak, but made no sound.

'Someone murdered her and buried her among the other bones on that island. And Declan Cleary ended up there, too.'

'You're wrong,' she managed. 'No one killed any of the children.'

'The post-mortem doesn't lie,' I said. 'The girl was killed.'

Her eyes began to moisten, the skin around her mouth tightening. I began to suspect that, despite her crimes in selling off the children she had been smuggling into the country, she had spent so long justifying her actions to herself that she truly believed she was helping the children involved.

'I don't think that you killed her,' I said. 'But I think you know who did. It was one of the Martins, wasn't it?'

She shook her head.

'If you really do love these children, you can't cover for someone murdering a baby,' I said.

Clark shook her head. 'Dominic,' she said. 'Dominic Callan did it, then O'Hara buried him. He must have done it.'

'Not Declan Cleary or Niall Martin?'

'Declan went to the RUC about the whole thing, for God's sake,' she snorted, before realizing she had gone too far.

Her brief, on the other hand, laid his hand on her arm. 'I need to speak to Miss Clark,' he said. 'Alone.'

Patterson and I stood outside the station door for a few minutes while I had a smoke, grateful for the break.

'So Declan Cleary went to the RUC about the children, rather than to tout on Dominic Callan,' Patterson said.

'Maybe they figured, when Dominic Callan got hit, they could use it to their advantage. Finger Declan Cleary for an informant and let the Provos do the rest.'

'Callan's father said he didn't kill Declan Cleary, though, back then,' Patterson said.

'Maybe he did, maybe he didn't,' I said. 'But I think the only people who had something to lose in this coming out now are the Martins. If O'Hara started talking to Sean Cleary recently and told him the truth, the Martins were the ones most likely to want them silenced. Sean goes to Jimmy Callan, who denies everything. Then he goes to O'Hara, who tells him what we know now; Sean challenges Niall Martin – we know he phoned him – Martin kills him. Martin realizes there's only one place Sean could have got his information from – O'Hara. So Martin pops him, too. Martin Senior is in no state to be going around shooting people: it must be the son.'

'So, Niall Martin, then?'

I nodded.

'We'll never get a warrant to bring him over for questioning,' Patterson said. 'We'll call the North and have them pick him up if she names him.'

'What about the child? The nosy neighbour in Drumoghill saw a couple waiting at the house, then later a woman collected the child from the house. It was locked when I arrived, so it was someone with a key. I think Clark missed the people who were meant to take the child; I'd bet the woman who came and got it was Martin's partner, Maria. Clark must have phoned him when we were after her and warned him. I'd bet the child is with him.'

'Call your friend in Strabane. Have them chase it up.'

I dragged a final few puffs from my cigarette, then nicked it and returned the stub to the box for later.

Chapter Fifty-two

WHEN WE RETURNED to the interview room, something had changed. The brief sat erect now, Clark herself slumped in her seat, as if the physical weight of her memories had worn her down.

'My client will assist you in your enquiries about the children you found on Islandmore,' he said. 'Obviously, to do so will require some form of recompense with regards to the issue of the adoptions mentioned.'

It was not a good deal to make. The children on Islandmore had been found during a dig for the Disappeared; the chances of any form of prosecution were small. But connecting Martin to those deaths would help establish a motive for the shootings of Sean Cleary and Seamus O'Hara.

'We'll see what we can do,' I said. 'It depends how useful the information she gives us proves to be.'

'We need to be sure she'll receive some form of quid pro quo for her help in this.'

'That depends on what we hear,' Patterson said. 'Now start talking.'

Clark clasped her hands together in front of her on the table. 'Alan Martin supported St Canice's with drugs and supplies for years. He had been adopted himself and he felt a degree of affection for the work we did. We never refused anyone's help.'

She preened herself, patting down the wild tangle of her hair.

'The summer Niall started working with us they offered us a skin cream for treating acne. A lot of the girls suffered horribly with it. They had approval for testing. It wasn't unusual in the homes for pharmaceutical companies to try out new drugs. We allowed the girls who suffered very bad acne to use the cream.'

'When did you know something was wrong?'

'The first birth following the start of the medication was okay, though the girl had started using the cream very late in her pregnancy. The next one was born with defects.'

'Jane Hillen's child?'

Clark shrugged. 'Maybe. I don't remember the names.'

'She kept the child.'

'She did,' Clark agreed. 'That's right. Her father wanted her to put him up for adoption, but she stuck with him, even with the . . . problems.'

'He's still with her,' I said. 'And he still carries those problems.'

She nodded, clearly not wanting to be drawn on any culpability she might feel for Christopher Hillen's condition.

'The next one was born the same way, but was already dead,' she continued. 'From then onwards, they were all stillborn.'

'All but the girl,' I added.

She swallowed dryly. 'We thought it would die when it came out, but it kept fighting. We could hear its cries. Dominic Callan took it out of the room, pushed it out in a little clear plastic trolley. He didn't come back. I thought it had died naturally, but . . . maybe not. Dominic and Seamus O'Hara buried it. Seamus said he knew where they could rest without being disturbed.'

'Without being found, you mean? So what happened with Declan Cleary?'

'His own partner got pregnant and he started to get squeamish about what was happening. We'd already told Alan Martin about the reactions to the drugs and he'd stopped the girls using them, but Declan wasn't happy with that. He went to the Martins about it.'

'The only one with a conscience,' Patterson commented.

Clark snorted derisively. 'He was trying to blackmail them. He needed money for his own kid coming and tried to get it off the Martins. Then when the army shot Dominic, the word went round that Declan had gone to the RUC and touted on him for money.'

'You don't believe that, do you?'

Clark shrugged. 'I don't know what happened.'

'Niall Martin killed him,' I suggested.

She shook her head.

'If he didn't, he at least put him in the frame for it.'

'Possibly,' she said. 'I stayed clear of that. The Martins arranged for children to be brought in from a home in eastern Europe that they supported, to cover up for the seven children who had died. It meant that there would be a paper trail.'

'But the mothers knew that their children had died already,' I said.

'The girls in those homes were usually told their children had died,' Clark said. 'Even when they hadn't. It made it easier for them to move on and forget the child. If they knew it had lived, they'd have gone looking for it. If they thought the child was dead already it would make the parting easier.'

'You really don't understand grief, do you?' I said.

'Grief is the cost of having loved,' Clark repeated. 'If they didn't know the child, they couldn't have loved it, so their grief would be easier.'

'All these platitudes about the cost of loving. You have no children of your own, have you?' I said.

She shook her head. 'Only the children I've helped to find new homes. And new parents to love them. I think of them often.'

'And the seven on the island. Do you think of them?'

'On occasions,' she said. 'They were never named, though. They never existed.'

'They existed,' I said. 'And still do to those who lost them. Ask Christine Cashell. Her son is Michael. She named him that to keep him alive in her mind. Because he was still her son. And that girl, the one that was murdered. Someone somewhere had a name for her, too. So, you tell yourself that what you did was good and right and helped people, but you were party to the killing of a child.'

She shook her head, but her features became pinched, her eyes glassy, her lips thin and purpled.

'Is Niall Martin still involved in the illegal adoption of children?'

'Yes,' she whispered, after a moment's pause.

'Will you testify that Niall Martin has been involved in the smuggling of children into the country for the past thirty-five years?'

She nodded her head, curtly, once; it was enough to dislodge the tears that had gathered in her eyes.

Chapter Fifty-three

I CALLED HENDRY and told him what we had learned. He, in turn, had assembled two squads and had already set out for Martin's home on Liskey Road.

When I arrived the PSNI were conducting a search of the property, though it was already too late. Niall Martin had left; presumably Clark had informed him that we were on to her and he had realized it was only a matter of time before we came looking for him. I suspected he was already making his way around whatever properties they had been using for the smuggled children, destroying any evidence which might link him to them.

Maria was in the house, visibly upset at the conduct of the police officers. She had resisted their attempts to search the bedroom which she and Martin had shared, until Hendry had instructed for her to be cuffed. She sat now on the sofa, watching her own reflection in the large plate-glass window that gave away nothing of its spectacular view due to the darkness beyond.

The team that entered the bedroom found that one of the closets was empty, the hangers lying on the floor, as if someone had removed the contents in haste.

'He's long gone,' Hendry said, standing with me, watching Maria staring at her reflection. 'She's refusing to speak anything but Russian or something.'

'No idea when he left?'

Hendry shook his head. 'He's taken a load of clothes, so either he's left for good, or else he's having to work out what he was wearing the night Cleary and O'Hara were killed and get rid of them.'

I walked over to where the woman sat staring impassively ahead.

'Where's the child you took from the house in Drumaghill tonight? Sheila Clark contacted you, didn't she? Where is the child now?'

She looked up at me disinterestedly, then turned away.

'I know you speak English. Where is the child? Clark is already talking. Help yourself now by helping us.'

She remained mute. I waited a moment, hoping she might provide me with something. Eventually, I moved back across to Jim Hendry.

'He can't stay away from here forever.'

Hendry nodded. 'His old man is getting back out soon,' he said. 'He'll have to come back for that. We'll pick him up as soon as he reappears. I'll leave a team on the house until then.'

I HEADED BACK over the border. On the bridge, the wind running down the river valley had torn down one of the posters advertising the commemoration march. It lay on the centre of the road, the passing traffic driving over it. I stopped and placed it against one of the bins along the pavement. Callan smiled jauntily in the image, carefree in his youthfulness.

I was getting back into the car when my mobile rang. I did not recognize the number.

'Inspector?' The voice was timid, hesitant.

'Yes?'

'This is Christine Cashell, Inspector.'

'Christine, how are you?' I said, shifting the phone to my other hand while I started the ignition. 'I meant to call with you again to see how things were going.'

'Mum said you told her I should phone you if . . .' she began. 'Andrew says I shouldn't bother you about it anymore, but you told Mum that I should call you if the woman across the way came back again.'

'I appreciate it, Christine,' I said. 'But we've found her already.'

'Oh,' she sounded disappointed. 'It's just that there's someone over there now.'

I PARKED UP a few streets back from where Clark had been living, so as not to alert whoever was there. I suspected it would be Niall Martin, cleaning up after Clark, destroying any evidence connecting him to the adoptions.

As I neared the house I could see Martin's car parked in the driveway. Just as I approached the bottom of the drive, the house door opened and Martin stepped out. He wore jeans and a light-coloured shirt which hung loose about his frame. Clasped in his hand was an object wrapped in a black plastic bag.

'Raise your hands where I can see them, Mr Martin,' I said. 'An Garda.'

He stopped moving and raised his hands to shoulder height.

'Step onto the driveway and lay flat on the ground,' I instructed him, moving forward with my gun trained on him.

He glanced around, trying to work out if I was alone.

'Lie flat on the ground,' I repeated.

His hands wavered slightly, dropping from shoulder-height, as he weighed up his options.

'Don't do anything stupid now. Support officers are on their way.' I edged closer to him as I spoke.

As soon as he realized I was alone, his stance hardened. His back straightening, he shifted suddenly sideways and, rounding the corner of the house, sprinted for the back garden. I set off after him, though he had a twenty-yard head-start on me. By the time I reached the fence at the rear of his property, he had already cleared it and was sprinting across the field beyond.

I took off after him, climbing over the fence, then following the path he had left in the long grass. I tried as best I could to keep pace with him, though he was undoubtedly fitter than I was. Not for the first time, I forswore cigarettes.

The wash of moonlight on the field meant that I could see him ahead of me. He seemed to be widening the gap between us, and I raised my pace, taking short deep breaths in an attempt to pump a little more power into my muscles. Instead, as I neared the broken-down pump house, I skidded on something and fell on my face. I thought of Peter O'Connell as I struggled to my feet, wiping away the detritus and setting off again, trying desperately to breathe through my mouth.

Ahead of me Martin was making a break for the river. I suspected I knew his intentions; he believed that if he could traverse the river onto Islandmore he could make it across the border and out of my jurisdiction.

The temporary bridge was still some way upriver, so I assumed Martin was hoping to wade across the hundred-or-so yards to the shore of the island. If that was his plan, he didn't know the river well. The edges of the river on both sides were mostly silt-beds, the mudflats exposed at low tide. If Martin attempted to wade out into the water, he might find himself unable to make it more than a few feet before he became bogged down.

I saw him drop from view as I set off in pursuit again. I knew that the field through which I was chasing him dropped down to rocks before the river itself. Martin had made it that far, at least. As I ran, the ground beneath me grew soggier, the waterlogged earth, still heavy with autumn rains, providing a squelching soundtrack to my movements.

As I drew near the edge of the field I could see that the tide was out. For perhaps twenty feet from the shore to the water's edge the land lay slick and smooth, the raw moonlight glinting off its surface. Grooves traversed the mudflats where streams of water ran from the sewage pipes from the shore into the river, while the mud oozed up between the rocks across which Martin was still struggling. He had clearly realized that his progress was hampered, for he stopped, staring around him wildly, trying to work out which route might offer him the best chance of escape.

'You can't go anywhere,' I shouted, dropping down myself onto the rocks. Martin twisted to look at me, then began to raise the object he held in his hand.

'Don't do it,' I shouted, unclipping my own gun-holster. But then I saw him lift the object above his head and fling it away from him.

As I drew nearer, I heard the plop as it struck the surface of the mud. It settled for a second, then was sucked beneath the surface, the mud oozing up around it to fill the void that it left as it sank.

'Stay where you are, Mr Martin. There's nowhere to go.'

Martin inched closer to the edge of the rocks, moving away from my approach.

'It's over. Sheila Clark has told us everything. About the acne cream, about O'Hara burying the children on the island. About Declan Cleary being set up because he tried to blackmail you. We have it all. Even if you get across to the North, you'll be arrested there for the killing of Sean Cleary.'

'Bullshit,' he shouted back.

'She's told us everything.'

'Don't come closer,' Martin shouted.

I was weighing up my own options, wondering how to bring him in. There was no back-up coming; my only hope would be to talk him into surrendering.

'Where's the child? We know Clark had one in the house at Drumaghill. Where is he now?'

Martin stepped gingerly from one rock to the next, ignoring the question. Then he launched himself out towards the mud, evidently hoping that, in a few strides, he would reach the water.

He landed in the mud, the impact marked with a loud sucking sound. His legs sank to halfway up his thighs. He seemed surprised at the depth of the sludge and tried to move forward, attempting to lift one leg. He stretched out his arms to balance himself but, in so doing, overcompensated and suddenly lurched to the right, falling prostrate onto the surface of the mire. I could see him scrabbling to stand again, his arms pushing against the thick slime to find purchase against the solid ground beneath. But the mud was too deep. His arms disappeared to the shoulder into the ooze.

He began to panic now, twisting his head out of the slime, shouting incoherently for help. His mouth was black with mud already, his face splattered by the ooze.

I ran to the edge of the rocks and tried to reach out for him. 'Take my hand,' I shouted, stretching out as far as I could. But he was too far from me.

He writhed now, his body sinking into the slime so that he had to twist his head around to keep his mouth clear of the surface. He began puffing, trying to catch a breath in case his face should go under.

I stepped down into the mud myself, its immense coldness taking my breath from me. It stank of salt and something more unpleasant. I tried to reach him, not lifting my leg out of the mud as he had done, but trying to push my way through the mire towards him. But it was too thick; I shifted only by tiny increments, for all my effort.

I reached out, my finger-tips grazing the fabric of his trouser leg where he lay. I leant forward, scrabbling with my fingers to catch purchase with his leg, in the hope it might offer him some incentive to keep fighting to stand.

He thrashed wildly now, his head twisting from side to side, though by this stage the mud had covered his face. I tried again to pull at his leg, even to pull myself closer towards him. Finally I managed to grip his trouser leg and began pulling him towards me. He twisted his head to the side, catching a breath, then began thrashing out with his foot, perhaps in panic, perhaps to force me to release him.

I tugged harder, pulling him closer, until I had good grip on his leg.

Behind me, I heard shouting and looked around. Andrew Dunne, Christine Cashell's partner, was dropping down onto the rocks, obviously having seen me arrive.

He ran to the edge of the rocks and offered me his hand to help pull Martin on to the solid ground. At first, I could not reach him. He leaned forward a little more, his fingers brushing the tips of mine. With an effort, I shifted my position towards him, until I felt him grip my hand and the tug as he tried to pull me from the mire. The sucking of the wet mud marked my progress, slow as it was, as I freed myself from the slime and allowed Dunne to pull me, with Martin in tow, onto the rocks of the shoreline.

Sunday, 4 November

Chapter Fifty-four

PATTERSON ARRIVED WITH the second team after I called for assistance. I explained to him how I had found Martin and that he had thrown something into the mudflats, possibly his gun. He directed a team to look for the gun while Martin was taken under armed guard to Letterkenny General for a check-up.

'What's happening with Clark?'

'We'll have to let her go,' Patterson said. 'We've nothing to hold her on.'

'She's a flight-risk, Harry. We'll not see her again.'

'We'll set a high bail, dependent on her staying in the state.'

'What about the child smuggling? The adoptions?'

'What child smuggling?' he said with exasperation. 'What child? You went to the house; there was nothing there. There is no child; there might not ever have been one.'

'You know there was,' I said. 'She admitted she had a child in the house.'

'Which she was watching for a friend.'

'The neighbour said she'd seen someone leave the house with an infant. At least, if we let her go, put someone on her for a while. She might lead us to the child.'

Patterson took a deep breath, then held it long enough for me to stop.

'Let's say she does,' he said. 'So what? What's the best that's going to happen? You find the child, take it from some poor saps who have paid through the nose for an adoption, and place it in foster care. Do you really think someone desperate enough to pay to adopt a child will not provide better care than the social-care system?'

'That's not the point.'

'Of course it's the bloody point,' Patterson snapped. 'Even if there was a child, someone has taken it, someone is looking after it. Leave it at that. You look at that bloody island, coming down with children's bodies. Someone wants this one; that's good enough for me.'

But I could not reconcile myself to what he had said. My issue was not with the child, but with the role that Martin and Clark had played, the impunity with which they had acted across three decades.

As I headed back to the car, I called Joe McCready.

'I need a favour,' I said. 'Patterson is releasing Sheila Clark. I want you to follow her, see where she goes.'

'Then what?'

'Just keep an eye. I need to go home and shower. I'll take over as soon as I'm done. She'll be taken from the station in the next hour, I'd suspect.'

McCready stifled a yawn at the other end of the line, as he agreed.

As I DROVE home, I suspected a car was following me. At first I dismissed the thought as a result of tiredness, but sure enough, as I pulled into my driveway, the car behind me likewise indicated and pulled to a stop in front of our gates.

I walked down the drive again to confront the driver. It was Jimmy Callan.

'Have you a minute?' he said.

Instinctively, I glanced around to see who else was about.

'I need to ask you something,' Callan said.

I nodded and, moving round to the passenger side, climbed into the car. I noticed, taped to the dashboard, an aged 'In Memoriam' card for his son. I wondered at the depth of the grief that Callan carried around with him that meant he felt compelled to keep a constant reminder of his loss before him as he drove.

'I hear Niall Martin went in the river,' he said.

'That's right. You hear things very quickly.'

'Always,' he agreed. 'Why did you go after him? Have you connected him with Declan Cleary's boy?'

'He'll be helping us with enquiries in that area. Why?' I said.

'Why him?' he asked, ignoring my own question.

'We think it connects with the mother-and-baby home.'

'St Canice's? What about it?'

'We believe that Martin's father's company was testing drugs on the girls there; acne drugs. It caused a number of the children to die before birth. They covered it up by burying them on the island. One child survived birth but was so badly disfigured they murdered her. Declan Cleary found out about it and threatened to go to the police unless the Martins paid him off. His girlfriend was pregnant, with Sean, at the time and he needed the money. We think that's why he was killed.'

'So he didn't inform on Dominic?'

I shook my head. 'Not as far as we know. I think someone used Dominic's death as a way to get rid of Cleary, by spreading the rumour that he had touted on your boy. They made him a target.'

'So what about my boy? Who actually touted to the Brits?'

'I don't know,' I said. I paused before continuing. 'But we've been told that Dominic was the one who murdered the infant.'

He gripped the steering wheel, his knuckles whitening.

'My turn for questions,' I said. 'Did Niall or Alan Martin kill Declan Cleary, or arrange to have him killed?'

'I can't tell you that.'

'Listen, we can't prosecute anyone on the Declan Cleary killing, it's so tied up in legislation.'

He considered my comment. 'An individual went to some of those in charge at the time and told them that Declan Cleary had admitted touting on Dominic. He was treated accordingly by volunteers, based on the information they were given. I was told this when I was inside.'

'So Niall Martin and Seamus O'Hara didn't pull the trigger?'

He shook his head.

'But they put him in the frame?'

'I can't tell you that,' he repeated.

'Well, whoever told you he touted on your son, they lied,' I said, getting out of the car.

'Devlin,' he said. 'How do you know all this?'

'A woman who worked with the boys. She was lifted earlier. She told us it all.'

'What was she arrested for?'

'Nothing, in the end,' I said. 'We're letting her go again.'

He nodded absently. 'We'll not be meeting again. I wanted to thank you for allowing me to get to my son's grave.'

I nodded. 'Stay out of trouble,' I said.

DEBBIE WAS STILL up, watching the end of the late movie on TV. 'Other women worry when their husbands come home smelling of perfume,' she said when I came in. 'It would be sweet relief for me.'

I stripped off in the hallway, bundling my clothes together and shoving them straight into the wash, then went and showered.

Then Debbie made tea and toast for us both while I called McCready. Clark had headed straight back to the house at Drumaghill upon her release and had not left since. I promised to get to him as soon as I could and let him get home.

I called Patterson next, to find out what was happening with Martin. It transpired that he was being held in hospital for the night. He would be released in the morning, when he would be taken into custody to be questioned about the shooting of Seamus O'Hara.

'The other stuff can wait. We'll look at the O'Hara killing first,' Patterson said.

'Any luck with the gun?'

'They couldn't get it. The tide is against us. We did find bags of clothes in his car. Forensics are testing them for anything that would place him at O'Hara's. Failing that, we'll have to hope he confesses.'

I stopped myself from asking him about the child.

IT WAS ALMOST 2.30 a.m. by the time I got on the road. I pulled into the estate at Drumaghill just before 2.45 a.m. McCready's car was parked up, its two left wheels on the kerb, with an unrestricted view of Clark's house.

As I approached the car I could see McCready's head pressed against the side window. I tapped a few times on the glass and he started. He stared ahead of himself for a second, blinking, as if trying to work out where he was. Then, using his sleeve to wipe his chin and cheek, he rolled down the window.

'Sorry sir,' he said. 'I must have dozed off.'

'Anything happening?

'Not as far as I know,' he said. 'Someone came to visit her. They were here about midnight. They were in for a while.'

'Who was it?'

'I don't know. A single man in a red car. I got the registration.'

I hardly needed to look at the numbers to know that the visitor had been James Callan. I told McCready as much.

'When did he leave? Did she leave with him?'

McCready shrugged sheepishly. 'I don't know. It must have been when I was sleeping.'

'For Christ's sake,' I snapped. 'All you had to do was stay awake until I got here.'

I could tell he was embarrassed, but my anger would not let me offer him any words of comfort.

I sprinted across the road to the house. The lights downstairs were still turned on. A sliver of light from the hall spilled onto the front step where the door lay ajar.

I stepped up and pushed the door open.

'Hello?' I called. 'An Garda. Ms Clark?'

There was no response. I was aware of McCready approaching behind me. I stepped into the hallway, half expecting to find Clark lying on the floor somewhere, like Seamus O'Hara. But the place was empty.

We moved into the living room. The TV still played, but there was no one there. In the kitchen, the kettle was plugged in. A black purse lay on the worktop. But there was no sign of Sheila Clark.

We searched the entire house, but it was clear that Clark had gone. Her clothes remained in the wardrobe, her purse and car keys lay downstairs. But she had simply disappeared.

Chapter Fifty-five

I SHOWERED AGAIN the following morning, certain I could still smell effluent on my skin. When I came down for breakfast, Debbie and Penny were in the middle of a heated row. Debs, it transpired, had borrowed Penny's mobile phone to make a call, her own being out of credit. She had, unashamedly, checked through Penny's text messages. There was a chain of messages between Penny and John Morrison, which had started two nights earlier, when he had sent her a video-clip. Debbie had played it, unprepared for what she saw. She replayed it for me when I arrived.

The footage was brief, running for less than thirty seconds. The picture was grainy and out-of-focus, but there could be no doubt about what we were watching. Stephen Burke lay prostrate on the ground while he was beaten repeatedly with a baseball bat by an assailant whose face was not shown. They struck him several times in the crotch, then whoever was filming focused in on Burke's face as he wept, and laughed.

Debbie held the phone out, staring at me.

'Dump that in the bin. Get it out of the house.'

Penny, on the other hand, was furious that her mother had read her messages.

'You were snooping,' she shouted.

'I'm your mother; I'm allowed to snoop. To make sure you're not involved in things you shouldn't be.'

'I didn't ask him to send it to me,' she said. 'I can't help it.'

'He shouldn't feel he can send it,' I said.

'That's not my fault.'

'Penny – you could get into real trouble for this. How many people has he sent this to?'

'No one. Just me. He said he did it for me.'

'How gallant,' I said.

'At least he did something about it,' she spat back.

'So did your father,' Debbie said. 'The right thing. He handed him over to the police.'

'For all the difference that made.'

Debbie gripped Penny by the shoulders. 'Do you not realize what this means? If John Morrison did that for you, what will he expect in return?'

Penny stared at her a moment. 'Nothing he's not already getting,' she retorted.

Debbie had slapped her across the face before any of us knew what was happening. Even Penny seemed shocked, both by the force of the strike, and the source of it.

'That boy never gets near the house again, Ben,' she said to me. 'And you're grounded,' she added turning to Penny. By that stage, Penny had already made for the stairs, stomping up to her room.

'Those people are going to bring us trouble,' she said darkly. 'I told you this would happen.'

Then she too turned and walked out of the room before I had chance to respond.

Shane was sitting at the table, his breakfast in front of him, his mouth open.

'Not Miss Perfect anymore, then,' he concluded, shaking his head, then spooning cornflakes into his mouth.

I CROSSED THE border before heading into work. I was not surprised to find Jimmy Callan's house empty, with no sign of his car. I stood at the living-room window, peering in.

'He's gone again.'

I looked across to where the neighbour I had met with Hendry stood, leaning over the hedge that separated the two properties.

'Any idea when he'll be back?'

The man shook his head. 'He asked me to cancel the milk for him. Indefinitely. I don't think he's planning on coming back.'

'That doesn't surprise me,' I said. 'When did you see him?'

'This morning. Just before eight.'

'Was he on his own?'

The man seemed puzzled by the question. 'Of course. He's always on his own.'

'CLARK MUST HAVE been spooked by Callan and did a runner. Either that, or he's done something to her,' I explained to Patterson in his office an hour later.

'You had a suspect followed without my permission,' Patterson said incredulously. 'What the hell did you think you were doing?'

'I thought she might lead us to the child.'

'I don't give a shit about the child,' he snapped. 'I don't care where it is or who has it, just so long as it's not one more thing for me to have to deal with.'

'I'm afraid that I do,' I said quietly.

'Regardless, I'm your boss, and you'll follow orders. Is that clear?'

I did not respond.

'You know where the door is, any time you want to use it, Inspector.'

He turned his attention to the papers on the desk in front of him, but as I stood to leave he looked up again.

'By the way, Lennie Millar contacted me.'

'And?'

'The feeling is that we'd not be successful in prosecuting anyone over the seven children. They were found as part of the dig.'

'But they're not Troubles killings.'

'Regardless, it's a loophole just waiting to be exploited. The DPP would only check with him if we tried to push for a prosecution, and he'll have to tell them the same thing.'

'So what now?'

'Forensics have been working through the night on the clothes they recovered. They've got nothing.'

'What about Martin?'

'Nothing,' Patterson said. 'No gun, no evidence, Clark's statement is useless if we don't find her. Nothing connects him to O'Hara.'

'We know Cleary called him the night they were both killed. And what about the other stuff, the kids and the drugs testing and that? The smuggling?'

'Have you not been listening? There's nowhere to go with them. No child, no gun, nothing.'

'We need to at least push him on the O'Hara shooting.'

'We can push, but I'd not be holding out much hope.'

IT WAS AFTER ten by the time Martin was released from the hospital. His solicitor was waiting for him in Letterkenny station when he arrived. I'd met the lawyer before; Gerald Brown worked out of Strabane. My suspicion that he represented every undesirable in the area was tempered slightly by the knowledge that the town was relatively small and Brown was one of its most experienced solicitors.

'Detective Inspector Devlin,' he said, nodding solemnly.

'Mr Brown, always good to see you.'

He said no more until we were settled in the interview room. Martin had showered in the hospital; his hair was still a little damp and he swept it back from his face. His skin was flushed around his jowls, as if he had recently shaved.

'I trust you're feeling better, Mr Martin.'

'My client would like it stated for the record that he has grave concerns about the way you have conducted yourself with regard to him over these past weeks.'

'Grave? That's an apt word.'

'He feels you have attempted to intimidate him, you have visited his house out of jurisdiction, you have harassed his partner, and then last night you pursued him with a loaded weapon, while he himself was unarmed.'

'I know you had a gun, Mr Martin,' I said. 'We will find it.'

'It was dark, I understand. You may have been mistaken in what you think you saw. Furthermore, in future, if you wish to speak to my client, you will apply to have him brought across under the European Arrest Warrant. Though, of course, to do so, you will have to provide good reason to arrest Mr Martin, something which, as yet, you have failed to do.'

'Sheila Clark made a statement to us last night that your father's drug company tested skin cream on girls in St Canice's home, as a result of which seven children were born with severe facial disfigurement. So severe, in fact, that six of the children died before birth. The seventh was found with evidence of violent death. Miss Clark tells us that you were aware of this and intimately involved in covering up the deaths.'

'That's nonsense.'

'Yet you were involved in her illegal adoptions.'

'No I wasn't.'

'She was living out of show houses on your estates.'

'She was a sad old woman. She had no family and no home. I allowed her to live out of houses which I am unable to sell. It was an act of charity for an old friend. Had I known how she'd repay me I can assure you she'd have been out of those houses long before now.'

'Can you explain to me again what you were doing in the property in Islandview?'

'I was cleaning it out. Miss Clark left quite a mess.'

'You were getting rid of evidence.'

'Of what?'

'Your involvement in the smuggling of children, perhaps? What about the child in Drumoghill? Where is he now?'

'There is no child. You should know; you already searched the place once.'

'Illegally,' Brown added.

'A neighbour saw someone leave that house with a child. I believe it was your partner, Maria Votchek.'

'Good luck proving any of that,' Martin sneered, earning a reproachful glance from Brown.

'Did O'Hara have second thoughts? When he discovered he was dying, did he regret what he had done, setting up Declan Cleary?'

I could tell from Martin's reaction that at least one part of my question was news to him.

'You didn't know he was dying, did you?'

'I had no reason to know, having not spoken to the man since we happened to work together in St Canice's.'

'You are grasping at straws,' Brown said. 'I believe that we're finished here.'

'I know you did it,' I said. 'I know you covered up those seven kids' deaths and used Dominic Callan's killing as a way to target Declan Cleary. Did you have Dominic Callan killed too? Did he threaten you, too? We know he killed one of the children. Did you set him up with the army?'

'This is ridiculous,' Brown snapped, standing up. 'You ought to be ashamed of your conduct in all of this. We will be lodging a complaint with your superintendent.'

'He'll expect nothing less, I'm sure,' I said. 'Before you leave, you'll need to give a statement about the events of last night. While you're here.'

To be honest, I was being petty in detaining him any longer, for any statement would be of little material use.

Martin was finally free to go in the middle of the afternoon, and Maria Votchek collected him from the station. Brown also left, satisfied that Martin was not being detained further. I contacted

Jim Hendry and told him about how events had unfolded, in case the PSNI wanted to pick him up over the border.

'We've nothing on him,' he said. 'We've searched the car and the house for forensics, but he's clean.'

'I believe he dumped the gun in the mudflats of the Foyle,' I said.

'Then so long as he keeps his nose clean, he's in the clear for now,' Hendry said. 'Galling as that is for both of us.'

I was packing up for the evening, when Joe McCready approached me. Whether by accident or design on his part, our paths had not crossed during the day.

'I'm sorry about last night, sir,' he said.

'Forget about it,' I said. 'I should never have asked you to go out.'

'I was knackered, sir,' he explained. 'I couldn't stay awake.'

'It's fine. Forget about it.'

He lingered a moment. 'Any sign of Clark?'

I shook my head. 'Nor Callan. I went to his house this morning. He's disappeared, too.'

'Why?'

'I'm not sure. I told him that his son was involved with Clark and the Martins in covering up the deaths of the children and that he killed the girl we found.'

'Why did he kill her? Why not just put her up for adoption?'

I shrugged. 'Maybe they thought no one would want her. Maybe they were worried that people might ask questions if two children with Goldenhar were born in the home within a few months of each other. I think Niall Martin got word to Jimmy Callan in prison that Declan Cleary had touted on Dominic. I think Callan had Cleary executed for it, though he'll not admit as much. Maybe he's realized now that he had the wrong man killed.'

'Maybe he's looking for the right man, instead.'

'Or woman,' I said. 'Clark's keys and purse were still in her house. If she'd done a runner herself, she'd have taken that stuff with her.'

THE COLD WAR was still in full swing when I went home, Penny sitting in her room, emerging only to eat her dinner in silence. She retreated back upstairs as soon as she'd eaten the last bite.

I went up after her, knocking on her door before going in. She was at the computer, quickly shutting down the page she was on when I came in.

'You need to sort things out with your mum,' I said, sitting on the edge of the bed, resisting the urge to quiz her about what she'd been doing before I came in.

'She hit me.'

'She lost her temper, Penny. You know she didn't mean it.'

'She snooped through my phone messages,' Penny said. 'I hate that.'

'She's worried about you. We both are.'

'I'm not a child,' she snapped petulantly.

'Yes you are, honey,' I said. 'You're our child. And you could be fifty, but you'll still be our child. Getting older doesn't make you less our daughter. We maybe need to look at how we treat you, but we won't stop worrying about you, or loving you, or wanting to protect you.'

'Right,' she said, folding her arms.

'I know you think I was wrong to not beat up Burke when I found him. But he'd already been beaten. He'd wet himself he was so scared.'

I was shocked to see a visceral glint in Penny's eyes at my comment. 'Penny, what type of a father would I be if I beat up a defenceless boy?'

'A decent one,' she muttered.

'Listen, love, I wanted Burke to suffer more than anyone. But I did what was right, not what was easy.'

'It's not right to snoop through my phone messages.'

'You know what? You're right. We shouldn't be checking up on you. But we care too much about you to let you get in deep with someone like Morrison.'

'Well, care less, then,' she said, turning her attention to the computer again.

MORRISON ANSWERED THE door on my second ring.

'Inspector Devlin. Always a treat.'

'We need to talk about something,' I said.

He called back into the house that he was stepping out for a minute, then closed the door and came out to join me. We walked around the edge of his property, to where the horses shifted uneasily in their stables. As we walked, we set off the motion-detecting security lights which Morrison had had installed around his property. His horses watched our progress, their wild, rolling eyes glinting under the glare of the lights, their breaths misting before them where they stood, heads hanging out over the half door of the stables.

'Your boy sent Penny footage of an attack on Stephen Burke.'

'Did he now?'

'You didn't know?'

He stared over my shoulder, then looked at me directly. 'I didn't say that.'

'I want him to stay away from my daughter.'

'I'm not entirely sure that's your choice,' he said. 'Penny is a young adult. Maybe you ought to treat her that way.'

'The day I need to take parenting advice from a drug trafficker, I'll know I'm in trouble.'

Morrison rubbed his nose between his finger and thumb, snuffling as he did so. 'You called here. I didn't ask you to.'

'Your son beat him until he pissed himself. I don't want someone like that around my daughter.'

'Why do you think John was responsible? Can you identify the person who's attacking the Burke boy in the footage?'

'John sent it to Penny.'

'Kids these days can access all sorts of stuff. That doesn't prove he actually did it. I'll tell you what I think is really going on here. You wanted Burke to pay for what he did; you just didn't have the balls to do it yourself. Now you're annoyed that someone else had instead. I can see why that might embarrass you.'

'Don't,' I said, struggling to remain composed. 'Don't get involved with my family.'

'Whatever you think, Inspector,' he said, stifling a yawn. 'We're done here; my horses need feeding.'

With that, he turned his back on me and strode across to where his horses waited, regarding his approach with wide, terrified eyes.

Chapter Fifty-six

I WAS HALFWAY back along the road to my own house when my mobile rang. It was Jim Hendry.

'Ben,' he said. I could hear the wind thudding against his mouthpiece as he spoke.

'Jim. Everything all right?'

'Niall Martin has disappeared. His partner called us. Someone broke into the house, tied her up and took him away.'

'Any ideas who?' I asked, though I already knew the answer.

'The partner said Martin had thought they were being followed the whole way from Letterkenny. A red Citroën.'

'James Callan?'

'We think so. Look, I need your help. We're at Callan's house but the place is deserted.'

'Right.'

'We can see the island from here. There's someone over there; we can see a torch moving about in the darkness. We can't access it from this side. We're waiting for a boat to be brought up from the docks in Derry with a crew to check it out.'

'You want me to take a look from over here?'

'It could be nothing; poachers or that. It's too dark to see from here, but we think there's two people there.'

'I'll check it out.'

I KNEW FROM my previous visits onto the island that the car's shuddering across the temporary bridge would make enough noise to alert whoever was on the island to my arrival. Therefore I parked up at the bridge's entrance; it also meant my car was blocking the route off the island. Grabbing my torch and my gun, I made my way across the bridge on foot.

If Hendry had seen a torch beam from Callan's house, it meant that whoever was using the torch must have been in the field where the Commission had been digging. Within a few minutes I reached the curve in the road that led to the field, and there, in the faint light given off by the sliver of moon above us, I recognized Callan's car parked at the side of the road.

I called Hendry's mobile.

'His car's here,' I whispered.

'The boat's on its way,' Hendry said. 'Sit tight.'

I pocketed my phone and picked my way down the embankment into the field where Declan Cleary's body had been found. Around me, mounds of soil from the various dig sites were piled in the darkness. I strained to see but could not discern any torchlight. I struggled across the field, stumbling over smaller mud piles, trying not to lose my footing. About halfway across I finally spotted the shifting glint of one torch. As I moved closer I realized that the beam had stopped moving. For a second I thought that Callan had heard my approach. Then I realized he had laid the torch on the ground.

The rasp of a spade sinking into the soil carried across the field towards me. In the dim light of Callan's torch, I saw his feet moving as he lifted one boot onto the lug of a shovel. Then he shifted and deposited the soil he had lifted off to his right. He was burying Niall Martin.

My gun already drawn, I moved quicker now, though still with some difficulty, being unable to turn on my torch lest Callan see me. I reasoned that, even if Callan were armed, he would not be holding a gun if he was carrying a shovel. Still, I wanted to get as close to him as I could before he realized I was there.

Just as I rounded one of the mounds of clay, I lost my footing and stumbled, falling against the piled earth. Though I held onto my gun, I dropped my torch. On all fours I felt around with my hands to see if I could find it. Then I realized that the sound of the digging had stopped.

I froze, trying to make out Callan in the darkness. His torch beam shifted suddenly upwards, then swept across the field as he scanned the area. I fell back against the mound, pressing myself against it as hard as I could and turning my face from him.

I held my breath, lest it condensed into mist and gave my presence away. For a moment the island was silent, then, in the distance, I could discern the low drone of the PSNI's motor boat running up the river. Suddenly I heard again the sound of Callan digging, faster this time, as if he too had heard the boat's approach and wanted to be finished. I wondered why he should risk finishing Martin's grave rather than making a run for it now, if he knew the PSNI were on their way.

I scrabbled in the dirt until my fingers found the hard casing of my torch. Standing again, I began making my way across to Callan.

He stopped and lifted his torch again, the beam cutting across the distance between us. In turn I flicked on my own, shining it on him, my gun held in my other hand.

'An Garda,' I shouted. 'I'm armed.'

In the broad sweep of my torch-beam I saw Callan ducking down, trying to use the mounds of clay for cover.

'You're surrounded, Jimmy,' I called. 'You can hear the PSNI on the river. They'll be here in a few minutes.'

'That's all it will take,' Callan shouted. 'I'm not going anywhere.'

'Hand yourself over now, to me, then,' I called, moving ever closer. I could see Callan reclining against one of the piles, perhaps thirty yards from me. The droning of the PSNI boat grew ever louder.

'I can't do that,' Callan called. 'He has to die. You understand that?'

'It's done,' I said. 'He's buried. Surrender yourself now. Please.'

Callan laughed mirthlessly. 'Dominic took hours to die. Hours. He's getting off easy.'

'Martin's still alive?' I shouted.

'Not for much longer,' Callan replied.

'Niall Martin didn't kill your son,' I said. 'The army did.'

'He set him up. He used him to kill children, then set him up with the Brits.'

I moved closer, rounding a mound of earth as I closed in on him. I could see Callan becoming distracted, his attention constantly being drawn to the river from where the noise of the boat engine reverberated. Suddenly he shifted behind the mound and I lost sight of him.

'I understand your anger, Jimmy,' I said, keen to keep him talking, if only to keep his attention from the shoreline behind him, where the PSNI would soon be arriving.

'You have no idea,' he said. 'You give your life to something. Your fucking soul. Killing children. Do you know what that does to you? Inside? And then you're no use anymore. The war's over and everyone goes home. He had my son killing fucking children. And that prick Seamus O'Hara telling people now. Taking my son's name away from him. Like they hadn't taken enough already.'

'You killed Seamus O'Hara?'

He did not respond. The river valley seemed to shudder now with the noise of the approaching motor boat. Suddenly, the sounds spluttered out and I realized the PSNI must have reached the shallow waters near the island's edge, at Tra na Cnahma.

'And Sean Cleary?' I rounded the final mound and reached the spot where Callan had been standing. The earth was still raw where he had thrown it on top of Martin, the spade lying off to the left.

'My Dominic's a hero. And they wanted to take that from me. The Cleary boy wanted to go to the papers and tell them the truth. The week of my son's death and he wants to tell the papers that Dominic killed babies.'

I dropped down and, holding my gun in my right hand, began pawing at the dirt with my left, trying to feel through the earth for Martin. If he was even still alive, he'd suffocate soon enough.

'You said you didn't care about all that. About the march,' I called.

'I don't give a shit about that. But he's my son. His life had to mean something. And they want to take that meaning from him.'

'And what about Sheila Clark? Where is she?' Callan had not compacted the soil and my hand sunk down into the loamy earth, cold and damp between my fingers.

'You're standing on top of a huge fucking graveyard, Inspector,' Callan hissed. 'This whole fucking country,' he added, his voice suddenly near.

I turned to see him standing above me, his gun, a silenced pistol, pointed at me. At that moment, my hand connected with cloth and flesh in the ground. I could feel Martin react to my touch, could feel him wriggling suddenly where he lay beneath the soil.

'The PSNI are coming,' I said. 'You heard them.'

'You should have left me alone,' he said, his gun lowering.

His body became suddenly illuminated with a number of torches.

'Drop the gun,' a voice shouted. 'Armed police.'

As Callan turned towards the light, blood spurted from his right arm in the same instant as the sound of the first shot rumbled across the Foyle valley. Callan twisted, dropping his gun and, as he did so, a further shot rang out. This one caught him in the neck with sufficient force to knock him from his feet onto the mound of earth behind him.

I scrambled across to him. He was already dying. I could hear the soft suspiration of air through the wound the second bullet had made in his neck. Blood bubbled on his lips as he tried to speak. I recited an act of contrition, though I could not tell if he joined me in the prayer.

I squatted next to him, pressing my hand on the wound to his neck, trying to staunch the flow of blood. Callan mouthed something dryly, pawing at me with his bloody hand. Then, his eyes shifted out of focus and his hand dropped to the ground.

'Hands where we can see 'em,' a Northern voice called. The torch beams were shining on me now.

'An Garda,' I shouted. 'DI Devlin.'

'We saved your bacon, Inspector,' the voice said. The speaker approached me, his hand out, to help me to my feet.

'Martin's still alive,' I shouted, scrabbling back to where I had been digging. I began pulling back the earth with my hands, while the PSNI men who had arrived dropped down and did likewise. Finally, we began to uncover his body.

His hands were bound with tape in front of him, his shirt clung to his stomach and was sodden with his blood. Callan had shot him in the stomach, just as Dominic had been, and left him to bleed out.

'Call an ambulance,' I said to the PSNI officer nearest me, handing him my mobile. I felt through the earth, gripping Martin's head and pulling his face free from the mud. His mouth was covered in duct tape, his eyes staring wildly from me to the officers opposite, who continued to dig him free from his grave. I ripped the tape from his mouth.

'Where's the child?' I asked.

His mouth gulped at the air, his eyes wide and fearful. I shook him roughly.

'The child that Sheila Clark had. Where is it?'

He looked at me dumbly, as if unable to process what I was asking.

'In the car.'

'What?'

'The car.'

'Where? At Islandview? When I caught you?'

He stared around him wildly. The car had been searched when Martin was arrested. It had been empty. I gripped his face, turning him towards me. My hands were slick with Callan's blood and his skin was tacky to my touch. I could hear one of the PSNI men mutter a comment to his colleague about my behaviour but I didn't care.

'Tell me. Which car?'

He nodded. 'At Islandview. The car,' he said, his body shuddering as it began to register the shock of all he had suffered.

I felt my stomach lurch as I realized, finally, the child's location.

Chapter Fifty-seven

CHRISTINE CASHELL WAS not at her house in Islandview when I called, though her partner, Andrew Dunne, told me that she had gone to stay with her mother for a few days. I would find her there. I believe he knew why I was calling and I suspected he felt a degree of relief at my visit.

I had not been at Sadie Cashell's house in Clipton Place since the death of her child, Angela, in 2002. The house had not changed much. The last of the summer's roses hung heavy on their stems in the narrow flower bed to the front of the house, their heads weeping their final few petals onto the soil.

Sadie came to the door when I knocked, but would not, at first, let me in.

'She's not here,' she said, folding her arms across her chest.

'I know she is,' I said. 'I know she has a child that's not hers, too.'

Sadie said nothing, though I could see the muscles in her jaw working beneath the skin.

Suddenly, from above, we heard the sharp, colicky cry of an infant, just for a second or two, then it went quiet.

'How long did you think she could keep it up, Sadie?' I asked. 'She has to start her life again, eventually.'

Sadie waited a beat, then stepped back, allowing me past into the hallway.

'She's in Angela's old room,' she said softly. 'Be easy on her.'

I mounted the stairs feeling a weight of dread settling in my gut, not in fear of what I might find, but in the certain knowledge of what I must do.

I knocked gently on the bedroom door, then opened it.

The room had changed little since last I had stood here, almost a decade ago. The window still dominated the back wall, facing out towards the rear yard. The carpet was still a shade of green, though the walls were painted cream now instead of the lilac they had been when Angela died.

Christine sat on the bed, bottle-feeding the infant. He was a little longer than her forearm, his head nuzzled against her breast, his mouth moving rhythmically as he drank.

'Christine,' I said.

She looked up, her smile bright, her eyes glinting.

'He's beautiful, isn't he?'

I looked at the baby. His fine fingers played at the edges of the rubber teat on the bottle, his legs kicking the air slightly as he drank.

'He is, Christine.'

'I found him,' she said. 'I lost him and then I found him again.'

'Where did you find him? In the car at the house across from you and Andrew?'

She nodded, smiling a little uncertainly.

'He was crying in the car. No one was taking care of him. He'd been crying for me all that time, all the time I'd heard him. He'd been waiting for me to come for him.'

'You can't keep him, Christine,' I said.

'Of course I can,' she replied quickly. 'No one will miss him.'

I tried to argue with that, but could not. She was right. No one would miss him. He had no family; no one who would love him the way Christine would. I realized, too, that I still had the birth certificate for the child, in Christine's son's name. She could give him the child's identity and no one would ever know.

As if aware of my thoughts, she said, 'We'd just disappear. It would be as if we had never existed.'

I recalled Sheila Clark's justification for the very same behaviour. And Harry Patterson's. Perhaps they were right. I wanted to convince myself that they were.

But I couldn't.

'I'm sorry, Christine,' I said. 'I'd love to, but I can't do that. It's not my place to make that kind of decision.'

'He's my child,' she said tearfully, wrapping her arms around the infant tightly enough that he mewed in response, kicking out with his legs.

'You can't stay in here forever, Christine,' I said. 'What about Andrew? And your son, Tony? He can't put his life on hold permanently. He's waiting for you, at home, to start living again. You can't do that if you've kept the child in this way. You know that.'

She began to cry suddenly, heavy tears that rolled down her cheeks with little effort on her part.

'It's not fair. Why can't I have my child? I didn't do anything wrong. I tried my best.'

I moved towards her. 'I know, Christine.'

'I'm a good mum,' she said, as much to herself as to me.

'I know,' I repeated. 'I know you are.'

'He's my son.'

'Let me hold him,' I said.

I heard the door creaking behind me, heard the heavy step of Sadie Cashell as she entered the room.

'Best let him have the baby, Chrissie,' she said. 'It's over now.'

'I deserve to be happy,' Christine sobbed.

'Not like this,' I said. 'You deserve to be properly happy. And you will be again.'

I reached out to her. 'Can I see the child?'

Sadie moved in beside me.

'Come on, Chrissie,' she said. 'It's time to go now.'

I reached out for the child, felt the coarse wool of the blanket which she had wrapped around him.

Stretching out her arm to me, she offered me the child. I took him, let him settle in the crook of my own arm and took the proffered bottle from her.

She sobbed as her mother put her arm around her shoulders and took her out of the room.

The baby nestled in my arm, nudged his head against my chest and nuzzled in further, twisting slightly. His fingers, fine and tapered, moved across my shirt front, then gripped the material at the gap where it buttoned.

I was reminded of Penny and Shane when they were infants and I had sat at night feeding them. At the time, I had complained of broken sleep, and had been constantly tetchy. Yet even then I had known that those moments were passing irrecoverably. The relationships I had enjoyed with them then had been simple, instinctive, free of guilt or remorse, free of judgement. Our relationships had been unconditional then; I could not help feeling that it was not the case now and that, despite my best efforts, I had failed in being the father they deserved.

As I considered the child, considered the vulnerability of its tiny bones, the simple need it had for someone to give it complete love and attention, I questioned what I had done. Christine Cashell would be a good mother to him, I had no doubt. But I could not make that decision alone.

I took him downstairs and asked Sadie to hold him while I reported his discovery to the Social Services team in the HSE. I explained that the child was at the centre of an illegal-adoption scam and had been found and taken care of by a member of the public.

As I had expected, they told me that their first action would be to locate a suitable emergency foster carer to look after the child.

I had a recommendation on that count.

Epilogue

ON 24 JANUARY, Declan Cleary was finally laid to rest. Following Requiem Mass, his remains were taken to the local graveyard and buried in the same plot as his son. Lennie Millar attended the service, as did all the other diggers who had helped locate his remains.

Afterwards I lit seven candles beneath the statue of the Blessed Virgin, for the seven children we had recovered. Despite my best efforts, the DPP in the south had decided that no criminal charges could be made against Martin. A civil charge, however, was a different matter. Christopher Hillen and his mother had started proceedings against Martin's company for compensation for Christopher for the disfigurement he suffered due to the drugs testing.

That afternoon, we attended the christening of David McCready. Joe McCready's wife Ellen had given birth to a healthy baby boy just after Christmas. Despite Joe's fears, the boy was thriving, although, if the state of his parents were anything to go by, he was not sleeping much.

Following the service, I went outside the church for a smoke. Debbie and Penny stood in the vestibule with Ellen, admiring the baby. Shane stood to one side, trying not to look out of place. When he saw I was looking at him, he smiled shyly. I noticed that Debbie slipped her hand through the crook of Penny's arm and pulled her closer to her. For a moment, I thought Penny would resist. Then she leaned her head towards Debbie's, until she was resting it against her shoulder. From behind, the two of them with their hair cropped short, it was almost impossible to tell them apart.

After dinner, I drove out to Islandview. Andrew Dunne answered the door when I knocked.

'Christine's in the living room,' he said.

In one corner sat a large pram, a blue blanket hanging from it onto the floor. Christine sat on the sofa, her son, Tony, sat next to her with the baby in his arms as he fed him.

'Inspector Devlin,' she said.

'Christine,' I said. 'I just thought I'd call and see how things are going.'

She smiled brightly. 'Great.'

'Your mum was all right with my suggesting her as an emergency foster carer, then.'

Christine nodded. 'She's not had much to do.'

'That doesn't surprise me.'

Andrew stood in the doorway, watching the child as it mewed for more milk.

'We've applied to be foster parents,' he said. 'Things are looking hopeful.'

I nodded. 'I brought this.' I handed him a small teddy bear which Debbie had bought for the child at the same time she'd been buying a gift for McCready's son.

'You're very kind,' Christine said, reaching up and taking the toy from Andrew and waving it in front of the infant.

'Michael, is it, then?'

Christine shook her head. 'We thought we'd call him Andrew, after, you know.' She gestured towards where Dunne stood, smiling sheepishly. 'We lost Michael. It wouldn't be right to either of them to give his name to this wee man.'

'That sounds just right, Christine,' I said. 'Whatever you do, just be sure to spoil him now. And this man,' I added, nodding to the boy by her side. 'I haven't seen this man since he was a baby Andrew's size.'

Tony beamed at me, holding the child with fraternal pride.

As I LEFT their house, before getting into my car, I stared across the fields at where Islandmore loomed out of the darkness, its outline just visible against the darkening sky.

Sheila Clark had never been found. If, as Callan suggested, she was buried on the island, Lennie Millar had claimed that the recovery of her remains would be almost impossible. Ironically, the dig for the Disappeared had created perfect conditions for the disposal of further bodies, for the recent disruption of the earth would make geophysical tests unreliable.

The island was quiet now, those nameless dead that still rested there seemingly content that one more had joined them in their eternal sleep, taking her rightful place on the Isle of Bones.

Author's Note

WHILE THIS NOVEL is fictitious, it is inspired, in part, by real events.

Two hundred and eleven girls in Mother and Baby homes in Ireland were used, without parental consent, to test trial vaccines during the sixties and seventies. This was to be investigated as part of the Commission to Inquire into Child Abuse in state institutions headed by Justice Laffoy. However, in 2003, following court action from doctors involved in the trials, the Commission's investigation in this regard ended.

Isotretinoin, used in the treatment of acne, does cause birth defects in the children of pregnant women using the drug. In the US, it is estimated over 2000 pregnant women who used the drug in the past thirty years lost their babies through miscarriage. At least 160 survived and were born with severe facial disfigurements.

The commission for the Location of Victims' Remains have, to date, recovered nine of the sixteen 'Disappeared'. For further information on their work, visit www.iclvr.ie

Acknowledgements

THANKS AS ALWAYS to my friends and colleagues in St Columb's College for their continued support.

Particular thanks to Bob McKimm; Geoff Knupfer of the Commission for the Location of Victims' Remains; Helen Guthrie, David Adamson, Eli Dryden, Jeremy Trevathan, Trisha Jackson, Will Atkins and Susan Opie at Pan Macmillan; Peter Straus and Jennifer Hewson at RCW; and Emily Hickman at The Agency.

As always, the McGilloways, Dohertys, O'Neills and Kerlins have supported my writing in innumerable ways. Thanks to all and, in particular, to Carmel, Joe and Dermot and to my parents, Laurence and Katrina, for all that they have done and continue to do. Finally, my love and gratitude to my wife, Tanya, and our children, Ben, Tom, David and Lucy, for their tolerance and support.

About the Author

BRIAN McGILLOWAY was born in Derry, Northern Ireland. He teaches English at St. Columb's College. His *New York Times* bestselling Lucy Black series is also available from Witness Impulse.

www.brianmcgilloway.com

Discover great authors, exclusive offers, and more at hc.com.